# AN UNDENIABLE ATTRACTION

Sabrina groaned and accepted his supportive embrace. This new husband of hers was not the doddering old duke on canvas, but a flesh-and-blood man, young, vibrant, and alive. A rare one who stirred her senses and became awed by the movement of her unborn child.

What had she gotten herself into?

In an effort to re-create the extraordinary connection she had experienced the night before, when he touched her burgeoning belly, Sabrina stepped back, took her husband's big, capable hands, and placed them flat against her child's cocoon. *"Will* you become his first pony?"

When Gideon's haughty, aristocratic features softened, so, too, did the brittle wall Sabrina kept erected around her oft-pummeled heart.

"Of course," he said with so easy a smile, Sabrina fancied they could both imagine the resultant giggles, and suddenly she dared hope that her bargain of a marriage might not be so unpleasant an arrangement after all.

Dear Romance Readers,

In July 1999, we launched the Ballad line with four new series, and each month we present both new and continuing stories set everywhere from medieval England to the American West—the kind of passionate, romantic stories you love best, written by the most gifted authors. At the back of each book, we tell you when you can find subsequent books in the series that have captured your heart.

First up this month is **Moonlight on Water,** the second book in the fabulous new *Haven* series by beloved author Jo Ann Ferguson. Will a young woman leave her familiar community behind for a steamboat's dashing captain? Next, talented Annette Blair takes us back to Regency England to meet **An Undeniable Rogue,** the first irresistible hero in her new series *The Rogues Club.* Marrying a fallen friend's sister is a simple matter of honor for one dashing rake newly returned from the war, until he meets the wildly tempting—and very pregnant—woman in question.

*The MacInness Legacy* continues with new author Sandy Moffett's **Call Down the Night,** as the second of three sisters separated at birth discovers her gift of second sight may lead her to a strange heritage—and keep her from the man she loves. Finally, talented Susan Grace begins the new series *Reluctant Heroes* with **The Prodigal Son** as one of the infamous Lady Cat's twin sons masquerades as the other—and finds himself falling for his brother's beloved . . .

These are stories we know you'll love! Why not try them all this month?

Kate Duffy
Editorial Director

The Rogues Club

# AN UNDENIABLE ROGUE

*Annette Blair*

Zebra Books
Kensington Publishing Corp.
http://www.kensingtonbooks.com

ZEBRA BOOKS are published by

Kensington Publishing Corp.
850 Third Avenue
New York, NY 10022

Copyright © 2002 by Annette Blair

All rights reserved. No part of this book may be reproduced in any form or by any means without the prior written consent of the Publisher, excepting brief quotes used in reviews.

If you purchased this book without a cover you should be aware that this book is stolen property. It was reported as "unsold and destroyed" to the Publisher and neither the Author nor the Publisher has received any payment for this "stripped book."

All Kensington titles, imprints, and distributed lines are available at special quantity discounts for bulk purchases for sales promotion, premiums, fund-raising, educational or institutional use.

Special book excerpts or customized printings can also be created to fit specific needs. For details, write or phone the office of the Kensington Special Sales Manager: Kensington Publishing Corp., 850 Third Avenue, New York, NY 10022. Attn. Special Sales Department. Phone: 1-800-221-2647.

Zebra and the Z logo Reg. U.S. Pat. & TM Off.

First Printing: July 2002
10 9 8 7 6 5 4 3 2 1

Printed in the United States of America

*To Robbie-Lynn*
*Bright and eager from the first*
*Who brought us the gift of love*

*To Scott*
*A surprise from the first*
*Who brought us the gift of laughter*

*I loved you when you were tiny and cuddly*
*And toddling and questioning and growing*
*But most of all, I love the people you have become*

*For every precious moment, I thank you*

# Prologue

*The Inn at Waterloo*
*June 19, 1815*

My dear Sabrina, weep not for me, for my time on this earth is short, yet the sun shines, truly, now that Bonaparte has been defeated, and you are settled. As I vowed, I found for you a husband. With time running out, I exacted from him a deathbed promise to wed and protect you.

He is the new Duke of Stanthorpe, honorable, and wealthy beyond your needs. Tell him of your enemy, I implore you, for he will help.

You suffered as the wife of my late and fiendish half brother, and for that I make recompense. I shall call you my beloved sister into eternity. Yours, Hawksworth.

# One

By this time tomorrow, he would be wed.

Gideon St. Goddard, Duke of Stanthorpe, was having second thoughts. Though he approached his Grosvenor Square home for the first time in months, more dread than anticipation filled him, for beyond the black enameled door of number twenty-three, his mystery bride awaited.

With a curse for fate and a tug on Deviltry's reins, Gideon slowed his pace, wishing the house stood empty of all but his few loyal retainers. Loyal—odd choice of words, especially for him. But, yes, they were, because he paid them well to be so.

Loyalty, constancy, fidelity; he did not possess the natural capacity to inspire those virtues, and he did not need another upon whom to test that ability and fail.

He did not *need* anyone.

Stanthorpe Place, tall, bright white, and inviting in the gentle winter sun, was not his best or his biggest home. But Gideon had chosen it to house the woman he had agreed sight-unseen to marry, because of its proximity to the pleasures of London. If worse came to worse and he found himself leg-shackled to an antidote, he could always send her to the country to rusticate and bear his progeny while he remained in town.

The realization that he need not bother with her more than once or twice a year might actually serve to relieve his anxiety, if the specter of his parents' almost-perfect marriage did not crook its come-hither finger so beguilingly.

At least, Grandmama was pleased about his marriage. After his estranged brother's scurrilous and untimely demise, her letter informing him of his unexpected ascendancy to the title had caught up with him in Belgium on the eve of battle. Even now, the Grande Dame believed that her letter insisting he, "hie thee home and get thee a bride," rather than Napoleon's fall at Waterloo, had ultimately brought him back to England.

In actuality, her promise to make him her heir if he did so had more to do with it than her insistence. That, and the mighty and mercurial hand of fate.

His coffers, while never empty, always needed topping off. His first bride—though she never got quite that far—ran off with a wealthier bridegroom, reminding him that as far as money was concerned, one could never have enough. And Miss Whitcomb, according to her brother, needed a husband to protect her from a life of indigence. "So," he told himself as he made his way 'round to the mews, " 'tis all for the best."

Nevertheless, as he left Deviltry to the eager stable lad's tender ministrations, Gideon's heart beat like a drummer boy's timorous tattoo.

In an effort to divest himself of travel grime and don his best armor before meeting his intended, Gideon chose the service entrance so he could take the back stairs to his bedchamber.

In the kitchen, Cook was not to be found, but a luscious wench looking set to pup shrieked when she saw him.

Arrested by an eerie sense of recognition, though he had never seen her before in his life, Gideon did not duck fast enough to evade the flour she tossed in guileless self-defense. Reduced to dusty ignobility, he bit off an oath that turned into a sneeze, and added *spirited* to *luscious* in his estimation of her.

Dusting flour from his shoulders, Gideon gave his attacker a slow, sweeping perusal. Judging by the manner, if not the style, of her dress, the nymph was no servant. Round in all the right places and then some, she obviously belonged to someone else. But who? And what was she doing in his kitchen?

"Where the devi—" A second sneeze diluted his vexation to the point that Gideon sighed and gave it up. "Where is Cook?"

His attacker's miffed mien turned sympathetic. "Oh, you must be hungry."

Yes, he was, suddenly and inexplicably, but not for food, he decided, chagrined over his reaction to her. He did not normally lust after women in her interesting condition, though there had been that one incredible time . . .

Gideon cleared his throat. "And you are?"

He must appear as wide-eyed and assessing as she, he mused even as he tumbled headlong into the bottomless depths of the most amazing green eyes he had ever beheld. Sultry. Beguiling.

"S-Sabrina," she said when the silence stretched nearly to snapping.

Shaken by the unlikely coincidence, Gideon waited for her last name, fearing, yet . . .

"Whitcomb. Sabrina Whitcomb."

For the first time since the Battle of Waterloo, Gideon's knees turned to jelly.

Behold his bride.

At first thought, the notion enticed almost as much as it appalled. Yet he knew instinctively that if he took this woman to wife, his solitary existence would end in flames, for she burned bright and alive, and had the power to singe if he got too close.

And he *would* get close, by God, especially if she were his. Be damned to the burn.

Gideon lowered himself to a chair.

"You *are* hungry," she all but cried as she hurried to gather bread, cheese, and fruit, and fill him a plate.

Gideon added *compassionate* to her list of qualities, but not graceful, at least not in her *delicate* condition. Then again, delicate was not the word he would use to describe her. Lush, ripe, and . . . blooming, he thought, yet with a naturally regal bearing, even now.

Soft and shapely, Sabrina Whitcomb possessed a body that would give a man ease and comfort. And despite every indication of perfidy—on the part of her brother, at the least—Gideon wanted, absurdly, to be that man and explore every gentle curve and rising crest.

Lust at first sight.

Suddenly dry of throat, Gideon drank the ale she placed before him.

He had hoped for passable looks in his bride, but he found this woman downright ravishing. By virtue of her . . . assets, he expected she would be a sweet and succulent bed partner.

But how came she to him with child? Or by whom? he should ask. And why had not Hawksworth prepared him for any of it?

Truth to tell, time had been running out for his friend . . . if Hawksworth could still be termed friend, after withholding certain "weighty" information, though Gideon supposed one did not quite view one's sister as other men did.

At least he could stop worrying about having to work up the necessary enthusiasm to bed a homely virgin, Gideon thought, consoling himself. There must be something to be said for experience in a wife, but what that might be, he could not precisely recall as having any import at this juncture. Given his bride's impending motherhood, however, he felt annoyed and . . . duped. "I assume you were widowed something less than nine months ago?"

She colored but raised her chin. "How do you know I am not married still?"

Explaining his knowledge would reveal his identity, which seemed precipitate and imprudent of a sudden. Perhaps he should wait a bit, at least until he regained his bearings and got a better grasp on the situation.

God's teeth, he wished honor were not at stake here, much as he wanted the delightful but surprising package before him, in the strictly carnal sense, of course.

Since hunger for food also gnawed at him,

Gideon cut a piece of cheese as he considered his answer. "Widow's weeds," he said after chewing thoughtfully, indicating her black bombazine gown. "If I do not mistake the matter."

Sabrina rolled a mound of dough from a tawny clay bowl and nodded. "You do not. I am eight months a widow. Perceptive of you."

Not perceptive enough, by damn.

So much for his wedding night. Gideon ripped a piece of bread from the warm loaf.

Good God, he was in danger of becoming a husband and father in one sweep. Not that children of themselves frightened him, but the notion of becoming immediately and directly responsible for one certainly did.

No wonder her brother had begged, as he lay dying, for Gideon to wed and protect her. How well he remembered that plea for her protection. But what Gideon's erstwhile friend had not said was that without his protection, Sabrina Whitcomb might be forced to a life on the streets.

Even without that knowledge, with the haze of smoke and the stench of death all about them, and Grandmama's letter in his pocket, Gideon had grasped Hawksworth's plea like a ticket to life.

Fulfilling his friend's dying wish became a call to honor, while caring for his sister would give Gideon purpose in a heretofore meaningless existence. Having suffered enough of ennui and regret, Gideon had, at that moment, stared his own mortality in its bony eye sockets and yearned of a sudden for an heir, someone to carry on his name. A small someone who might fill the emptiness and accept him without condition.

He had simply not expected that small someone to arrive quite so soon.

Since the begetting of heirs fell into line with his favorite and most accomplished sport—he had practiced diligently for years—the offer of a fresh and virginal bride upon whom to get his heir had seemed a gift from above, though hell had needed to be faced first.

Hawksworth had breathed a great sigh with Gideon's promise and all but expired in his arms. Then Gideon was forced to rejoin his regiment in the thick of battle.

By the time he returned, his friend's body had been taken away.

Weeks after Napoleon had been routed, Gideon had finally been able to send letters offering Sabrina Whitcomb his hand and arranging to have her brought to Stanthorpe Place. After weeks aboard the *Bellerophon* in Torbay Harbor, guarding the conquered Frenchman, he had then sailed on the *Northumberland* to St. Helena to stand guard there till his tour of duty ended.

Not until Dover's cliffs finally came into sight did Gideon have the time and freedom to worry in earnest about the pitfalls in his promise, namely, the bride herself.

He had reasoned then that a poor and homely spinster should be particularly grateful for his name and protection, and therefore amenable and . . . easy to the bit. But the bemused goddess watching him could in no way, even in her interesting condition, be compared to any creature he might master. Nor, he suspected, would she ever be easy—to the bit or anything else. And yet, something about her answered a need in him, a longing he could not even name.

Gideon scoffed inwardly at his idiocy.

While Grandmama had dubbed the alliance romantic, and destined, he had called it daft and wondered if he was not sickening from something. Not that he had any choice in the matter. Honor dictated that he not deny the friend whose blood thinned the mud beneath them. No more than he could deny this remarkable woman who called forth in him a bizarre and unexplained need to care for and protect.

Moreover, it was entirely possible that despite her temporary indisposition, Sabrina Whitcomb, with her gull-winged brows and sable-thick hair, might actually make him an acceptable wife.

And who was he trying to fool? He was eager for her. He had heard it said that expectant women glowed with vitality, but he had never witnessed the like.

Until today.

What he should do, Gideon thought with derision, was take himself off to Bedlam to get fitted for a straitjacket. Never mind that this challenging mix of seductress and virgin, child and woman, could be said to fulfill every male fantasy. Never mind that his longtime mistress, svelte and skilled, awaited his arrival even now.

"Are you unwell?" his intended asked, her brows knit with sincere concern.

"Unquestionably," Gideon replied in bad humor. "Positively dotty. I must say, you do not seem particularly overcome with grief at your husband's passing."

Sabrina's eyes darkened to liquid emerald, and

Gideon regretfully expected her to shrink before him. Instead, a tigress emerged, all bright fire and unsheathed claws. "I suppose your bad manners are understandable," she snapped, "begging at the back doors of your betters as you are, but you might at least pretend a degree of polite gratitude."

Claws that could draw blood, he must remember. Gideon suppressed an unnatural and frightening urge to break into a smile. And did he resemble a derelict so much that she did not realize who he must be?

His bride's stubborn chin rose a fraction. "For your information, not that you merit any, my husband was . . . less than a good man, but I do grieve, though even more for a dear friend."

Gideon heard the truth of it in her voice, read sincerity in her eyes, and was shamed. "Please," he said. "Accept my apology. You have had a bad time of it and did not deserve a show of temper. I do thank you for the meal." He began to eat in earnest. "Tell me about your friend."

The tigress nodded, claws instantly sheathed, seeming surprised at his humble reaction to her scold. "The friend for whom I mourn was the Duke of Hawksworth," she said, love and sadness etching her features. "And I do not know how I shall go on without him."

Friend? Something dark, possessive, and ponderous rose up in Gideon. The liar had called her sister. Why would a man lie about his relationship with a woman, unless—

Good God, had Hawksworth been looking to give his bastard a name?

No, and again, no.

It was true that he, Hawksworth, and a few others,

had been friends for no more than a matter of months, their friendships forged by circumstance, camaraderie, and shared patriotism. Their whimsical "club" had been formed in a tent, in time of war, so life-stories had been dispensed with, and Gideon knew little of Hawksworth's family, less about his taste in women.

Nevertheless, his friend had been, without doubt, a man of honor. That, and some strong but nameless instinct about the woman before him, made Gideon believe he must be wrong. And yet . . .

Less than twenty-four hours remained until his wedding and would have to suffice as time enough to learn what he must. If his groundless suspicions proved true and he found the prospect of marriage to this woman insupportable, he would call off the wedding and she would never know "Stanthorpe" had been here.

For now, however, since he obviously appeared as much a derelict as he felt, he had best get himself upstairs to wash. Blast and damnation, how the devil would he manage that without revealing his name?

Feeling caged of a sudden, Gideon rose to stare out the window as if an answer could be found upon the sudden summer gale.

"Please Mr. . . . I do not know your name."

Gideon turned, read her bewilderment, and resigned himself to revealing his identity. "You may call me Gideon."

When she made no sign of recognition, he began to hope for a reprieve. He bowed. "Gideon St. Goddard, at your service."

"Mr. St. Goddard." She curtsied, inasmuch as

she could, bestowing upon him a genuinely delighted smile. And when the deepest dimples that
ever felled man tugged at his cold rogue's heart,
Gideon feared there would be no reprieve for him.
None.

"Ah, Mrs. Chalmer," Sabrina said as they turned
as one to the woman who had just entered the
kitchen. "Mr. St. Goddard here will be staying with
us for a while. Please have your husband put him
in with the others."

*The others?*

Mrs. Chalmer's brows arched. But when Gideon,
imperceptibly, shook his head, his wizened old
cook set her mouth, narrowed her eyes, and led
him wordlessly up the stairs.


Sabrina Whitcomb had never felt more gauche
or nonplussed in her four and twenty years of life.
Never had she come face-to-face with such a vital
and disarming specimen of manhood.

True, his dark shadow of a beard, his obsidian
eyes, gave a stark first impression. True, he regarded her as if he were a hawk sighting prey.

Yes, that thick hair flowing away from his face,
like waves in a midnight wind, had served only to
enhance the image, and he had frightened her.

But despite all that, she had also been fascinated
by his every unexpected facet. His demeanor had
seemed at differing moments to shift from beggar
to baron, scamp to sorcerer, champion to charmer.

Here was a man who might protect her from all
comers, even from the likes of the vile creature she
was afraid still searched for her. Not that Homer
Lowick would ever find her in as safe and unlikely

a location as Stanthorpe Place, a blessing for which she had Hawksworth to thank.

But Gideon St. Goddard was another matter entirely. Lord, that such a bold, capable one should arrive at her door the day before her wedding to another. Which made no account, because the man was penniless, she must remember, a situation she could no longer tolerate, for herself or her children.

Hawksworth had kept his promise with his last breath. For that reason, first, if not for her vow to herself, she must remain true to Stanthorpe. Forget that his assessing regard turned her to pudding, that St. Goddard's melting midnight eyes appeared almost to smile even when he did not. Never mind a mouth shaped to reveal an inborn cheerfulness that inevitably tugged at her own.

And when St. Goddard had finally bestowed his first true smile upon her, full and deadly, before following Mrs. Chalmer up the stairs, the sculpted grooves in his cheeks had deepened, revealing a rogue undeniable, handsome as sin and rife with promise.

Well, Sabrina thought, kneading her dough to India rubber, palpitations over a charming rogue did not belong in the breast of a woman engaged to another. Especially not one past the blush of youth and due to give birth at any moment.

The doddering old Duke of Stanthorpe would do very well for her, thank you very much. With his money, he would be as able to protect her as any broad-shouldered pauper.

Tonight, after dinner, tomorrow at the latest, she would tell the handsome St. Goddard that he must leave Stanthorpe Place at once.

She had no room in her life for a seductive lady-killer.

More's the pity.

# Two

Sabrina Whitcomb's ocean-deep green eyes and generous spirit played in Gideon's mind throughout his bath and shave, so much so that he once called his valet Sabrina, a slip he would not live down any day soon.

And since Chalmer had had the good sense to show him to his own apartments—where he dressed as befitted his bride's current impoverished impression of him—he did not even wonder about "the others" until he met them at dinner.

The first of Sabrina's "boarders," a sixty-nine-year-old rag lady, had lost just enough of her sight to ruin her living. And her hearing, he discovered at dinner, was not much better. During Sabrina's journey to Stanthorpe Place, she had found Miss Minchip wandering outside a posting inn and took her along.

When Gideon heard the story, he formed a mental image of his intended as a child, all big eyes and dark curls, bringing home a kitten in her pocket and telling her mother that it followed her.

Mr. Oscar Waredraper, young at sixty-two, had driven his peddler's wagon of sewing notions into the path of Sabrina's carriage three weeks before, and ended the collision with a sprained back.

While Sabrina herself escaped harm, Ware-draper got taken home as well and had been installed, it appeared, as the new seamstress. Gideon did not know if the title was a sop to his pride or if the well-mannered older man actually performed that task for the household. Either way, like the rest, he was treated as an honored guest and joined them for dinner.

Doggett, of that suspiciously singular name, seemed to have appeared most recently inside the house—much as Gideon had done, Sabrina chidingly pointed out. And judging by Doggett's colorful Spitalfields vocabulary, Gideon surmised that the man had either been a pickpocket or a fence, though at seventy-seven, he seemed harmless enough, Gideon hoped.

After introducing Gideon as her latest boarder, and a seeker of fortune down on his luck—to Chalmer's chuckle-cum-cough—Sabrina entertained them throughout dinner with intelligent and witty conversation. Gideon learned, through carefully sprinkled questions, that she had attended finishing school, married young and foolishly, and paid the price.

She was generous—sharing even that which was not yet hers to share—thoughtful, captivating, and as the meal progressed, Gideon could more and more easily envision her fulfilling the role of duchess. His. Yet despite all her genteel qualities, Sabrina radiated an amazing depth of spirit and fire of passion that bore more than a trace of obstinacy.

Though her clothes were not in the first stare,

her poise and beauty would carry her through any social encounter. She would, he decided, appear graceful in a sack, a near thing right now, considering the size of her expected burden.

The man who wed Sabrina Whitcomb would never be bored, Gideon decided, but neither would he rest easy. The disturbing notion actually shot a frisson of anticipation through him, to the point that he could not seem to remove his gaze from her.

When dinner came to an end, he eschewed port and rose with the ladies. And after they were joined by the rest of the gentlemen, the "others" decided on a lively game of *vingt-et-un* for ha'pennies, Doggett their self-proclaimed dealer. Hmm.

Sabrina opted for a walk in the picture gallery in lieu of a wet garden, and Gideon, eager to know her better, offered her his arm.

Awareness sizzled between them as they strolled beneath the seemingly knowing eyes of his scapegrace ancestors, and before long Gideon felt compelled to break the silence and ease the tension. "My compliments on your home," he said. "I find the house to be in surprisingly good order, given the short duration of your stay. I did understand from Miss Minchip, did I not, that you have resided here a mere month?"

Sabrina nodded. "We scrubbed and polished the whole time. The others helped." She beamed as she gazed about. "After I dismissed the housekeeper, of course."

She had discharged his housekeeper? Indignation rose in Gideon on the instant, and he had to struggle to keep his temper in check.

Sabrina stopped before his grandfather's portrait. "Hopefully," she said. "He will be pleased with the results."

That turned Gideon's ire. "He?" Unfortunately, the remnants of his annoyance laced his inquiry.

Catching and shrugging his pique away, Sabrina indicated the man in the picture. "Behold the owner of Stanthorpe Place. The man I am pledged to marry."

Good God. Gideon regarded the engraved plate beneath the portrait. "Harold, Duke of Stanthorpe. But there is no date. Do you not think his clothes a trifle out of fashion?"

Like fifty years or more, Gideon thought.

"Do you think so?" Sabrina tilted her head to examine his grandsire in more detail. "I am not a member of the fashionable set, so I must admit that I would not know this year's court dress from yesteryear's."

"I see." Gideon placed his hands behind his back to resist a strong and inexplicable urge to reach for her. It seemed that her guileless naïveté, combined with the candlelight playing across her flawless features, was wont to make him forget her offering of his home to strangers. Not to mention her high-handed dismissal of his housekeeper. But he was being petty, and he knew it.

Still, his irritation rose again, and he ignored it again.

"So, what do you think of him?" Gideon nodded toward the portrait. "As your intended, that is. If he is, indeed, the current Duke of Stanthorpe." Why the devil was he dropping hints? Did he want to set the cat, so soon, among the pigeons?

Sabrina gave the portrait another thorough

study. "He is. And I think if he cannot be handsome, then it is better he is rich."

Like fingernails across slate, her words raised the hair at his nape while the prickling of foreboding racing up his spine further threatened his equanimity.

So much for naïveté.

Gideon composed himself so as not to give his agitation away. "You seek a rich husband, then? May I ask why?" Foolish question.

An impish grin slivered her eyes to crescents and revealed the slightest glimpse of calculated intent. "For the same reason you should seek a rich wife," she said. "Money."

Honest and artless even in her cunning, Sabrina Whitcomb remained true to the paradox he had already come to expect. Still, Gideon bristled. "Considering, as you say, you are not of the fashionable set, how became you so fortunate as to end up here, pledged to marry a peer?"

"The Duke of Hawksworth found Stanthorpe for me."

"Did he indeed? Again, may I ask why?"

"I think, Mr. St. Goddard, that you ask too many questions."

"Perhaps I do," Gideon conceded with a hard-won smile. "Again, my apologies. Nevertheless, will you humor me and answer just one more?"

"Why should I?" Headstrong, as he expected.

Gideon almost wished he could warn that her future, and that of her child, depended upon her answer. "Let us just say that I was . . . intrigued the moment I set eyes upon you. And I find myself wondering how it has come about that I have lost all opportunity to get to know you better, before I ever had the chance, my, er . . . temporary lack of funds aside, that is."

"Ask, then," said she, her voice like fluttering velvet, her regard less certain of a sudden, more vulnerable, or sorrowful, perhaps.

"Why the Duke of Stanthorpe?"

In due course, across her perfect features, marched embarrassment, a thought to prevarication, then resignation. Eventually, she sighed. "To be totally honest, Stanthorpe is rich and he was convenient."

"Convenient, by God." Gideon bristled—he could not help himself—but he sobered posthaste lest he waste a God-given opportunity to learn more about this siren fixed to fleece him.

She had given him the worst possible answer, though he did not know what might have been better. Convenient indeed. "Are you telling me that you need money so badly, you would sell yourself?"

Her expeditious, and unexpected, slap echoed forever through the long gallery. And as his cheek and his dignity stung, Gideon decided that a scheming bride's handprint might be a fitting brand for her fool of a bridegroom at their wedding.

A silent pall of tension hung in the air after that, and they regarded each other in stunned disbelief. Magnified night sounds—the creaks and groans of the old house—had Gideon imagining his ancestors uniting in his defense . . . or hers.

He cleared his throat. "My word choice was . . . unfortunate," he said. "I suppose I owe you an apology."

"You suppose?" Her voice no longer velvet, but ice, Sabrina turned on her heel and walked away, but she slowed, faltered, stopped, and looked back. "I have . . . responsibilities," she said by way of a tardy explanation, regret, apology almost, paling her agonized features. And like a Madonna, she stood there regarding him, soothing her babe with soft, unconscious strokes.

Gideon recognized and ignored his ridiculous inclination to soothe both mother and babe. "In other words, you would do anything for your child. I commend and admire the sentiment, but what about caring, Sabrina?" He began to approach her with caution, intending to offer amends and what little comfort he could, but was arrested by her babe's movement.

"May I?" he asked, his hand hovering. And when she nodded, he placed it gently upon the site in fascination. "Amazing," he whispered, riding a wave of unborn movement, gazing into storm-sea eyes and feeling suddenly closer to this woman than he had to any other in his life.

A faint stirring of alarm assailed him then, for the sentiment had come so strong, but he ignored apprehension as he had done with his promise to wed. "Would you not rather give this little one a father who would care for it?" he asked. "Do you even know whether Stanthorpe likes children or not?"

A spark of distress, quickly vanquished, managed to shatter her composure, as it did their fleeting connection.

Sabrina stepped from his reach. "You speak foolishness. I know firsthand that life can be gotten through without love, but it cannot, believe me, without money."

She was right, of course. And what the bloody

devil was ailing him? Why talk her out of marrying his more desirable persona—that of the duke rather than the pauper—when, if he would but be honest with himself, he would take her any way he could have her.

Would he? Did he want this siren of a goddess at any cost? As in, purchasing her, fidelity and all, the way he purchased his servants? Or, as in . . . love at first sight?

Gideon stopped himself from scoffing outwardly. Either way, he was an idiot deserving of nothing but her scorn. Gad, but he was more like his grandmother than he expected, except that he did not even know the meaning of love.

He did not think he could do "love."

He could do "like," definitely "lust." He could even throw in courtesy and respect to make things comfortable. But love?

For the life of him, Gideon did not understand what was ailing him. From whence had come this perverse need to believe a woman he had known for less than a day would take him as a pauper?

What he should do is ride to Drury Lane tonight, find a willing wench, purge Sabrina Whitcomb from his blood forthwith, and cancel his ill-advised wedding.

Pertinent notion notwithstanding, he wanted nothing more than to continue doggedly in pursuit of a woman he felt duped into marrying . . . a woman he wished would want him as much as he wanted her.

Tomorrow, Bedlam and a straitjacket.

Tonight, pursuit.

"Let us examine the possibility of 'like' and 'attraction' or 'lust' between us," Gideon suggested, his voice a croaking rasp. He stepped a hairbreadth nearer . . . and promptly fell into the shimmering verdant depths of her eyes once more.

Minutes—or hours—later, when he recovered, barely, he fought good sense and grazed her cheek with the back of a hand.

Sabrina swallowed, she trembled, but she did not seem able to turn away, and neither did he. In that moment, Gideon fancied that they were adjoined by some hot, invisible current flowing from one to the other of them and back, like heat lightning, sizzling without sound. "Though I have no right," he whispered, awed and encouraged by the openness in her countenance. "I felt those things. I felt them the minute I saw you."

Like a doe in lantern light, Sabrina stilled.

Silently denying his statement? Or rejecting a similar admission?

"Frivolous sensibilities have no place in my life," she said after another tension-fraught span and with no conviction. Then she moved again from his reach. "I am engaged to marry another. And what you felt this afternoon was hunger."

"Yes," he said, taking now one step forward for each of hers back.

When the wall stopped her retreat, Gideon placed tentative hands on her shoulders, and when she made no attempt to shrug him away, he slid his hand upward to cup her face and contemplate her full, ripe lips.

"As you say," he whispered. "Hunger, pure and simple."

While he waited for a subtle invitation to touch her lips with his own, Sabrina stood still as stone—

cold, hard, and unyielding. Yet he caught her inner struggle in the pulse at her throat and in her fists clenched tight and trembling against his chest.

Only when he flattened her hands over his hastening heart did she begin to thaw. But she pulled away nevertheless, breathing as if she could not get enough air, leaving him disconnected and floundering.

"No wonder you have had no luck making your fortune," she said, soothing her unkissed lips with her tongue and bringing his body to erect and rigid attention. "You believe in fairy stories."

No one had ever accused him of *that* before. "I was not speaking of happily-ever-after, my dear Sabrina, but of physical hunger." Was he, really? "Women are the romantics in this world, not the men," he said for his own benefit.

"Not me," she responded with a rueful laugh. "I cannot afford to be. I am sick unto death of poverty. I must keep food in my children's bellies, clothes on their backs, and a roof over their heads."

She could have no idea how much he respected her resourcefulness and determination, but he was mightily frustrated that she resisted the attraction sparking nearly to flame between them.

"Children?" he asked, only now absorbing her words. "Plural? Do you think, perhaps, you will have twins, then? You certainly seem bi—er capable enough, though I am no expert."

Her eyes widened to saucers. "Not a—I hope not."

For his own sanity, and to keep from kissing her, after all, Gideon placed her hand on his arm and started them strolling again. "When is he due?"

"Two weeks."

Gideon stopped, surprised. "Your bridegroom is not due for two weeks? I, ah . . . must have misunderstood."

She smiled. "Oh. No, my baby."

Gideon cursed his revealing slip and sought to recover himself. "You hope for a boy, then? That surprises me. I would think that with no heir required of you in this instance, you would long for a girl.

"My sister-in-law adores dressing her daughters in lace and ruffles and setting them out to be prodigiously admired by the rest of us. Said daughters, however, manage always to ruin their perfection with spilled jam and paw prints. And sometimes, I must confess, I become too spirited a pony for them and jiggle their curls askew."

Sabrina's laughter effervesced Gideon's heart in the way their near-kiss had quickened his body, yet something different, longing perhaps, hazed her eyes for a blink before she checked it.

Score one for him.

"Perhaps after your marriage," he said, bringing home his point. "The Duke of Stanthorpe will become your son's first pony . . . if Stanthorpe is capable . . . at his advanced age."

Sabrina released him and returned to studying his grandfather's portrait. "Even if he does not . . ." She sighed audibly. "Today is nearly over. He said he would arrive today."

Gideon stepped behind her. "What would you do, Sabrina, if he did not come?"

"Wait for him," she said, turning. "What choice do I have?"

"Would it be so very terrible if he never came?"

That stubborn chin of hers went up again, and all trace of vulnerability disappeared from her expression. "If the Duke of Stanthorpe refuses to marry me, Mr. St. Goddard, I will be forced to bring forth this child by the side of the road."

"Poor as a church mouse, are you?"

His jest did not in the least ease the lines between her brows, as he intended. Instead, she nodded in all seriousness. "A mouse without as much as a feather for a nest." Fact, plainly stated, with no room for self-pity.

Gideon's respect for her increased tenfold, as much as his hope for himself dwindled. He had set out to inspire a degree of attachment in her, for him, without monetary cost, though he should know better than to expect success on that score. Fine, then, their relationship would have to remain on a par with every other in his life.

Gideon stepped back, disconcerted by a sudden wild notion that theirs, of all relationships, merited better.

He shook off the burdensome fancy, ran a hand through his hair, and bowed. "I pray then that he will come."


Left alone in the huge picture gallery, mourning a loss she could not name, Sabrina sought the nearest gilt chair. Lowering her trembling and ungainly body into it, she did not allow herself the luxury of resting against its tapestried back.

Strong. She must remain strong.

Stanthorpe would come. He would come.

She regarded the duke's portrait without emotion. Tomorrow would be their wedding day. She would marry a . . . mature, dependable man, and see an end to her struggles.

Nevertheless, panic rose in her like bile, and when a vision of Gideon St. Goddard came to her as a possible form of rescue, she forced herself to rout his chiseled features from her mind's eye.

The man made her think of a deceptively docile dragon, one that would rise up and breathe fire when least expected. Rescue from such a quarter, she suspected, might be as much a hardship as the threat from which one needed delivering.

No. Neither magnificence nor charm would put food on her table. And no man was worth starving for. All were essentially the same, brutes out to appease their beastly appetites. The gentlemanly manner in which one comported himself before those appetites were satisfied would in no way resemble his deportment afterward.

No member of the male persuasion had ever made her doubt that before. Most simply verified it. Sabrina wished only that one had not come along to make her doubt that truth today of all days.

Had the man's dark eyes seemed almost to smolder when she thought he might kiss her?

No matter if they did. The future was out of her hands. Which was just as well, for she was in a fair way to making a muddle of it.

Ah, but his smile . . .

Would not be worth the price.

Her foolish musings were brought to an abrupt but welcome halt by the suddenly cavorting antics of her expected child.

Grateful for deliverance, Sabrina rose to make her way to the nursery, and her purpose for everything.

# **Three**

The note Gideon had written after a long and sleepless night, and had sent round to the front door only minutes before, arrived in the breakfast room on a silver salver.

Unlike the others present, Gideon pretended disinterest as Sabrina read her missive, while he made a show of deliberating between poached eggs and boiled.

"Stanthorpe isn't coming," she wailed with more distress than he would have liked or expected, and he dropped his pretense of indifference to rush to her side.

"Oh, wait," she said, stopping him in his tracks and allowing her guests to release their collective breaths. "He has suggested a proxy wedding, provided I can find someone to stand in for him."

"I would be happy to oblige," Gideon offered, forestalling Doggett, who appeared at the ready to make the offer and ruin Gideon's plan.

In the small hours of the morning, Gideon had remained wakeful and aware, body and mind, that he had but to open the connecting door between his bedchamber and hers to find the remarkable Sabrina in her bed. Heady knowledge, that.

More than once, during those hours, he told himself he was a hundred times a fool, yearning to marry a woman he had just met. Especially one big with child. His instant and inexplicable attraction to this woman suggested an immature weakness, a gullibility he thought he had lost a dozen years before.

He knew better. She was used goods.

Younger, more malleable women, virgins all, would fall at his feet for a smile, he kept reminding himself.

He owed Sabrina Whitcomb nothing, whether she had been Hawksworth's friend or his sister . . . or whatever else she might have been. Except that he had made a promise to Hawksworth . . . who had, of course, been dishonest in extracting it. But just because Gideon had not stumbled across many honorable people in his lifetime did not mean he could not be honorable himself.

Furthermore, Grandmama was right; it was time he got him a wife and an heir.

Sabrina Whitcomb eased his soul just by walking into a room. He could not help imagine how she would ease his body as well. Yet simple physical attraction alone had not inspired his fantastical plan.

Sabrina was a woman who gathered and nurtured strays. And during the dark and lonely hours of the night, he had thought for one weak moment that he just might be among the most "lost" she would ever encounter, that he had been for more years than he cared to admit.

No, she did not love him. But neither did he love her. Yes, she calculated his worth in coin of the realm. But why should a wife be any different from anyone else in his life? Sabrina wanted the security that his name and money offered, and he wanted a purpose in life, someone to care for and protect. He wanted to be needed, to be cherished, if only for what he could provide.

He wanted . . . no longer to be alone.

He wanted Sabrina Whitcomb.

So he would buy her.

Marrying her would sever a pattern of unwelcome solitude and satisfy honor at one and the same time. They could wed today, as planned, so she could await the birth of her child with no worry for her future. And while she ostensibly awaited "Stanthorpe's" arrival, they could come to know each other, without expectation.

Despite her cost to his pocketbook, and his pride, Gideon had found himself considering Sabrina's needs in this final decision. She must have suffered in her short life. One did not become so pragmatically focused, so jaded, for no reason. Though she was not hard and unfeeling as regards to her strays.

Gideon did not know the particulars of the unsavory first husband or the motivation behind her mercenary choice of him as her second. He still worried about Hawksworth's hand in that, but life sometimes forced less than exemplary choices. In time, he hoped she would willingly reveal all of it.

He hoped . . . for more than he could ever have.

In time, if a relationship between them did not seem feasible, "Stanthorpe" could always write that he had had a change of heart and was having the marriage annulled. If it came to that, "Stanthorpe" would leave her with a comfortable competence and she would never have to sell herself again.

If all worked out to Gideon's satisfaction, however, they could consummate their union at any time that seemed the right time.

Either way, for a while, at least until after her babe was born, he was doomed to spending more "hard" nights, like the last.

Except that he would no longer be alone in his bed, or in his life.

"Mr. St. Goddard?" Her words brought him back to the present and everyone's eyes upon him. "Thank you," she said.

Gideon straightened, wondered how long he had been woolgathering, and saw immediately that Sabrina's smile did not reach her eyes.

Dare he hope that she pined for the penniless wanderer before her? Or that perhaps she might, eventually? She might even come to request an annulment of "Stanthorpe," at which point Gideon would tell her who he was and make her deliriously happy.

And pigs would fly.

She was right; he was a romantic. He should take to penning his Gothic machinations, like some fanciful novel by Mrs. Radcliffe, and profit at least from his suffering to win her.

Especially since he need not win her at all.

A simple financial acquisition would do.

"This delay can only be good," she said as he helped her from her chair and she regarded her stomach ruefully. "In a month the duke might gaze upon me, for the first time, at my best, rather than at my worst."

And if this was her worst, Gideon imagined he had a treat in store.

"If you will all excuse me," she said to the room at large. "I shall go and prepare for my wedding."

At the bottom of the stairs, she stopped and released his arm. "Thank you for your offer to stand in. The new vicar, who has only just arrived to take over the parish, sent a note first thing this morning to say he would be here at three."

"The banns have been posted and the license procured?" Gideon asked, glad he had taken care of everything by messenger from Sussex before the new vicar's arrival.

"All is in readiness," she said. "You need only stand in Stanthorpe's stead and say 'I do,' then affix your name as his proxy in the parish register."

"I expect I can do that without error. Here, let me walk you up. I, too, would like to dress as befits the occasion."

He would not sign himself as proxy, of course— pray God he would get away with shutting the book before the vicar took a look. Then he would distract the man with an offer of libation. As a ruse, it was weak, but it was all Gideon had.

Bilbury, his valet, tut-tutted disapprovingly, in that way dared only by the most longstanding of retainers. "A proxy wedding, your grace?"

"As you say."

"But . . . standing in for yourself?"

Gideon raised a brow. "Is there a problem with my decision?"

The question brought sudden color to his starched valet's paste complexion. "Certainly not, your grace, but she *is* a right one, if you will pardon me saying so."

Gideon nodded. "It appears a distinct possibility."

"Everybody below stairs says so, even Mrs. Chalmer. So I am to suggest that you be nice to her—your bride, that is, not Mrs. Chalmer."

"I shall even be nice to Chalmer. You as well, though you, none of you, deserves it."

Bilbury nodded as he adjusted the form-fitting shoulder on Gideon's frock coat of clarence blue. "Mind, we do not see why you must lead her on, but we suppose it is for you to say, since you are Stanthorpe."

"If you expect me to thank all and sundry for that reproachful concession," Gideon said. "You may all find new employment on the morrow."

"Yes, your grace." Bilbury pretended a search for "that scapegrace stickpin," to cover his lack of proper horror.

Gideon raised a brow, certain that his man had not quite finished with him.

"You just be nice to her," his intrepid valet repeated as he tied Gideon's neckcloth fit to strangle.


Miss Minchip and Mr. Waredraper performed a miracle, transforming the drawing room into a wedding chapel, complete with silk-carpeted aisle and flowered canopy. The hothouse jasmine, lilacs, and roses that graced the tables had been Doggett's addition.

For their contribution to the wedding arrangements alone, Gideon was willing to support the three of them to their dying day.

While he awaited his bride beside the vicar, Miss Minchip sat at the pianoforte and began to play a Bach sonata with surprising skill and no sheet music.

As a bride, Sabrina was beautiful, and blushing, which was a surprise to Gideon, considering the nature of this union, and the bride's delicate condition. In addition, he had imagined her as far too stubborn to allow for a show of emotion. He liked that about her, her fight. But he also liked her honesty, even of emotion, even when the truth could be painful.

Sabrina Whitcomb would give as good as she got, in and out of bed.

Gideon liked most women, he admitted to himself, especially the pleasure derived in their beds, but as a wife, this one appealed to him in myriad ways. And he suspected he had not yet discovered a fraction of them—an adventure he anticipated with surprising relish.

Gideon looked about him with amazement. This was his wedding day. Yet everything seemed hazy and dreamlike, reminding him of a fantasy, or a nightmare—it was yet to be determined which. An event not wholly within his grasp, much as he suspected he would look back upon it in the years to come.

He wondered how Sabrina would remember this day twenty years hence, when they were an old married couple with a score of grandchildren. Would she blush all over again at her scheme to net herself a rich and eligible husband, knowing she had confessed all to him in advance?

Gideon knew how the *ton* would regard the proceedings. They would see Sabrina walking down the aisle, big with child, as infamous, a marriage "of necessity," and a poor alliance at best. She more than he would become grist for the gossip mill.

As a peer, he was foolishly considered a prize on the marriage mart and was down in the betting books as slated to come in dead last to the altar, paradoxically making him a prime catch.

Gideon scoffed inwardly, relieved to keep society at bay, at least for today, glad no one of note was expected, particularly since his bride had come to a dead stop midway up the aisle.

She stood rooted and wide-eyed, frozen nearly in . . . horror?

"Sabrina? Did you change your mind?"

"You—"

He went to her. "Are you unwell?"

She looked him down and up, shining pumps to diamond stickpin and touched the pin's crystalline jewel with trembling fingers. "You look so . . ."

"Groomly?" he asked. "Is there such a word? Groomlike, then?"

Her eyes filled to brimming. "Yes. That. And—"

"I thought you should have a wedding to remember."

"But your clothes . . ."

Oh, good God. Gideon wordlessly sought aid from those around him.

Bilbury eradicated his smile posthaste.

Mrs. Chalmer gave Gideon an I-told-you-so smirk, for which Mr. Chalmer pinched her, for which the man would be getting his ears boxed later.

Gideon cleared his throat of the laughter lodged there and returned his attention to his uneasy bride. "I borrowed the clothes from the duke. Do you mind? I should have asked."

Sabrina released her breath and nearly stopped trembling. "Oh. Oh, I see. Well, then . . . that is to say, I suppose . . . though I wish . . . Fine." She placed her hand on his arm when he offered it, and he indicated to Miss Minchip that she should begin again to play.

Gideon walked his bride to the vicar with dispatch, afraid she would turn tail and run otherwise. Not that he needed her, or anyone, but now that he had set his course, he wanted it done.

After that, Miss Minchip sang like a nightingale and the service moved along smoothly enough. Except for the point at which the words "till death do you part" were spoken, and the length of time Gideon's life, and therefore his hasty marriage, might last, came as a near-paralyzing shock to him.

By the time the ceremony was over and the assemblage applauded, however, Gideon realized there was no turning back. His fate had been sealed and he was strangely pleased after all.

Sabrina regarded him with trepidation, or expectation, and so he took her into his firm embrace and kissed her witless.

With the act, his apprehension turned to anticipation.

His bride went weak in the knees and Gideon all but crowed, because she was so overcome by his kiss, he needed to hold her up when it ended.

His life, his future, seemed suddenly splendid, and he congratulated himself on this brilliant plan.

The vicar commented wryly, and pointedly, that in the case of proxy weddings, it was *unnecessary* for the bridal kiss to take place. Then he told Sabrina to sign the register, first with her maiden name and then her married one—the name she did not yet know. His name.

Gideon bit off an oath.

His frantic mind-search for a solution ended with a familiar screech that severed his final thread of elation and plummeted his euphoria straight to hell.

"Stop this wedding at once!" Lady Veronica Cartwright, his former mistress—no, drat, he had forgotten to go and break it off with her last night—appearing the tart in crimson watered silk, charged up the aisle like Wellington before the Life Guards. "Gideon St. Goddard, what do you think you are doing?"

"What are you doing? Here? Now?"

"A good thing I am, and just in time to stop this farce. When your grandmother told me—"

Gideon raised a staying hand. "Let me make the introductions. Sabrina, this is Lady Veronica, a childhood friend. Ronnie, my wife. You are, I am pleased to say, too late to stop anything."

"Not at all. You can have the marriage annulled."

Gideon squeezed Sabrina's hand and stepped from his protective stance to reveal her in her full blossoming glory. "Too late for that too." And in the event anyone could possibly have missed the imposing sight, Gideon patted Sabrina's middle with a possessive hand. "We suspect it must be twins."

Ronnie screeched theatrically, and Bilbury, who had referred to her as "that toadying trollop" for as far back as Gideon could remember, chuckled inelegantly.

Veronica shot his valet a withering glance before she regarded Sabrina with similar venom. "He is mine," she announced with slow precision, punctuating each word with a poking finger to Sabrina's swollen middle. "Do you hear me?"

"The world hears you," Gideon said, bored for the first time in twenty-four hours as he moved Veronica's offensive digit aside. As all the world and his brother would hear, as soon as Ronnie quit these premises and got the gossip mill grinding, he thought.

Veronica slapped his hand aside before turning back to his wife. "I have planned to be the Duchess of Stanthorpe since I was six, and I will allow no dowdy upstart to displace me at this late date."

Well, there went the cat among the pigeons, Gideon thought, not daring to regard his wife, who had stiffened perceptibly beside him. Damn. "You must have planned to marry my brother, after Cartwright's death, then," Gideon told his former mistress. "Since I never expected to inherit. Or did you know something that I did not?"

Veronica's eyes widened and her nostrils flared for one terrible moment, and then she shrugged with forced nonchalance. But it was too late, because she had given herself away. Gideon realized, then, that Lady Veronica Cartwright was likely more dangerous than he had ever suspected.

"You would have inherited eventually," his formidable new enemy said.

Gideon shook his head. "You have not been content with anything less than 'immediate' in your entire life."

"Well, you have the title now, and I would be more than content."

He doubted it. "Listen, Ronnie, this cannot come as a surprise to you, since I have told you a score of times, but I never planned for us to marry.

AN UNDENIABLE ROGUE 47

You are a very resourceful and desirable woman, though, and I am certain you will soon find another . . ." Deep pocket with a coronet attached, he had nearly insultingly said, but he did not want her any angrier than she was already. "I am sorry to disappoint you, but I will not be seeing you again, now that I am married."

"What?" His former mistress gaped like a Drury Lane actress.

Gideon did not repeat himself; he could see that she had heard him clearly enough.

"We shall see about that!" she snapped into the ponderous silence. Then she turned on her heel and exited the room, and the house itself, in regal splendor, each and every door slamming in her wake.

Gideon regarded Sabrina's heightened color, no match for her white-knuckled grip stopping the blood flow to his arm. "I will have to speak with my grandmother about the company she keeps," he said, but his bride did not smile.

She turned, in fact, to the vicar. "How, sir, did you say I should sign the register?"

"First, your grace, as Sabrina Whitcomb, and then as Sabrina St. Goddard. Then you, your grace." The vicar drew Gideon's attention from his wife's cold and rigid expression. "If you would sign your own name and title, I believe a special wedding supper awaits you."

Gideon had not expected Sabrina to sign so readily. He had supposed that she would be angry and intractable. But she wanted Stanthorpe after all, and he was Stanthorpe, so why should she change her mind now she had him?

When everything seemed in order and he and

his bride regarded their guests, everyone returned to Sabrina a glance of concern, even sympathy. But toward him, each retainer looked reproachful and each boarder suspicious.

Nevertheless, Gideon invited them to celebrate his nuptials with a toast in the library before the bridal supper. "My duchess and I will join you in a moment," he said, seeing them out.

Then he squared his shoulders, prepared himself for battle, and closed himself and his seething bride inside.

# Four

As soon as the drawing room door clicked shut, Sabrina's eyes blazed, except that she also seemed frightened. Perhaps she feared releasing the anger Gideon could plainly see seething beneath the surface of her feigned calm.

"Well?" he asked.

"Well . . . you tricked me into marrying you."

"Hah! Do not pretend that you were not prepared to trick me into marrying you, except that you thought I was a rich old man instead of a rich young one. So, what do you have to say about this marriage of ours?"

Sabrina raised her chin. "I am satisfied, as I hope you are."

"Oh, my dear, sweet Sabrina, it will take a great deal more than stepping into a parson's mousetrap to satisfy me."

Again, emotion flared in her eyes. Again, she held her tongue.

"Being married to me does not mean you cannot say what you think," Gideon pointed out. "You had no trouble baring your claws yesterday, when you thought I was an ungrateful wretch, begging at the back doors of my betters."

His bride winced.

"So, please, tell me what you truly think of this unexpected turn of events."

"I think—" Her breasts heaved and her fists clenched, and as Gideon watched passion simmer within her, he could think only of getting her into his bed. "I think . . . you lied to me."

"Well, you discharged my housekeeper."

"And you tried to talk me out of marrying the duke."

"I *am* the duke. I tried to talk you out of marrying for money. And I did not lie. I simply omitted my title."

"Your pardon, your grace, but why the ruse? You do not even want me."

He did, physically at any rate, but that did not seem a clever weapon to place in her hands at this juncture. "You cannot imagine how difficult it is to find a good housekeeper," he said foolishly. "For what reason did you say you discharged her?"

"You did not *have* a good housekeeper. You had a brandy-faced gabble-grinder. You should have seen the state of your poor home when I arrived. Why did you not tell me you were the duke?"

"Rich and convenient?" Gideon quirked a brow. "Shame on you."

His bride had the good grace to pale and cover her face with a hand. "I cannot believe I told you that."

"Fortunate, am I not?" he said in sincere self-mockery. "That I can afford to purchase anything, even love."

"No." Sabrina's head came up at that. "No one can buy love. Not even you, your grace. And I do not have a heart to give, or sell, make no mistake on that score." That organ she would retain, intact, Sabrina had promised herself. For if she so much as offered it, and another rejected it—which this charming rogue most certainly would do—then she would have lost the last trace of self remaining to her.

Brian Whitcomb had stolen almost everything worth having from her, including her pride and self-respect. All she had left at his death was her heart. That, and her children, the only good to come from the union. But children carried an awesome price, precious though they were; they required a lifetime of responsibility.

If not for them, she would never have entered into this arranged marriage. Oddly, though, now that the bargain was sealed, she was not nearly as fretful as she had expected to be.

After all, her father had sold her into marriage the first time, and she had no say in the matter. Certainly, a marriage of her own choosing, an arrangement that would actually serve her and her children well, could be no worse.

"Why did you go ahead with the marriage once you understood my intent?" she asked her handsome, and annoyed, new husband.

He scowled. "I can be an idiot sometimes."

An idiot, perhaps, but a man of honor nevertheless. Sabrina knew that already. She was quite sure he would not set her aside now that the marriage had taken place, no matter how much he might rue his actions. Especially since his note suggesting a proxy wedding had come this morning, after he had learned almost everything about her last night. She wished only that she had told him then about the children. Now was certainly not an appropriate time, after everything. Though telling him was going to become ever so much more difficult as time went on.

"Why *did* you marry me?" she asked again. "If you regretted your promise to Hawksworth upon seeing me."

He took her arm, led her to a chair, and knelt before her. "You are with child, for heaven's sake."

"You married me because I am with child?"

"And beautiful." He took her hand.

*He* was beautiful. *"Do* you like children?"

"And I promised Hawksworth."

"That you would like children?"

*"He* lied. He led me to believe that you were a virgin."

Sabrina chuckled, surprising even herself. "Hardly."

"No bloody fooling."

He looked so annoyed, she laughed again. "I knew you were too self-assured to be a penniless wanderer, your grace."

"And you were too . . . everything. Call me Gideon."

Encouraged by the warmth in his gaze, Sabrina wanted to ask him to define "everything," but she might not like his answer.

"And you bring home stray kittens and feed penniless wanderers," he added.

"Hawksworth did not lie," she interjected. "He simply failed to tell you everything."

The man who could stir her with a look scowled once more. "He *said* you were his sister!"

Sabrina sighed. "I should have married him instead of Brian."

Gideon scoffed inelegantly. "Just what a bride-groom wants to hear on his wedding night."

"Wedding night? I . . . you. . . ."

"Out with it. How many times must I tell you that I will not beat you for speaking your mind?"

Sabrina decided then and there that she must begin as she meant to go on. She knew, firsthand the pitfalls of not doing so. Once burnt, twice wary. So she squared her shoulders, raised her chin, and faced her newest, and, perhaps, her greatest challenge thus far. "I would rather we did not share a bed."

Her new husband actually growled. "Were you going to tell my grandfather that?"

"Your grandfather?"

"The man in the portrait."

"Oh. Well, he would have been too old to care."

"Not *my* grandfather. 'Twas death alone kept him from bedding every female in the kingdom."

Dismayed by his ribald statement, Sabrina wanted to fan the heat rising in her face. "Tell me you do not take after him!"

Gideon flashed a grin that held the power to enslave her, which it might have done were they discussing any other subject.

"I hate the physical side of marriage!" she cried. Then she covered her mouth with a hand, horrified at her revealing statement.

Her bridegroom reared back, no less horrified, his grin gone, his utter astonishment comical. In slow measure, he seemed to recover his equilibrium, until only a slight frown remained. "When you set yourself to speaking your mind, wife, I must say you succeed with a vengeance. But I do believe you must have been with the wrong men. I promise you will like the physical aspect of marriage when I am the one to—"

All warmth deserted Sabrina, as if the blood drained from her body, and she shivered.

Gideon went for the pitcher of water.

Tense moments later, she gratefully accepted the glass he brought her. "You may be right," she said after a slow sip and too long a silence. "But we will never know."

Gideon tensed for a moment before gathering his wits about him. "I believe I should be given the same opportunity that you afforded your first husband, to prove myself. I deserve that much, and more. I, at least, can afford to support you, and if I precede you in death, rest assured you will not need to seek support elsewhere. You owe me a husband's due."

"I cannot give it to you." Sabrina rose with the alarming pronouncement, a riot of emotions pummeling her—nervousness, panic . . . anticipation?

She was so agitated, she took to pacing.

She could not believe they were having this infamous conversation. Whatever happened to sweeping such indelicate issues beneath the proverbial carpet?

"Sabrina."

Her husband's determined voice halted her mid-step.

"I *will* sleep in your bed. Beginning tonight."

"All night? Every night?"

"I promise you will enjoy it."

"You will not."

"I will too." He stood as well and approached her. "I always enjoy it, and so do the w—er . . . so will you."

"That is the most conceited—so do who?"

"Accept my word. We will both enjoy it."

"I meant that I did not want—"

"I know what you meant."

"Oh." She blushed.

"You would have accepted a tired old man in your bed, but not me? I do believe that might be cause for annulment."

"Too late for that. You told the strumpet this was your baby." And why she did not feel the least threatened, even by her bridegroom's perfectly clear threat, Sabrina could not imagine.

"Oh, no one will believe Ronnie."

Sabrina quirked a questioning brow.

"Unsavory reputation," he explained.

"A reputation *you* gave her."

Relief flooded Sabrina when he shook his head in denial. "I hate to admit this," he said, looking abashed, "but she initiated me."

Relief vanished. "But she is a woman and she seems younger than you."

"I had to work hard to catch up. I was heartily ashamed of myself."

Sabrina nearly choked on her sip of water. She coughed to catch her breath while Gideon removed the glass from her hand.

"What if we were to compromise?" she asked when he returned.

"Compromise?" He stepped near enough for her to detect the subtle fragrance of wintergreen amidst other enticing scents of brandy and man. The blend made her head spin and her body tighten.

"I can help you catch up too," her seducer whispered, his lips so near her ear, she felt the warmth of his breath to her thrumming center.

If he climbed into her bed tonight, she just might melt on the spot. "About . . . sleeping . . . arrangements . . ."

"Sabrina, I am paying a premium price to bed you."

She reared back, stunned. "That is a crude way to characterize marriage."

"Perhaps, but I should receive some compensation for being 'rich and convenient.' "

Sabrina groaned and accepted his supportive embrace. This new husband of hers was not the doddering old duke on canvas, but a flesh-and-blood man, young, vibrant, and alive. A rare one who stirred her senses and became awed by the movement of her unborn child.

What had she gotten herself into?

In an effort to re-create the extraordinary connection she had experienced the night before, when he touched her burgeoning belly, Sabrina stepped back, took her husband's big, capable hands, and placed them flat against her child's cocoon. *"Will* you become his first pony?"

When Gideon's haughty, aristocratic features softened, so, too, did the brittle wall Sabrina kept erected around her oft-pummeled heart.

"Of course," he said with so easy a smile, Sabrina fancied they could both imagine the resultant giggles, and suddenly she dared hope that her bargain of a marriage might not be so unpleasant an arrangement after all.

No matter her previous experience, in marriage or in life, this enigmatic man deserved an agreeable if not an enthusiastic bride. Nervous, however, about committing herself to the overwhelmingly physical being before her, and uncertain as to how to phrase her cautious bravado, Sabrina toyed with his cravat. "Your grace. . . ."

"How much of a compromise?" He looked down upon her as if he might discover what beguiling trick she contemplated—as if he might eat her alive.

"We . . . sleep . . . in the same bed," she said, taken aback by the question when she had been prepared to grant . . . everything. "But no . . . touching."

"We touch," he quickly countered, then he stroked the skin above her bodice, setting word to action and claiming her by branding her. "Everywhere. But no actual—"

"Fine," she said fast enough to halt the knee-weakening word, but not fast enough to stop anticipation from coursing through her.

Her husband regarded her with knowing eyes, then, as if he could see her nipples tighten beneath her gown and the scurrilous skitterings within her traitorous body. "Fine," he conceded. "No consummation, in fact, until after the baby."

"Wait a minute," she said with no small degree of panic. That would be no more than a matter of weeks. Too soon.

Not soon enough.

"You would rather not wait until after the baby?"

"Yes," she amended. "No. Fine. Until after the baby, then."

Gideon slid his hands upward, from the mound of her child, to rest lightly beneath her breasts, and as she watched, he skimmed the tight, aching nubs with his thumbs, shivering her to her marrow and flooding her with need.

"Now I begin to anticipate our wedding night," he whispered, nipping her lobe. "Within the allowed perimeters . . ." He laved and suckled that skittery spot. "There are any number of ways"—he kissed a trail to her lips—"to amuse ourselves."

Sabrina shivered again. "There are?" Her voice came out a squeaking croak and she swayed on her feet. "Oh." She covered her belly with her hand. "I think the babe must be hungry."

Gideon steadied her and walked her to the door. "I suggest a relaxed wedding dinner and then an early night."

Perhaps if she seemed tired enough and was agreeable to retiring early, Sabrina thought, denying the sparkle in her rogue bridegroom's mesmerizing eyes, she might shut herself safely away from him and his alarmingly resolved wedding night.

She might also grow wings and fly, but she would not place a wager on either. Still, she must at least try to turn the tide. "I *am* exhausted."

"It has been a busy day," her husband said as he led her into the hall, stopping her before the library door. "Let us finish our discussion later." He kissed her temple. "In bed."


Gideon had no sooner dropped Sabrina at the door to her bedchamber, than she was pacing. She could not believe her ill luck. She had married a man she was more attracted to than to any other in her life, a man she was also more angry with.

Just minutes after Gideon left her, Sabrina opened her door to a knock and found Miss

Minchip, come to deliver a wisp of a white lace night rail.

"I designed this myself," she said, coming inside, "for your coloring and delicate condition, dear, and our dear Mr. Waredraper stitched it. Is it not splendid?"

How could Sabrina refuse such a gift when she did not even have the heart to refuse to be helped into it when Miss Minchip offered?

The virginal white gown gathered beneath Sabrina's breasts to drape elegantly, if that were possible, over her blossoming figure. The white lace confection also made her feel the fraud for the first time since she accepted Stanthorpe's proposal.

"No need for the vapors," said Miss Minchip, noting her sudden lack of color. "Your bridegroom is not hard on the eyes. The only thing hard on that one will be what counts, mark my words."

Sabrina gasped and the old woman giggled. "Well, it is not as if you are untouched," she said, echoing Sabrina's thoughts. "I would not have made so bold, if that were the case." The old woman patted Sabrina's hand and kissed her cheek. "Relax and enjoy."

"Enjoy?"

"Do not sound so incredulous. Ah, I see. You have never . . . well, well, you do have a treat in store." Miss Minchip grinned and winked as she left, shutting Sabrina inside.

And what could the woman possibly have meant by that cryptic remark? Did she, too, believe, as Gideon seemed to, that enjoyment could be had even for a woman in the marriage bed? Or outside of marriage, given the fact that the woman had never married, and neither had Gideon, and the both of them certainly seemed to know something Sabrina did not.

Either way, she thought, she had no intention of staying here and becoming a sacrificial lamb to a scapegrace bridegroom who withheld the truth about himself upon meeting her.

Checking the corridor to be certain all was deserted, Sabrina made her lumbering way down the servants' stairwell toward the main part of the house.

Rooms that were big and airy by day appeared ghastly and intimidating in the dead of night, she discovered. But she found, finally, that Stanthorpe's grand library was not among the worst of them.

Illuminated by the silver glow of the moon, the elegant room, with the smell of beeswax and lemon-polished wood, old books and fresh flowers, radiated a welcoming quality even now.

Deciding to peruse the books closest to the moonlight streaming through the big bow window, Sabrina placed her candle on a table by the door.

She hoped that by the time she went back upstairs, the duke would have given up waiting for her and retired to his own bedchamber.

There were hundreds of books to peruse, and she took her time, seeking a title to suit her mood. Nothing so Gothic as Mrs. Radcliffe's *The Mysteries of Udolpho*, but rather something more fairy-tale-like or Austen-ish. Perhaps the story of an aristocratic bridegroom and the apprehensive bride with whom he falls madly and irrevocably in love.

Sabrina bit her lip on a surge of grief at the foolish sentiment, but much to her consternation, the banked emotion escaped as something of a sob.

Blast it, she must remain strong.


When Gideon knocked on the door adjoining his bedchamber with his bride's, he received no responding answer. "Sabrina?" he called. "Are you ready f— May I enter?"

He listened carefully for at least the sound of a scuffle that might reveal her as unprepared to receive him as yet, but he heard nothing.

"Sabrina, are you in there?" Another minute of silence and Gideon opened the door, only to come face-to-face with a sea of black pitch.

After he went back to his bedchamber for a candle, he illuminated his bride's maddeningly-empty chamber. "Where the devil?"

Taking up the candle, while attempting to keep his composure, Gideon set out to spend his wedding night on a bloody foolish bedtime chase for his new and decidedly-difficult non-virgin bride.

Truth to tell, the mettle it took for her to flee almost made him like her the more. It certainly added a degree of respect to his estimation of her. Frustration as well, not to mention his anticipation of rising to the challenge she presented. But he should be angry.

He was angry damn it. He was furious. Where the devil had she run off to?

If the tale of this wedding-night folly ever got out, he would be dubbed the sorriest wretch ever to indulge in sensual gratification. His reputation would, in fact, be ruined. *He* would be ruined.

After nearly an hour of searching, frustration

and vexation at an all-time high, Gideon entered the library's upper balcony on his way to the lower level for the decanter of brandy.

If he ever got his hands on his fugitive bride, he swore that he would not be held accountable for his actions.

# Five

Gideon had no sooner entered the library's wraparound balcony, than he caught sight of Sabrina in the main library below. Her exotic beauty, enhanced by the moon's soft glow, stole his anger as well as his breath.

His bride was extraordinary, and Gideon could do nothing for the moment but drink in the sight of her.

She stood in full profile before a tall bow window, the moonlight flowing through its mullioned panes casting a carpet of bright blocks on the floor at her feet. The same light revealed, in shadowed profile, through her lace and gossamer night rail, the shape of her, heavy with child, her breasts, large and full, her legs long, slim, and shapely.

The almost quixotic sight of her, every layer of defense peeled away, nearly stopped Gideon's heart. Afraid even to breathe, lest she become aware of his presence, Gideon willed himself to remain still and silent, so as to continue his clandestine observation.

He had yesterday, and earlier, seen her hair, twisted and plaited, arranged to be flattering and beautiful. But the silken mane of sable that he beheld at this moment, in its full radiant glory, cascading in magnificent splendor well past her waist, appeared long and lush enough to blanket them both through the night.

Her features in profile were no less exquisite.

Recognition again swamped him, much as it had the first time he saw her, as if they were connected in some fantastical way.

Never with another living soul had Gideon experienced such a heart-stopping awareness. And seeing her unguarded beauty, now, for the first time, he found himself doubly awed.

She had vowed to withhold her heart, and he respected that. He might have promised the same, for he had none. But for all his mystery bride's bravado, he could not help wonder—

She gasped, straightened, and placed her hands to the small of her back, and as if her sudden physical pain combined with some hidden desolation inside her, she sobbed.

Gideon's unprecedented flight down the carved circular stairs revealed his presence in no small way. "Are you in pain?"

In turn startled and astonished, Sabrina reacted as if he were on the attack, as if she could not comprehend his presence.

When he stopped before her, her emerald eyes wide in dismay, she held a hand to her throat, looking for all the world as if she were prepared to die.

"Are you in pain?" he asked again.

"No. Yes, my back. It aches sometimes, which is n— Which is, I am told, normal for a woman this far along. It is nothing for which to become alarmed."

With the intention of easing the ache at the base

of her spine, Gideon made to place his arms about her, but his bride reared back, as if he might do her harm. "No," she said. "Do not."

Fighting a welling of anger, Gideon willed himself to still and school his features. "You are my wife," he bit out.

Her eyes filled but she blinked the moisture quickly away. She caught her lips in her teeth to keep them from trembling, he perceived, and despite all that, she raised her chin. "Our bargain," she said. "I apologize. I forgot."

"Well, I have not," he said louder than he should. "I will not, by God, forget such a scurrilous wedding pact any day soon. If you cannot so easily afford me the courtesy due a husband, then please remember, Madam, that purchasers have rights too."

His bride paled, nearly undoing him, shaming him. Except that he, Gideon righteously reminded himself, had nothing for which to be ashamed.

She alone had planned dishonesty . . . and . . . well, so had he, he supposed, now that he thought on it, for a time at least. But— "We find ourselves on common ground," he said. "With a bargain between us. If you keep to your portion of it, then I promise I shall keep to mine. Will you?"

His reluctant bride released her breath, her color returned, and she nodded.

"Very well," Gideon said, releasing his own breath.

He attempted again to place his arms around her and, finally, without her recoil, he slipped his hands beneath the silken fall of her hair to knead her lower back.

The sound she made, of regret or relief, or even,

God help him, of pleasure, did not help him forget that this was his wedding night.

"Place your hands on my shoulders," Gideon said, his voice soft enough to soothe her and firm enough to assure her compliance. "I seek only to ease your pain, nothing more."

Their gazes held as she complied.

Her abdomen, huge, taut, hard, pushed against him as his fingers worked the small of her back.

His stroking eased her to such a degree that her frightened look vanished, as did the furrows upon her brow and the panic in her eyes.

Sabrina closed her eyes, floating of a sudden in some strange netherworld, thinking she must be dreaming, wishing, if she were, that the dream might never end. This man, more handsome than her imagination, in black brocade dressing gown and leather slippers, with his thick, dark waving hair and long, sooty-black lashes, could not possibly be her husband.

Her nemesis, more like. Her judgment.

When she opened her eyes, however, the devil remained, though the crinkles at the outer corners of his eyes, not quite a smile, neither quite a sneer, altered his angular features to reflect . . . concern?

That enigmatic look engendered hope in Sabrina's tired breast. Almost too much to be borne and then lost, and yet the unlikely possibility of his caring warmed her just the same.

Comprehending that her bridegroom did not intend to beat her for her mad dash from their marriage bed, her apprehension slipped slowly away, leaving Sabrina relieved but shaken.

"I suspect your little one could become a pugilist of some renown, judging by his efforts to dislodge me at this moment," her bridegroom said without lessening the pressure of his stroking, perhaps even deepening it.

Reminded of her babe's antics, Sabrina relaxed to the degree that she smiled, surprised to find herself capable.

"Perhaps I should step back and allow him his way?" he suggested.

Disappointment filled Sabrina at the thought of relinquishing her new husband's surprisingly gentle attention, to the degree that self-disgust filled her. How could she allow herself to become such an easy mark? Scoundrels of this caliber captivated women in such a way all the time. And this one, it appeared, was more practiced in seduction than most.

In self-protection, Sabrina stepped from his reach. "My child shall have to learn that he cannot always have life as he would. He shall have to compromise and settle for less than he might wish, as we all do, your grace."

He took her reminder of their bargain as she expected, as if she had slapped him. His brow darkened to an anger as dark as his day's growth of beard, though he bit down on his rage, if she did not miss her guess, for a tic worked vigorously in his cheek.

Uneasiness and exhaustion, combined with the weight of her burden, all mingled to betray Sabrina in that moment, and her knees buckled beneath her.

Gideon caught and lifted her in his arms, distress once again creasing his brow. "I should not have kept you standing for so long." He searched her face, for what she did not know, and carried her to the settee.

He lay her upon it, easing her to her side and lowered himself to lie facing her.

Her shock at this scene, so closely resembling any number of foolish girlhood fancies, set up a trembling within her. Their bodies fit together like two halves of a whole. Their lips, scant inches apart, would meet if one or the other of them moved so much as an inch.

This lying so close, in so small a confinement, in so public yet unlikely a place, where anyone could come upon them, must be considered indecent, Sabrina reflected. Except that they were husband and wife.

What should she do? How should she act?

Her husband gathered her hair and lay it across them. Then he placed his arm behind her to continue his undulating motion, widening his span to knead her upper back and shoulders, to the base of her spine and beyond.

Sabrina gave up trying to make decisions and simply absorbed his touch, her senses heightened, her limbs growing heavy and weak. She dared to place her hand against his chest near the V of his dressing gown, noticing that he caught his breath when she did.

Gideon had not expected his bride to make such a bold move; neither had he expected her to beg for his kiss. Did she even realize she was doing it? Could she know how invitingly parted were her lips?

In a moment, he would know.

He parted his own, fitting them to the invitation

of hers, discovering a treasure of cool silk and warm, welcoming woman.

As the kiss went on, he continued stroking her back, with some force now, pulling her closer against him, as close as could be given her current condition.

Gideon realized that the cadence of his touch had turned sensual, in the way he stroked her to her bottom, along the side of her breast, and in his arousal, hard against her, and he wondered at her thoughts. "What are you feeling and thinking right now?" he asked.

"I—I think we should go upstairs," she said.

"Yes," Gideon said. "Let us go up to bed."

That was not what she meant, Sabrina thought, almost frantic as he lifted her off the settee and carried her up the library stairs.

But when he left her at her bedchamber door, for the second time that night, relief filled her and she bid him a good night.

Back in her bedchamber, she nearly fainted with relief, then she saw herself in her mirror. If not for the antics of her child, she could almost imagine herself a new bride, so innocent did she appear— from her breasts up at least.

Still, the lacy confection seemed almost too dangerous a temptation, as if she were inviting trouble just by wearing it. "I have got to get out of this gown," she said.

"By all means do," said her bridegroom, framed by a portal previously unseen by her, cut in the wall as it was. So much steely intent brightened his hunter's eyes as to rob Sabrina of breath before he was even close enough to reach for her.

And when he did reach, to unfasten the silken

frogs at her bodice, she allowed that he must hear her heart pounding in the same way she could hear it echo inside her head.

"Do you feel better?" he asked.

"Much, thank you."

Her bodice scandalously undone, her breasts nearly spilling free, he took her hand and sat her at her dressing table.

Regarding him in her mirror as he stood behind her, Sabrina shook her head, not certain what he wanted but sure she must say no, and he nodded, just to be contrary, she thought, judging by the dubious twinkle in his piercing eyes. "Relax," he said, anticipation deepening the dimples in his cheeks and chin and darkening his eyes to midnight.

He combed his fingers through her hair. "Silk enough to cover us both," he said almost in reverence. "Had I known about this last night, I fear yon door would not have remained sealed."

Sabrina knew then just how much trouble she was in, for he had but stroked her hair and her weak body shuddered.

"Tell me how you feel, Sabrina."

Did he honestly care? She knew of only one way to find out. "Nervous," she said, licking her lips and waiting for him to turn on her, but he did not. Dare she reveal the whole? Though he did not know of her concern, his open countenance invited her to do so.

"And frightened," she added.

"Good God." He sat beside her, facing her, his back to the mirror, took her hand, and examined her face. "You tremble. In fear of *me*?"

And why should that surprise him? She turned away.

"Look at me."

She tried, but her gaze dropped to their clasped hands instead.

With a gentle finger, he tilted her chin upward and looked into her eyes in such a way as to suggest he could read her emotions there.

Thank God he could not.

"Need I remind you that you ran from me." He raised a brow. "On our wedding night, and no evil has befallen you at my hand."

"Not yet," she said.

Gideon cocked a brow. "There will be no reprisals," he said. "My word on it. It is finished. Now tell me what else frightens you."

"That . . . pleasing you . . . might . . . harm my child." And cost me a piece of myself, she did not say.

"But I promised I would not penetrate."

An inferno consumed her at his bold words. "But you said there were other ways," she all but cried. "And I—"

Her agitated husband rose to pace.

She stood to plead with him but stopped when she saw his thunderous expression.

"Do not recoil from me," he snapped.

"I cannot help myself. You look furious."

"I am, damn it, but not at you. My fury is directed toward the man who frightened you."

Sabrina looked away, ashamed of cowering.

Gideon walked her back to her dressing table, sat with her, and took up her brush to run it through her hair. "You do not need to look at me right now if you had rather not," he said. "But you do need to listen. I have never hurt a woman in my life, and not for lack of opportunity."

"An understatement, I think."

He nodded at her reflection in the mirror, but no pride laced his look, only fact, plainly stated. "When you and I climb into that bed, which we *will* do . . ." He sighed and faced her. "When we are intimate and you want me to stop—whatever I am doing,—beginning now and until the moment death parts us, you must simply say 'stop,' and I will do so. Do you understand me?"

"You do not even want me. Why are you being . . . kind?"

"I can see that I will need a great deal of time to prove my humanity to you, but I take courage in the fact that it is not just me who frightens you. It is any man, is it not?"

"Except Hawksworth."

Her husband sighed. "Ah, yes. Hawksworth." He slapped his knees with the flat of his hands and stood. "And on that sobering note, I will take my bride to our marriage bed."

Why sobering? Sabrina wondered. Was her husband jealous of a dead man? Oddly, the notion calmed her as nothing else had since the ceremony. That sign of insecurity in him was more a proof of humanity to her than kindness, for the latter could be falsified, the former, no proud man would own. And this man was prouder than most.

When Sabrina had settled herself against her pillows, however, her husband remained standing, there, at the side of the bed, as if he were waiting for something in particular.

Sabrina sat up. "Your grace?"

"I expected you to remove your gown."

"Not in this condition, I will not."

Her husband sighed, disappointed, she thought,

and unfastened his splendid black dressing gown, beneath which he wore nothing but the skin God gave him.

Sabrina squeaked and turned her face to her pillow.

The sound he made was something of a strangled chuckle. "Scoot over a bit," he said.

She did, appalled that her naked husband wanted to share her bed at all, never mind climb onto her side of it, when he had an entire side of his own to occupy.

He settled in behind her nevertheless. Close. Too close. Did the bed seem smaller suddenly? The covers warmer?

Skin, she felt along her legs. His legs, hairy, hard, abrading and . . . incredible, slid against her own. Sabrina assured herself that she did not warm to the sensation, not even a little.

Her rogue of a husband found the hem of her gown, lifted it, and stroked her ankle, the underside of a knee, the inside of a thigh, his insolent hand moving too quickly, yet too slowly to be borne.

She trembled, she shivered, then suddenly he was stroking her big naked belly and Sabrina groaned in mortification, but in relief also. He had not touched her where she expected and she was grateful, though a strange lethargy assaulted her at his simple touch of her belly, bringing a heaviness to her limbs and breasts.

She wanted somehow to stop him, but she could not.

The bed, which had not seemed empty on nights previous, seemed now to be filled properly, with the wicked-as-sin Duke of Stanthorpe wrapped warm and snug around her.

Sin notwithstanding, Sabrina found herself almost able to breathe again, for perhaps the first time since climbing into the bed.

Slowly, sensuously, as if he must know intimately every inch of her child's haven, the knave who owned her smoothed his big, impertinent hand along her girth.

With the quickening beat of his heart at her back, and his gentling whispers at her ear, he told her she was beautiful in her maternity, aglow, the most wondrous of God's creatures . . . with child.

Unable to keep herself from falling under the unrelenting spell of his practiced touch, Sabrina relaxed to the point that, several mesmerizing minutes later when he sought her embarrassingly moist center, she jumped and squeaked in surprise, protestation, or, God help her, in jubilation. Nevertheless, she grabbed his hand and brought it back to her belly.

"I will not hurt you," he whispered, his mouth at her ear, enhancing his spell. "Pleasure will not hurt you."

"It will do you no harm either," Sabrina snapped.

# Six

Men were the same the world over, Sabrina thought as she tried to ignore the—something— her clever husband stirred, there, where no man had ever touched her before, though he was not even touching her there now.

"I seek your pleasure, Sabrina, not mine."

She craned her neck to look back at the scoundrel. "Do you think I was born yesterday?"

There, that strangled chuckle again.

"Are you laughing at me?"

"Not at all," said he, all wide-eyed and feigned innocence. "I merely find myself thinking that your not having been born yesterday is a fact for which I shall remain eternally grateful."

As if to prove his words, he planted kisses at her shoulder, her collarbone. Unusually skillful kisses. And while his one hand played lower along her belly, in an oddly soothing yet agitating way, the other came around to cup her breast and finger her nipple, adjoining the separate actions with a charged filament of sizzling fire.

Liquid heat pooled inside Sabrina, there, where he might have stroked had she let him, spiraling to and from places where his hands, and other parts of him, met and sparked off complimenting portions of her.

Sabrina moved her legs, just to sense the full length of his, from thighs to arching feet, and when she did, she unwittingly opened for him and he made to take advantage.

She jumped when he touched her, crying out involuntarily, and again she brought his hand back to her belly. But in the back of her mind, Sabrina knew that she was being dishonest with herself.

She had cried out at the wonder of his touch, however fleeting.

Who was this woman living inside her skin? Sabrina asked herself. This woman who took a man to her bed and gloried in his touch, after everything. Never mind that he was her husband, that he would care for and protect her children. Who was *she?*

As if he understood her sudden need to be soothed, he gentled her as he might a skittish mare, with sweet, tender words and soft, amiable strokes, making her deliciously drowsy, yet amazingly alert at one and the same time.

Afraid to forgo some new and momentous sensation, Sabrina refused to succumb to sleep, but neither would her treacherous past allow her to succumb to exhilaration. One seemed a waste and the other a danger. And yet, she felt as if there was something of this experience she was missing, and she coveted the unknown.

"Your grace," she said, barely recognizing the soft, lazy voice as her own.

"Yes, Sabrina."

How sweet her name sounded on his gifted lips. How foolish she was becoming for reasoning so. "I have never experienced anything quite like this before."

"Never?"

Sabrina caught a suggestion of cocksure satisfaction in her new husband's hypnotic voice, and as a result, she experienced a disgraceful surge of gratification at having pleased him.

"Do you like this new experience?" he asked, his breath against her ear, warm and shivery, raising the hair on her arms and the temperature in the room.

"Is it . . . terribly wicked, do you think?"

"Terribly," he said on a nipping half-chuckle against her neck. "But did you not know that wickedness is suspended in the marriage bed?"

She sighed. "Then God must surely be a man."

A moment later, she felt rather than heard a hint of mirth in the ripple of her husband's chest at her back and in his weakening arms around her.

At another time she would challenge his ridiculous notion of suspended wickedness, but she had rather float as talk. How amazing that his hands on her skin, almost everywhere, could feel so fine.

"Shall we remove your gown?" her undeniable rogue of a seducer asked in such a way as to insure compliance, the last traces of mirth not entirely missing yet from his voice.

"Yes," she said, knowing herself for a weakling and wishing she cared.

Her night rail was gone before she quite understood the forfeit. But her bridegroom had been right; every touch felt better, richer, tighter, skin to silken skin. Then his mouth covered her breast, pulling pleasure from her deepest recesses in undulating waves of pure sensation. Touching her in such a way, and in such places, as to make her arch and reach in an anxiety of expectation, and yet she could not bring herself to open for him.

She would not make that mistake again.

When she found herself turned toward him, and his shaft hard against her thigh, rigid and prodding, sparked a memory, an old and frightening discomfort, Sabrina whimpered and pushed at that invasive portion of his anatomy.

"Yes," he gasped at the accidental stroke of her hand, the single word bearing a plea, hoarse and urgent, but not harsh or demanding, as she would have expected. And the very absence of threat helped her to recall his promise, which she grasped like a lifeline as she called him on it. "Gideon, stop."

Gideon stopped—breathing nearly—though his heart pounded fit to burst, as if he had run up against a door of steel, his body screaming for denied release.

He pulled his arm from around his trembling wife and fell back against his pillows, perplexed and aghast.

Embarrassed at his prominent arousal, he raised a knee, as if he could hide that throbbing evidence, and rested his arm along his brow. Closing his eyes, he waited for his breathing to catch up with his pumping heart.

He felt a dip in the bed as his bride moved beside him. He felt her breath against his arm, sensed her concern.

"Your grace?" she queried. "Are you unwell?"

Almost warily, Gideon opened his eyes, and met the bright green gaze of his tremulous bride. A single droplet of true remorse hung suspended from one long sable lash.

Gideon released his breath on a last fading glimmer of hope, bowing to another inevitable night of discomfort. " 'Tis nothing a romp to the finish would not cure," he said, but he knew better than to expect it.

"Oh." His untouched bride took her full bottom lip between perfect, white teeth.

Gideon groaned inwardly as he watched, while he contemplated soothing the poor beleaguered lip by sacrificing his own for her nibbling pleasure. But he contented himself with gently prodding the abused lip free with his index finger. "Do not. You will hurt yourself."

She bit down on his finger, tugged it playfully, and a shaft of white-hot lightning shot straight to his groin. Startled by the unexpected jolt, Gideon winced and moaned as if he had been struck.

"Your grace?" Sabrina's face became a study in naive disquiet.

What spell had this frustrating mix of seductress and saint cast upon him that she could leave him in such terrible shape, hard and needy as all hell. And instead of getting upset at a teasing bride who halted him at the worst possible moment, he wanted to smile just for looking at her.

"Do you worry about me?" he asked, amazed that he could think as much.

Sabrina nodded, all wide, exotic eyes, and needy in her own right, except that he could not put his finger on her need exactly. He could not name or imagine it. But he sensed its existence keenly.

Twirling one of her thick raven curls around his finger, his hand hovering above her breast, just inches away, Gideon enjoyed the silken warmth of it, even as he was engulfed by a strong wave of serene possession. "Why did you stop me?"

For a minute, Sabrina seemed to consider her answer. From the multitude and diversity of expressions that marched across her rich, perfect features, he imagined her reaching a conclusion, then pondering a choice somewhere between fabrication and truth.

Finally, she nodded. "I was testing you."

Gideon could only gape and wonder what the devil he had gotten himself into. Then all thought fled when his bride leaned toward him, as if she would confide a secret, and the blanket fell from her breasts. Heavy with milk and ripe for suckling, her tantalizing nipples, with their dusky aureoles, stood proud and mouth-watering.

"Good God, woman," he said, salivating at the sight while heat pooled in his loins. "Forgive me for saying so, but I have this sudden and horrific fear that you will test me to my dying day."

In self-preservation, he covered the enchantress up to her neck.

Wide-eyed with understanding, she grasped the blanket tight against herself.

"Did I frighten you badly?" He had to know.

The innocent siren licked her lips. "Almost."

Gideon barked a laugh. "Almost, by God. Did I, at least, pass your test?"

A shrug, a nod, and a sidelong glance toward the location of his incessant throbbing. "I guess."

"God's teeth, woman. If you have another trial in mind, give it to me now, or watch me perish in a blaze of nervous anxiety."

The sound she made was nearly a giggle, or a

gurgle, he supposed he should say, and still she stared at his burgeoning erection. "Staring will only make it worse, Sabrina."

"Can I do anything to make it less . . . inconvenient? It seems to be getting huge."

"Why, thank you, sweetheart. And yes. Touching it would help."

Damned if she did not reach right out—and pull as swiftly back. "I am sorry. But I . . . cannot."

Gideon released his breath. 'Twas probably for the best that she did not touch him, for if she did, he would burst into flame and embarrass them both. Simple as that. Just the idea drove him about as close to the edge as a man could get.

"Come here," he said, and when she complied, innocent that she was, he settled her on her side in front of him spoon-style. "If you can ignore the 'inconvenience' for a while, we can just settle down to sleep. Comfortable?"

She nodded. He liked that she was using one of his arms for a pillow. His other he rested against her belly, where her little one seemed totally unwilling to settle in to rest.

Despite his hard discomfort, contentment stole over Gideon in slow, soothing measure, while the old emptiness that had long been his companion seemed somehow to be missing from the softening mist of drifting night-shadows.

He thought he just might be able to sleep then, until his bride did something wondrous. She turned in his arms, reached over, and curled her hand around him.

Gideon sucked in his breath and moved involuntarily within the glove of her grasp. "God's teeth, Bree, you try me to my limits."

"Is that bad?"

"Bad can be good. Much too good." He tried to pull away, but she would not allow it. Since coming was a near thing, Gideon stopped struggling, wondering how a woman about to deliver a child could be such an innocent at one and the same time.

She began to move her hand along his length and he could barely breathe, so incredible did her touch transform him. "What . . . ?" He shuddered. "What are you . . . planning to do?" he bit out, determined not to embarrass himself with the release he craved.

"I think . . . I *might* be ready now to . . . do what you started."

"The devil you say? All of it?"

Like a hot poker, she let him go. "All of what?" Suspicion. Dread.

"I think you do not really wish to do this," Gideon said, fighting disappointment.

"Why do I not?" Sabrina asked, snuggling against him, relaxing, and taking him into her hand again.

Sweet, sweet torture.

"Could we not continue?" she asked.

"Like this, you mean?" He could not keep from nudging her blanket away and taking her nipple into his mouth once more.

She gasped and she sighed, and her legs shifted and stirred, as if she were seeking . . .

In answer to the need she failed to recognize, Gideon again tried to touch her, there, at her core, but, again, she would not have it, would not open for him.

She must have been frightened once, badly. Perhaps more than once. In that case, there was only one way to go about this seduction business—from the beginning.

After that, he touched her everywhere—almost. Never at her center, but nearly there. When finally she allowed him to cup her—legs still closed tight against him—she sighed and relaxed. And he thought perhaps she floated at least.

She sought his chiseled mouth with her own.

Amazed at her boldness, Gideon complied and gave her his. He took command of the kiss, and to his shock and delight, she allowed him to use his tongue in such a way as to mimic the act he most wanted to perform.

She used him as her anchor then, her grip like a vise, a tourniquet, until he lost all feeling in his ill-used shaft. But never one to shy away from a challenge, Gideon became resolved to bestow a lightness of pleasure upon her, while denying his own need, and oddly enough, he barely minded at all.

"I could make you fly," he whispered when he sensed that she craved but fought his final touch with equal panic. "Let go, sweetheart. Open for me," he kept asking, but she would not.

Instead, she kissed him again.

"Let me touch you," Gideon whispered at her ear a few minutes later.

"I cannot. I cannot. Do not make me," she cried, but she did not let him go or push him away. Indeed, she seemed for all the world as if she were trying to climb inside his skin.

Even as he cupped her and allowed her to move against his hand, Gideon got as close as she seemed to want him. "You are a fine and beautiful woman, Sabrina—a wife, my wife—exquisite, precious. And

I am the man destined to deliver you to a new and wondrous place. A place you have never journeyed, never imagined. Come with me to a summit higher than the clouds, and all the way to the stars."

"I cannot," she whispered.

Gideon let her set the pace, then, a gentle touch for a gentle rise. He would not ask her again, not this night.

Somehow, she must have sensed his surrender, for she seemed to relax and float, slowly, and more slowly, and he saw her smile just before she slipped into sleep.

And Gideon was left speechless, battered of pride, and hard as a pikestaff.

Minutes, or hours, later, Sabrina moaned and turned on her side, and Gideon woke.

She must be uncomfortable with such a burden to carry, he thought. Yet this might be her best night's sleep in months, despite the fact that ultimate satisfaction had escaped her . . . escaped them both, he could not seem to forget.

Imagine getting himself a pregnant, yet innocent, bride.

Imagine him failing to satisfy her.

Imagine waking on the day after his wedding with his marriage yet to be consummated.

Gideon groaned. His ego could not take much more of Sabrina St. Goddard. "Till death do them part" be damned. Being married to this woman would surely kill him.

Why, then, did being married to her give him no end of satisfaction? A puzzle as intricate as Sabrina herself.

As enticing.

As exasperating.

Already, he ached to stroke her again, to bring her back into his arms, but he would forgo that pleasure to allow her sleep. With her burden, comfort in sleep must be difficult enough to attain without him disallowing her rest at his whim.

Even he was not so selfish as that. Not quite.

Gideon turned on his side to resettle himself . . . and came face-to-face with . . . a child?

"What?" He sat up and regarded the location by the bed where the boy had just stood, but it lay in shadows, empty and undisturbed.

While he tried to decide if he had been asleep or awake, seen or imagined a child, he heard the squeal of a door hinge, and then silence.

Could one of the servants' children be sleepwalking? He would inquire in the morning as to which child might have taken to wandering.

Ignoring his state of semi-arousal, yet absurdly content with his previous day's work, considering the abysmal failure of his wedding night, Gideon curled himself around his bride and drifted back into sleep.


Sabrina awoke disoriented, surprised to find herself pinned to the mattress, and sought to identify her ravager.

Ah, yes, 'twas the penniless wanderer who had charmed her—until she realized she had married him. The rogue who talked her out of her night rail and seduced his way into her bed. Yon dragon with his prodding staff tucked against her backside even now—the staff, she discovered to her surprise, that was harmless after all.

Such a slow, sweet warmth had built inside her at his tender touch, she had thought she might burst into flame, almost hoped she would. But she did not. Instead, she simmered until the contented heaviness of half-sleep beckoned. She remembered smiling when she realized she was drifting, wrapped in her new husband's gentle arms.

For the first time in a marriage bed, she had reveled in the gentleness of a husband.

Peace had claimed her then, as it did now in memory. And because she understood already that Gideon St. Goddard just might be that rarest of creatures, a good and gentle man, Sabrina almost wanted to give him what he sought. Almost.

When she considered the price—herself—she decided that consummation would have to wait. Perhaps forever.

She supposed she might someday trust him enough to give herself to him, body and heart, free and clear, but she knew he would have to earn it first. And in this case, earning was a state of mind— hers. Even she did not quite understand the proof she sought. She simply knew that she would recognize it when she found it.

She wondered, then, about their life, what a future with this puzzling man might possibly hold.

Gideon St. Goddard, Duke of Stanthorpe, her husband—sweet one minute, tart the next, first hot, then cold. He had frightened her witless and stirred her senses . . . and they had only just met the day before.

Tonight, she had drifted to sleep, naked and content in his arms . . . and left him wanting.

She would never be able to look him in the eye again.

# Seven

"Mama? Are you sleeping?"

Sabrina sat up, clutching her blankets to cover herself. "Damon?" she whispered frantically. "What are you doing here?"

"It is Rafferty, Mama. Damon is still sleeping, but I cannot, because I am thirsty."

"Where is Miss Minchip? Why did you not ask her for a drink of water?"

"She is snoring so loud, she cannot hear me. I think her ears are too old," he whispered, all serious concern. "She does not hear very good."

Sabrina smiled at her son's observation. "Go back to the nursery, Sweet, and Mama will be right up."

"But that man, he—"

"Go, Sweet, I will be up right behind you. Move now."

She should have realized right away, if he was quiet, he was Rafe. Damon would have climbed into bed with her and spoken afterward, and he would not have whispered.

She told the twins, of course, that they could no longer come to her during the night, that they would have to see how this man would deal with two noisy little boys.

But how could two four-year-olds who had already faced the devil in their short lives understand the appearance of what they must perceive as another fiend, after the first had frightened them senseless?

Sabrina slipped from her marriage bed, somewhat sorry to be leaving her new husband's embrace, a circumstance she would not have thought possible a short twenty-four hours before.

She groped for her night rail, found it, and slipped it over her head. Two nights before, she had gone to sleep foolishly wishing that the penniless wanderer and the Duke of Stanthorpe were one and the same, and now that she discovered they were, or, rather, he was, she was not certain how she felt.

Somehow, Stanthorpe had seemed safer as a figment of her imagination than as a flesh-and-blood man with wants and needs of his own.

When she had discovered his perfidy, in company with the others at her wedding, she had experienced relief, gladness, annoyance, any number of new and strange emotions. But right now, she was too comfortably lethargic to examine her careening feelings.

Besides, she had best see to the twins before they instigated a midnight insurrection fit to wake the dead, thereby revealing to her new husband just how large a family he had taken on.

Shivering at the very thought, Sabrina tied her serviceable wrapper over her burgeoning middle. She cut through her dressing room and slipped out the servants' access into the hall. Then she stole through the house like a thief in the night.

She should have told Gideon about the twins already, she supposed, as she made her way up the servants' stairs toward the third-floor nursery. And, she supposed, she should tell him sooner, rather than later, before he discovered their existence on his own. Horrifying thought.

But perhaps she was worrying uselessly, for he seemed sincerely to like children. Had he not become his niece's galloping pony, a steed so spirited he had knocked his rider's curls askew?

But had he not also suggested that she should discover whether her intended even liked children? Did he mean the words as a warning? If so, would he not have cried off at the mere sight of her impending motherhood?

Her maternity had certainly not deterred him in their bed earlier tonight. Not at all. Her very condition seemed actually to . . . stimulate him.

Then again, a quiet expectancy and an unquiet pair of striplings were entirely different kettles of fish.

Sabrina heard the twins' laughter before she stepped into their bedchamber off the nursery, where, she just now realized, Gideon must once have played.

A pillow hit her in the face as she entered their cozy room. And her sons' giggles escalated.

As she approached in the darkness, something dropped down before her, and Sabrina sat on the bed rather than fall on her face. "Damon Whitcomb!"

A gratified giggle.

"I did nothing. Those were Rafferty's legs com-

ing down before you. *He* is the drawbridge. I am
only the toll booth."

Sabrina grinned. "Do you really want a drink of
water, Rafe? Or just someone to play with?"

"He woke me up," Damon accused.

"I did not."

"Did so."

"Jinglebrains."

"Paperskull."

Sabrina shook her head, lit a lamp, and poured
them each half a glass of water from the pitcher
high atop a nursery shelf. And like centuries of
male travelers at every village inn the world over,
her men guzzled their drinks to a lusty beat, until
both empty glasses were handed back with corre-
sponding thanks and sighs of relief.

She ruffled one dark, curly head, then the other.

Damon stood the taller of the two, and the
broader, by as little as only a mother would note.

Rafferty bore a wiry whip-strength that Damon
lacked, but you would have to hold them each in
your arms to discern the trifling difference.

"Ready to go back to sleep," she asked when one
of them yawned.

Damon climbed on his miniature bed to stand
face-to-face with her and reached out to stroke her
cheek with his little hand. "Are you all right,
Mama? That man did not hurt you, did he?"

"If he did, we would protect you," Rafe said,
climbing up beside his twin.

"As I would protect you," Sabrina returned,
pushing them down one by one to land with a giggling bounce. Then she lay between them, both
boys snuggling in.

She hugged them close and kissed each precious

head, thinking she must like them best scrubbed clean and in their flannel nightshirts, all warm, soft, and open to a mother's love.

"I would scale a mountain to protect you," she said, beginning the game they had played, once upon a time, to comfort each other when they had all rather have cried.

"I would climb the highest mountain to protect *you,*" Rafferty said.

Sabrina kissed his nose. "I would sail the seven seas."

"I would sail the biggest sea," Damon said.

"The coldest," Rafe countered.

"The deepest." A yawn.

"Stormiest."

In minutes, they were quiet, and Sabrina relished their deep and even breathing and their small hearts beating against her.

For nearly four years, these two amazing gifts, these identical miracles, had given her strength and purpose and a reason for living. As they would in the days and years ahead, and she would let nothing, and no one, harm them.

"I would catch me a dragon to protect you," Sabrina whispered. "And hide you in his cave."


The dragon rose at dawn, aroused and hungry for more than food; it was easy to see, as he stood in glorious relief, stretching his most amazing body.

That was when Sabrina realized what a challenge would be this peer of the realm, this fine-sculpted Corinthian who claimed her bed and shivered her spine.

As if the mythical beast sensed her watching, he

turned and looked right at her, his obsidian eyes direct and probing, pleased, if she did not miss her guess, at the shiny new bauble he had bought for his bed.

With a grin, he approached the four-poster. And with a squeak, Sabrina launched herself up and out of it, in as ungainly a manner as she could manage, given the fact that her burden seemed actually to have dropped during the night.

Her dragon's expression went from fire to ice in a blink as he leapt.

Sabrina reared back and cowered.

Gideon caught and braced her. "Are you all right?"

Embarrassed at her fear, Sabrina silently chided herself. "Of course I am all right," she snapped. "Why would I not be?"

"One minute I thought you might fall, and the next, I could swear that you were afraid I would strike you."

Sabrina raised her chin, but she could think of nothing to say.

"You *have* been struck in the past, have you not?"

He was pressing a point she had rather perish than reveal. "My past is not your business."

A shutter seemed to descend over his expression. His eyes, his very aspect, shut down. "Correct," said the suddenly haughty Duke of Stanthorpe, all regal splendor, arrogant condescension, and hard-eyed fury.

He let her go. "I have purchased you for the present and for the future. And a tidy price I paid."

In silence, he strode toward his own bedchamber, controlled anger in every step. At the door, he turned. "You will meet me in the breakfast room in one hour, precisely. Good morning to you, Madam."

The door between their rooms closed tight.

So, too, did Sabrina's hope.

"A child, your grace?"

Typical for Bilbury. A question for a question. "Yes, man, who of the servants has a child?" Gideon asked for the second time in as many minutes.

"Why, none that I know of. Would you like the bottle-green, the celestial-blue, or the Devonshire-brown frock coat this morning?"

"The blue. Does a close neighbor have a child, then?" Gideon asked as Bilbury helped him on with the coat and smoothed the shoulders.

"I wonder, your grace, if you saw this childlike apparition late last night, after, say, a brandy or three, when you were half in your cups? Or in the early morning, when you were still sleeping?"

"Damn it man, are you saying that I imagined the child?"

"Actually . . ." Bilbury placed a sapphire stick-pin in Gideon's mathematical-styled neckcloth. "If there was a lad, he might be a chimney sweep turned to burglary."

"That, at least, is a sane explanation. Thank you, Bilbury. That will be all."

After his valet left, Gideon checked his pocket watch to see how long he must cool his heels until meeting Sabrina. Seventeen minutes. She had better be on time.

He snapped the watch shut.

But when he arrived in the breakfast room, he

found no breakfast, no wife, but his servants were all shivering in their shoes.

Someone had entered the library during the night and had searched desks, knocked books off shelves, and taken paintings from walls.

"Looking for a safe, no doubt," Chalmer said as Gideon stepped into the room.

"Inside the books?" he replied, raising his brows at the preposterous notion.

"Some people hide paper money and even bank drafts in books," Doggett said, though that sturdy character was trembling like a leaf in an English gale. His knowledge of money hidden in books, however, would seem to confirm Gideon's belief that he might have survived as a rookery cutpurse, or some such, in his former life. Except that his certain fear also seemed to negate same.

"Searching the library makes no sense," Gideon said. "Would a robber not search bedrooms for jewels or the long gallery for paintings?"

"Oh, none of the paintings are missing, your grace. Nothing is, actually. Everything is simply 'disturbed.'"

"As am I." Gideon took in the dishevelment of his favorite room. "I believe I shall send a note to see what the Runners have to say about this."

"Very good, your grace." Chalmer bowed and left the room.

Doggett sidled up to him. "You think the Runners are necessary, your grace?"

"Do you have another suggestion?"

"I would like to offer my services for the night watch, if I might. I have some . . . little . . . experience in these matters."

"I see."

"I would do anything for her grace. And for you, of course," he added in a rush, almost as an afterthought. "I promise to keep your home safe from any and all comers. My honor as a . . . peddler."

"You think you know who might have done this?"

"I know the type."

"Very well, Doggett. You are officially assigned the night watch."

"Thank you, your grace."

Gideon squeezed the older man's shoulder. "I am depending upon you."

Sabrina would not let emotion rule her, she vowed, not for the first time, as she lowered her awkward body into a slipper bath of warm lilac-scented water, placed before the fire in her dressing room.

She did not need romance, just a husband, a man to house her and her children, to give them a sense of belonging, of peace, and to put food in their bellies.

That Stanthorpe could control his ire stood to his credit. That she dared want more than control from the man angered her inordinately.

Her first marriage had remained turbulent, unpredictable, and grim. For the better part of her life, she had known hunger and abuse, betrayal, treachery. She remembered well the humiliation of being sold to the highest bidder, the hopelessness of being tossed in the trash.

Now she craved stability and predictability for herself and her children, and in today's world, nothing but unrestricted wealth could purchase such rare and expensive commodities. Yes, *she* had sold herself to the high bidder this time, but if anybody deserved to do the selling of her, 'twas she, thank you very much.

She did not bloody well care what his royal haughtiness thought about her decision not to share her past. That horror was hers to bury, and bury it she would, as deep as the sea if she could.

This sudden need for . . . happiness, for a man she knew nothing about, husband or not, was misplaced, foreign, totally out of character. An aberration.

Sabrina knew better than to allow her heart to become involved within marriage. The Duke of Stanthorpe might have purchased her body, but there existed no purse in all the kingdom large enough to purchase Sabrina Whit—Sabrina St. Goddard's heart.

And her husband knew it. She had already told him so.

So why could *she* not remember?

What ailed her today? How could she possibly forget such a hard-won lesson?

'Twas her own nurturing body giving her trouble, Sabrina mused as she soaped her big belly in soothing circles. Her mind and body worked unpredictably these days, and sometimes, even, independently of each other.

'Twas the babe made her feel unsettled, emotional, needy.

She suffered weakness and craved strength. Of course she would be tempted to turn to the first man to show both strength and gentleness. She had never come across the likes of Gideon St. Goddard in her life. But just because a man acted gentle in bed did not mean he would act anything like out of bed.

Regard the stodgy duke himself just this morning. Demand this and demand that, without a by-your-leave, if you please. Be there or be damned, he had all but said.

Well, be damned to him. She would *not* be there.

Sabrina dressed in her second-best black bombazine empire-style gown, wondering again why she wore mourning for a barbaric brute of a man she had wanted to murder herself more times than she cared to recall, a man she still feared somebody must have murdered.

Somebody, she also feared, whose name she knew.

A short while later, looking in on her children, she remembered the reason she wore black. She did it for them. Respectability, it was called. She would do anything to earn that for them. Even marry a doddering old man, or worse, a virile young one.

After she left the boys in Miss Minchip's able care, she took the servants' stairs to the kitchen, conferred with Cook, and set out for a walk toward Old Souls Church. There she would seek guidance from a higher authority as to how she might best deal with her mystifying rogue.

She had not waddled half a block, however, when a closed carriage pulled up beside her, and to her surprise, the door was thrown open by an unseen hand. "Come in, your grace, and rest from your burden."

The voice prickled the hair on Sabrina's arms and sent a chill down her spine. Familiar, yet not, and even as the words invited, the voice struck terror.

"Come," it coaxed. "I will convey you wherever you wish to go."

Though Sabrina was certain she must have heard the voice somewhere before, she could not seem to recall it.

And she believed she should.

Oh, she was certain she should.

# Eight

Sabrina faltered as she tried to decide whether to turn and run or peek into the dark, forbidding interior of the nondescript conveyance. But her decision was taken away by a top-of-the-trees Corinthian out for a stroll. In his many-caped greatcoat, his curly black beaver at a jaunty angle, and tipping his gold-tipped cane her way, the rogue offered her his arm.

Almost at once, the door of the mysterious carriage closed and the driver pulled the vehicle smoothly into traffic.

"Who was that?" her husband asked.

Sabrina looked down her nose at him, but she took his arm nevertheless. "Someone looking for directions, I expect."

Damned if her duke did not resemble the devil incarnate this morning, wicked as sin and elegant as ever. Amazing what a bath and a change of clothes, or clothing at all, could do for a man.

Not that he appeared a fragment less than magnificent without his clothes.

"Do we feel better after our bath?" he asked, both patronizing and annoying.

"If you mean, by we, do I?" Sabrina asked. "And

does the baby? Yes, we do. If you are asking after you and me, then I suppose you will have to answer at least part of the question yourself. Do *you* feel better, your surliness?"

His bark of laughter surprised and delighted Sabrina. She had heard it only in the dark, in bed, and supposed that any and all playfulness on his part would be kept strictly in the bedchamber.

Glad to be found wrong on that score, Sabrina smiled, relaxed, certainly for the first time since she annoyed him by refusing to share her past with him.

"For some odd reason, despite the nature of our wedding night," he said with a wink. "I feel incredibly well rested this morning. But I must admit that I find myself concerned about your missing breakfast. You are eating for two, you must remember."

"Mrs. Chalmer force-fed me toast and milk in the kitchen when I went down to approve today's menu," she said. "But thank you for your kind concern."

"Balderdash!" he said.

"Balderdash?"

"You mock an honest emotion, Sabrina. I am genuinely concerned for you. While you may not always like what I have to say, you may be certain that I will always speak in earnest."

"I see."

"I am glad to hear it. Let us then proceed to the dressmaker, shall we, and get you out of your blacks?"

Sabrina stopped walking. "In this condition? Now?"

"If you had rather go out of mourning after the baby—"

"Honestly? I had rather bury the blacks now, but I find myself weary and feeling rather exhausted, I am appalled to admit."

Sabrina had no sooner spoken than Gideon snapped his fingers and bundled her into his carriage, which must have been following at a discreet distance, for the two-block trip back to Stanthorpe Place.

Mr. Chalmer reset the breakfast room posthaste, and half the household rallied round to be certain "the little mother" consumed enough "good healthy fare" to recover herself, while Gideon relaxed and partook of the breakfast he had been too remorseful to enjoy without her.

He gave her a sidelong glance as he buttered his toast, and wondered if she realized the importance of the lessons they had taught each other today.

He had showed her that she could not run anywhere he would not find her. And he hoped she noted that he would not let his temper get the better of him, no matter how much she annoyed him.

Direct orders, she had demonstrated, like surly behavior, she as much as said, would not be tolerated or obeyed by her.

Gideon grinned as the implication sank in. As he had suspected, his bride did indeed make for a worthy opponent, in and out of bed.

Anticipation filled him at the thought.

He liked nothing better than a proper challenge, except, perhaps, winning.

"What, pray tell, do you find to amuse you?" she asked as she regarded him, perhaps a bit worried, but more than a trace smug as well.

So, she did comprehend her power, or she thought she did. Gideon gave her a grudging nod

of approval while she had the audacity to acknowl-
edge what amounted to her rebuke of his high-
handedness with a vainglorious grin.

Round two to Sabrina.

"Oh, my," Miss Minchip said.

Gideon saw that "the others" had been watching
and likely bestowed a somewhat sensual bent to
their individual translations of the silent byplay between him and his new wife.

Gideon chuckled but did not reveal the source
of his humor, even when pressed. Instead, he
sought to change the subject. "I had a remarkable
experience during the night."

Sabrina squeaked and nearly choked on her
eggs. Miss Minchip's eyes grew huge and eager, and
one of Mr. Waredraper's bushy white eyebrows rose
high enough to kiss his bald pate.

To halt speculation, Gideon held up his hand.
"You will pardon my poor word choice," he said,
winking at Miss Minchip, then fearing she might
swoon. "I awoke," he said, starting again, "and
could swear that I came face-to-face with a child, a
lad, I believe."

Doggett sat up as if he had been called to attention. "Did he have a mustache?" he asked. "Or a
gold hoop in his ear?"

Everyone's head turned swiftly in that man's direction.

"You know a child who looks like this?" Gideon
asked.

"Er . . . no, but you can never be too careful with
the silver."

"We do not keep the silver in the bedrooms. Most
people do not." Perhaps that lack in Doggett's edu-
cation was the reason he seemed not to have suc-

ceeded in his chosen profession. If thievery was his chosen profession.

"Perhaps I *should* call in the Runners," Gideon said.

Doggett blustered and cited any number of aristocrats who hid their "baubles" in as many varied and unusual places.

When his recitation ended, Gideon thanked him for the lesson, pondered from whence Doggett's knowledge had come, and turned to the others at the table. "Do any of you know who our midnight visitor might have been?"

If their previous reactions could be called "rapt," then their current expressions could only be termed "wary." Interesting, indeed.

"Who? The child, or the intruder who made that mess in the library?" Doggett asked.

"Oh, no," Sabrina said. "What happened in the library?"

"Not to worry," Gideon said. "Nothing was taken. But if one of the servants is keeping a child without my knowledge," he added, more to Sabrina and the hovering Chalmer than to his boarders, "all his mother has to do is come to me and we will discuss the matter and see that her child is properly housed and schooled. The boy should be given an opportunity to flourish, rather than stagnate."

Silence, ponderous and bleak, served as his answer. And the nature of that quiet, or disquiet, he should say, ruffled Gideon's feathers. What the deuce was going on?

"You must have been dreaming." Sabrina laughed, not sounding nearly as lighthearted as she pretended.

"Yes," Waredraper said, too eager by half. "Last night's supper gave me vile dreams too. Er . . . pardon to Mrs. Chalmer," he said, nodding toward Mr. Chalmer, who had ceased pouring Gideon's tea.

Rather than bristle, Chalmer released his breath. "Apology noted. She will not hear a word from me."

"There, that is settled," Sabrina said as she rose.

Gideon concluded his meal as well and took her arm. "Perhaps," he said, "the child made the mess in the library."

"No," said every member of his household, from his wife to his butler.

"Well, that is an end to that," he said, tongue in cheek.

What dire secret lived in his own damned house, Gideon wondered as he escorted his wife from the dining room, that kept everyone from revealing it?

Whatever it was—and he would bet fifty guineas there was a child nearby who might or might not be a thief—he had best nip this little intrigue in the bud before suspicion destroyed the foundation of his household.

What could the lot of them possibly have to keep from him anyway? And what could a child he had not even been certain existed have to do with it?

That he was being kept in the dark rankled, and Gideon bloody well wanted to know why.


Sabrina discovered that very first morning that as Stanthorpe's expeditious and unexpected bride, she had become the newest form of entertainment for London's beau monde, an experience she had rather have done without.

The gears of the gossip mill must have started grinding the moment Lady Veronica left their wedding, Sabrina mused, because all and sundry seemed to be working those gears into a powerful head of steam.

Almost the instant her first collection of morning callers arrived, they began to regard her as if she were a rare specimen under glass, or an exotic creature in a zoological exhibit.

As the unique display in question, Sabrina began to entertain an absurd image of herself roaring, or crouching—to the horrified delectation of her audience—like one of the tigers brought from India and kept on display at Exeter 'Change.

In her maternally girthed widow's weeds, however, Sabrina very much feared that she more closely resembled one of the ill-kept beasts at the Tower's Royal Menagerie. She dearly wished, now, that she had felt up to visiting the dressmaker earlier, for she might well be there still.

The one boost to her pride and confidence was Stanthorpe Place, particularly the drawing room where she received her visitors. A veritable showpiece, the room boasted twin fireplaces of topaz marble, carved cypress-wood ceilings, and six wide, full-length windows that admitted just enough illumination to spotlight its luxurious appointments.

Buttercream damask covered the walls, with the same pale yellow, robin's-egg blue, and soft fern green picked out in the upholstered furniture, cushions, and curtains. Subtle scents of beeswax and citrus freshened the air and complemented the serene atmosphere.

Bright, welcoming, and subtly beautiful, the room had already become Sabrina's favorite in the house. The first time she had seen it, she had experienced the most wonderful sense of having arrived home, safe finally.

At this moment, she reveled in the sentiment, wrapped it around herself like a mantel of spun gold and wore it with her head held high.

She needed all the help she could get.

Her guests were so much a drain on her self-confidence as to be more likened to weapons of utter destruction.

Claws bared and innuendo at the ready, refined ladies in silk and satin—vultures in disguise—tore her up one side and down the other, barely stopping long enough to collect the bloody shreds. They simpered and they smiled, wielding compliments like swords.

As each party left, Sabrina sighed in relief, but if she thought her first group of visitors concealed lethal talons, they were nothing to Lady Veronica Cartwright and her toadying train of twittering trollops.

"Congratulations, your grace," said one mawkish matron. "So you are the new Duchess of Stanthorpe. . . . Quite a rise in station, I should say. Would that we were all so fortunate." Her bristly brows rose with the last, giving her the look of a startled porker. "An heir apparent as well," she simpered, examining Sabrina's middle through her lorgnette. "You certainly know how to *procure* that which you fancy, do you not, my dear?" The woman smiled artfully and raised her teacup in salute. "No matter the rest of the world's opinion, I say, well done!"

Verbal swordplay must be a form of entertainment with the scandal-broth set, Sabrina mused, offering her tormentor more tea, wishing she could tip the pot and drench yon feathered bonnet. She thought it amazing, really, and sad, that she had imagined herself the tigress, and her guests the innocents, when all along things stood the other way round.

Lady Veronica herself acted as if upon a theater stage, an edgy desperation stiffening both manner and movement, like a marionette, clumsily worked. As if her very life depended upon the success of her performance.

Not many minutes after thinking so, Sabrina began to understand what Lady Veronica might actually be attempting.

Society must perceive her as pitiable—suddenly and publicly abandoned, as she was, by Stanthorpe. So to maintain her social rank and associated power, the poor woman needed to show the *ton* why she had been displaced, or, replaced,—please God—in Gideon's affections.

How better to prove one had not been thrown over lightly, or even willingly, than to reveal the "true" reason for one's abandonment—the imminent possibility of an heir.

Sabrina smiled knowingly and raised her chin higher. Rather than being embarrassed by her delicate condition, she wore her maternity like a medal of honor.

'Twas she, not Lady Veronica Cartwright, who bore the title Duchess of Stanthorpe. In the eyes of the world, at least, Sabrina—not the ruthless Lady Veronica—carried Stanthorpe's child.

Unfortunately, Sabrina could not shake the notion that she should not underestimate the lady. Not only had she married the man Veronica had chosen for herself, she was afraid she had made a powerful enemy in the bargain.

When the requisite time for the visit was up, Veronica and her entourage rose as one—a covey of bright, chattering birds startled into flight.

Before departing the room, however, Veronica, the head "mistress," narrowed her eyes and stepped close enough for Sabrina to detect the acrid scent of hate. "I will have Stanthorpe yet, one way or another," she promised. "He desires me, not you."

The way Veronica preened before her friends made Sabrina want, for all the world, to slap the smile from the woman's face.

"Do not forget that Stanthorpe was still bedding me," she went on, looking down her nose at Sabrina's figure, "when he put *that* in you."

"Odd you should say so." Sabrina placed a hand on her belly. "For I believe our child is proof to the contrary."

"As do I," her husband said from behind Sabrina's tormentor, turning the woman on her heel with a gasp.

"Lady Veronica mistakes the matter." Gideon regarded Sabrina. "My tastes have matured. Improved, I daresay."

He returned his gaze to his former mistress. "I now prefer sweet to . . . tart."

# Nine

Gideon stepped around his dumbstruck mistress, kissed his wife's hand, and gazed with adoration into her eyes, a move for which Sabrina would remain forever grateful.

Then he placed her hand on his arm and covered it possessively with his own. "It took no one less powerful than Napoleon Bonaparte himself to keep me from marrying Sabrina sooner."

He encompassed Veronica's intimates in his smile. "Surely you, dear and lovely ladies of the *ton,* understand the sacrifices war demands." By the time he bowed to them, he had made conquests of them all. "We shall bid you a good day." He swept Sabrina from the room.

"Chalmer," Gideon snapped as they crossed the hall. "Her grace is not 'at home' to visitors for the rest of the day—no, for the rest of the week. He examined Sabrina's face, his brow a study in concern. Amend that; she will not be receiving for a fortnight."

Sabrina smiled gratefully.

Lady Veronica Cartwright had overplayed her hand.

\* \* \*

Lady Veronica Cartwright's dislike of his wife was beginning to worry Gideon. He knew her too well not to be concerned.

They *had* been childhood friends of a sort, and he had seen her at her worst, or what he hoped was her worst. At the age of eight, he had failed to keep Veronica from strangling the life out of a baby bird whose only crime had been falling from its nest and landing in her lap.

As an adult, he had fooled himself into thinking she had outgrown her ghastly childhood antics. He told himself she had changed and proceeded to use her body as she used his.

In retrospect, Gideon was ashamed of his ongoing liaison with the viper. He hated to admit, even to himself, that keeping her as his mistress had satisfied him, because he could bed her one minute and walk away without looking back the next.

He had, God help him, reveled in the disconnectedness of their alliance.

As he escorted Sabrina up the stairs for a rest after Veronica's fateful visit, he berated himself for having placed his wife in danger by virtue of association. Veronica must be declawed, he knew, so that he and Sabrina could get on with their lives.

"Here we go," he said, accompanying Sabrina into her bedchamber. "Let me help you out of your dress."

Sabrina laughed. "Do you never stop trying?"

Gideon grinned. "Never."

"I suppose I should take that as fair warning." She drew her hair over her shoulder and turned to present him with the row of buttons down her back.

Gideon regarded this woman, who had caught

his imagination the first moment he saw her, as something of a gift to unwrap. And like an excited child at Christmas, he hardly knew where to begin.

In fact, he did not begin. He stepped close behind, put his arms around her, and rested the flat of his hands upon the haven of her child. What would life be like, he wondered, if this were his child too?

But he could not imagine it. Not yet, at any rate.

"How is he?" Gideon spoke softly at Sabrina's ear.

She lay her head back against his shoulder and closed her eyes. "He is sleeping now. He performs only during the night."

"Performs?"

"Acrobatics, jigs, reels . . ."

"Then this should be a good time for you to catch up on your sleep. I will undo your buttons quickly, shall I, before he wakes?"

"Yes, please."

Gideon especially admired her beauty as she lay back against her pillows, wearing nothing but her shift. He sat on the bed beside her and took her small hand in his, liking the notion that together they alone belonged to this intimate moment.

He supposed that he simply liked her attention, however and whenever he could get it. He had wanted her from the first after all.

Never having had an opportunity previous to this to examine his bride at his leisure, Gideon feasted to his heart's content.

He found her flawless and marveled at the richness of her beauty. Exotic eyes, green as an island sea and just as deep. Lips, full and pouting, exceptionally kissable.

But what Gideon decided intrigued him most about this new wife of his was the sparse dusting of wayward freckles that danced beneath her eyes and across the top of her nose. With his fingertip, he skimmed each beauty mark, as if connecting them one to the other.

Without them, she would seem altogether too perfect, untouchable. Imperfect as she was, she presented a surprising blend of porcelain doll and flesh-and-blood woman, vibrant and alive.

Allure and vulnerability, all in one package.

Gideon wanted to touch . . . and more.

"You make me want to pull the blanket up over my head," she said.

Gideon shook his head at her cryptic comment. "Do I, by God? And why would you want to do that?"

"To save you from having to look at me."

"From having to?" He knuckled the crest of a breast, at the edge of her shift. "My darling wife, no one, not even you, could stop me from feasting on your beauty."

Her laugh reminded him of a songbird that brings joy to all who hear it. "Does that kind of talk work on your other women?"

Gideon wrapped himself in dignity. "Excuse me?"

"Ah, the haughty duke returns."

All his life, his aristocratic arrogance had served to put people in their proper places. And now, behold his bride, happily oblivious to his awesome presence.

Gideon released an exasperated breath. "Let us set your mind at ease concerning my . . . er . . . other women, shall we?"

"Oh, yes. Let us, please."

Gideon raised a brow but refused to respond to her caustic gauntlet. "I have employed—one at a time, mind—several mistresses over the years—"

"How many is several?"

Gideon raised a brow. "Five."

Sabrina nodded. "A good conservative number," she said. "I approve. Go on."

Gideon coughed and cleared his throat. "As it happens, I dismissed my latest, and my last, in your presence, after our wedding yesterday. Unfortunate timing, that. Again, I apologize."

"You are forgiven. Did I not say so then?"

He quirked a brow, and his bride closed her mouth and schooled her features.

Gideon kissed her hand and held her gaze. "I am now devoted to one woman—you. And I shall keep only unto you till death parts us."

Gideon watched keenly for his bride's reaction to his vow, but he perceived nothing in her demeanor to reveal that she had heard him. "You doubt me." It was a statement, not a question, and the only possible reason for her lack of response.

"I doubt . . . me," she said after a moment, and he suspected she was being as honest as she could, given their situation.

But he was confused. "Explain, please."

"I have never managed to inspire . . . fidelity in a man, so I . . . worry that this marriage will be no different."

"Then we are of like mind. Identical, actually."

Sabrina rose on her elbow. "I vow that I will remain faithful to you."

If only he could believe it, Gideon thought, regarding their clasped hands, because he did not want her to see how deeply her naive declaration affected him.

After he collected himself, he raised her hand to his lips and returned his gaze to her. "I promise the same, Sabrina. I would inscribe and sign the vow in blood if such would help you believe me."

Sabrina let go of his hand, lay back against her pillows, and closed her eyes. But after a minute, a single tear escaped from between her lashes. And Gideon knew that she could no more believe him than he could believe her. Had she also lost her ability to trust after having it stripped carelessly away?

If so, perhaps they could heal together.

Gideon rose and pressed his lips to the tear trail on her cheek. "Sleep."

Gideon went to his bedchamber to change, then to the mews. He wanted to take Deviltry out and run him fast and furious, faster and farther than his need—his desire, damn it—for a wife who frightened him with the strength of her inscrutable hold on him.

As he neared Deviltry's stall, Gideon stopped in his tracks. There, stroking his steed's silken muzzle was the child he had seen in the night. "You, there. What is your name?"

The child bolted faster than a jackrabbit, and disappeared just as quick.

Where was the stable hand? "Harry! Har— Oh, there you are. The lad who was just here? Who is he? What is his name?"

Harry scratched his head, his chin, beneath his arm, and he was going for his ballocks when Gideon ran out of patience. "Damn it, Man, take a bath!"

The shocked expression on the stable hand's

face drained the pique right out of Gideon. " 'Twas a simple enough question," he said. "Surely small boys do not wander in and out of my stables at will. You must know who he is."

"Well, sure, I know him well enough, I just don't know his name is all."

"Well, where does he live?" Gideon asked, losing patience again.

Harry made to scratch his head, caught Gideon's expression, and stopped. "As to where he comes from, your grace. I am sure I . . . cannot say."

Gideon cursed and turned to leave.

"Were you wanting to ride, your grace?"

"No. I changed my mind. Thank you."

To Gideon's surprise, not five minutes later, he spotted the boy outside the servants' entrance to his own bloody kitchen. And this time when he approached, the urchin did not bolt.

Gideon bent on his haunches to address him. "How did you get back here so fast? I could swear that I saw you disappear in the opposite direction."

The boy shrugged. He had dark hair and darker eyes and so much dirt on his face, you could hardly tell where the grime ended and the freckles began. His serviceable, nankeen playsuit looked to be as dirty as his face and hands, as was his short serge jacket. Gideon could not help think that the boy reminded him of someone, but he could not, for the life of him, imagine who. "Are you from around here?"

"No, sir." The boy shook his head, not seeming the least inclined to scamper.

"Funny, I could have sworn I saw you in my bed-chamber last night."

The boy laughed, a happy little-boy sound. "Not

me, sir. If I did such a thing, Mama said she would— 'Twas not me, sir."

Just from his ease of speech, Gideon knew the boy was speaking the truth. "Where is your mother?"

"Right now? I cannot say for certain, but I do know she must be working. She works all the time."

Taking in laundry and such, most likely, when she should be caring for her son. Gideon wondered how far the lad had wandered to get here. "I am on my way to the small kennel we keep here in town," he said. "Would you like to come and see the puppies?"

The boy shrugged but fell into step beside him. Along the way, they talked about dogs, and Gideon was glad he had been inspired to offer the impromptu outing.

If only to prove to the members of his household that there was nothing they could, or should, keep from him, Gideon very much wanted to unearth their secret, and he was certain that this boy held the key.

His name was Damon and he was four. Cute little tiger. Bright. Loved the puppies, and they loved him. Giggled in the way all little boys should, easy and free, without restraint, the way Gideon had never dared.

This child was loved unconditionally, unreservedly; that was clear. Gideon need not worry about Damon's upbringing or the momentary absence of his mother. He lacked nothing but a recent face-wash. Hell, little boys needed their faces washed about every ten minutes, did they not?

A shrill whistle split the air, and Damon stood

like a shot. "Gotta go," he said even as he ran. "Thank you," he called back.

Gideon found himself smiling from ear to ear as he returned to the house, looking forward to seeing, well, he was looking forward to talking with . . . someone—anyone would do. Though Sabrina was his wife now, and he supposed she would be the logical choice.

He took the stairs two at a time but slowed at her bedchamber door. He went softly in, disappointed to find that she was still sleeping.

Not disappointed, actually. It was not as if he needed her, or anyone. He had simply hoped to lie down and wrap his arms around her, perhaps attempt a bit of playful seduction, to keep his skills honed. He did have a challenge to rise to after the baby was born, and he needed to learn all he could about this new wife of his, like what was most likely to melt her resolve.

Damn, he had become hard just watching her sleep.

Gideon backed away from the bed and carefully closed the door between their rooms. She needed to rest. He needed to cool down.

He stripped out of his clothes. He may not have returned smelling of horse, but the pungent aroma of puppy clung.

One of the beagle pups, to his absolute horror, had lifted a leg and drizzled on his boots. Even Gideon's inexpressibles had been sprinkled in the onslaught.

When it happened, Damon had fallen to the ground in a paroxysm of giggles.

Gideon chuckled now, just remembering, his heart lighter than it had been in some time.

# Ten

Sabrina awoke from what turned out to be a three-hour nap, dressed, and slipped up to the nursery to check on Damon and Rafferty. While Miss Minchip dozed in her rocker, the boys sat in the far corner, spillikin sticks scattered on the floor between them.

Unfortunately, they looked less like they were playing and more like they were conspiring. "What are you two whispering about?" she asked.

Just their tight faces and tighter lips told her that she had reason to be suspicious.

"Out with it," she demanded, hands on hips.

"With what, Mama?"

At what point had they conquered the art of apparent innocence? "Damon?"

"Mama, can I have a puppy?"

Sabrina allowed herself a great mental sigh. Her life was complicated enough, keeping two energetic little boys entertained and quiet, never mind throwing a yapping pup into the mix. "What brought that on?"

"The kennel man showed me the puppies."

"I see."

"He said they need homes."

"I am sure he did." Wonderful. For her boys' sakes, she would inquire of Miss Minchip, later, which of the servants cared for the kennels and whether the man dealt well with children. Meanwhile. . . .

Sabrina sat in the nursery rocker and took a hand of each to pull the boys closer. "Boys, listen, I am sorry, but we cannot have a puppy, not right now. I am not even certain you should go back to visit the kennels."

"But, Mama?" Identical twins, identical entreaties, quadruple the maternal guilt.

Sabrina sighed. "Tell you what. Perhaps we can hunt you up a cat. Cats are quiet. And perhaps we can come to a compromise on the kennels. If Miss Minchip approves of the kennel man, and if you promise to always tell me where you are going, I will let you visit the puppies again."

That concession earned her two kisses and four hugs. Not bad for half an hour's work. Before she left, Sabrina kissed both boys one more time and woke Miss Minchip to inquire about the kennel man and give her decision concerning puppy visits.

Once she knew the boys were settled, she went in search of her husband.

She found him sitting on the settee in the library, reading the London *Times*, but he looked up and rose when he saw her, folded the paper, and tossed it on a table. "Good," he said. He checked his pocket watch. "Dinner will be ready shortly. I was just about to go and fetch you. Come. Sit beside me." When she reached him, he surprised her by kissing her cheek rather than her hand.

She sat on the settee, he beside her, and she wished she could tell him how nice she found the experience of anticipating her husband's company rather than dreading it.

"What?" he asked.

But she shook her head. "Woolgathering," she improvised. "Sorry."

"Still sleepy? Did you not have a good rest, then?"

"I did . . . until the baby started doing the Highland Fling."

"Smart little tiger. Is he still flinging?"

Sabrina carried her husband's hand to her belly. "See for yourself."

Gideon winced as he felt and saw her child's wild contortions. "Does that not hurt?"

"Not at all."

"I think he is trying to break out."

"Soon enough, he will. How do you think you will feel about having a little one in the house?"

"A babe could make life interesting."

"No emotion stronger than interest comes to mind?"

"Such as?"

"Pleasure, panic, anger, elation, dread?"

"I assume the babe will not be leaving puddles on the carpets, or anything like . . . correct? The reason I ask is because a hunting dog lifted a leg against my boot this morning."

Sabrina laughed. "In that case, I will be very careful that the baby does not do the same."

"Then I am still open to the experience."

"Open to the experience," Sabrina said, considering. "I like that far better than plain old 'interest,' because interest can result either positively or negatively, you know, and sometimes we do not even—"

Gideon kissed her, and when he had her silence, he crossed her lips with a finger. "I know you are not willing to share your past yet, but I perceive in you an emotion akin to fear. So let me give you my promise that you have nothing to fear from me, and neither does your child."

Before Sabrina could respond, she needed to swallow the emotion that welled up in her at his unsolicited vow. "Thank you, Gideon."

"Gideon! She calls me Gideon. Finally. And not just to stop me in our bed. We make progress, I think."

"Yes," Sabrina said, blushing. "I believe we do."

"Good. Now I am going to pour myself a glass of sherry before dinner. Would you care for one?"

"No, thank you, but go ahead." Sabrina could not help remembering the two of them wrapped in each other's arms, on this very settee, and how frightened she had been.

"Woolgathering again," he asked from beside her, and she jumped.

But she turned to face him. "I was remembering how frightened I was last night, especially when you came charging down the balcony stairs."

"Are you saying you are less frightened of the marriage act now?"

"No. I am saying that I am less frightened of you now."

"I suppose that must suffice as a beginning."

"I expected you to be terribly upset when I informed you of my feelings concerning . . . the intimate side of marriage, but you were not."

Gideon barked a laugh. "I shall take that as a compliment to my equanimity. But for your information, I was very, terribly bothered, for about ten minutes, then I decided to handle the situation in the way I usually do. Did I not make my intentions clear to you at that time?"

"Uh, no, I do not believe you did."

Her husband shrugged. "I considered your telling me that you dislike marital intimacy as a form of throwing down the proverbial gauntlet, and I decided I should take it up."

Sabrina raised a brow.

"Accept your challenge? *Change* your mind?" Gideon set his drink on the table and decided to show his wife what he meant, by taking her into his arms. "I am going to make you ache for me, Sabrina St. Goddard. And when we do consummate this marriage of ours, you are going to enjoy the remarkable experience so much, you are going to beg for more."

Sabrina did not know whether to laugh or cry, but when she made to speak, Gideon opened his mouth over hers, and his sculpted lips worked magic.

Her first kiss ever, a mutual and spontaneous burst, had taken place the night before on that very settee, in the heat of passion, but it was more of an inferno than this slow, sweet sizzle.

This kiss went on and on, while temperatures escalated, and Sabrina happily sizzled.

Before she knew what Gideon was about, he was lying on his back, her draped over him like a rug— a lumpy rug—her knee soothing his erection, his face between her breasts.

Sabrina pulled away a bit, and they regarded each other with more of the heat lighting sparks between them than had visited them the night before. "Hefty blanket you have here," she said when her breathing caught up with her heart.

"I feared crushing the baby, so I reversed our positions."

Sabrina raised a brow. "You planned this? I do not even know how we got here."

"Good," he said. "That means I am going about this seduction business in just the right way."

Chalmer cleared his throat.

Sabrina started and felt her face warm.

Gideon grinned.

"Dinner is served," the manservant said, almost without expression, except for the smile Sabrina caught as he turned.

Sabrina was terribly uncomfortable by the time they retired that night.

Gideon seemed so in tune with her discomfort that he helped her off with her shoes and stockings and left while she finished undressing and got into her night rail. When he returned, she was shifting in the bed, trying to find a position to suit her.

"What can I do to help you?"

"Not what you want to do."

"I fear I agree," he said, coming to stand by the bed. "Tell me what you would like and I will comply. I will even go and sleep in my own bed if you think you would be more comfortable."

Sabrina shook her head. "Honestly? I was more comfortable with you at my back last night than I have been for weeks."

"You shall have me at your back, then."

"Can you rub it, just a bit?"

Gideon placed his hands at her back and gave

himself over to the unexpectedly stirring experience. It was more sensual even than in the library the night before, given the fact that he was now in her bed with her, and he knew her body a vast deal better than he had then.

"Ah, yes, like that," Sabrina said. "Down lower. Mmm. Oh, yes. Oh, God, that feels so good. Harder. A bit lower. Yes, just there."

"Damn, you are getting me excited."

His statement surprised and tickled Sabrina so much, she could not seem to stop laughing.

Her mirth was so contagious, Gideon took to laughing with her, though he never stopped soothing her sore back.

The thought occurred to him, as he absorbed the sound of her laughter, that he had never before enjoyed a woman—beyond sexual gratification— in or out of bed. He had never laughed with a woman, talked with her as he and Sabrina had talked before dinner.

He liked the experience, the easy camaraderie, as if they were a world unto themselves, the two of them alone. Amazing how shared laughter could make life seem . . . sweet. Good.

Sabrina calmed after a while, but every so often she would take to giggling again. One of those times, Gideon was so wholly charmed, he could not stop himself; he bent over and kissed her cheek. "Damned if I do not find myself liking you, Sabrina St. Goddard. Welcome to my life."

For a minute, he thought she might cry, but she brightened instead, almost as if she needed to correct her errant emotions and set them on the proper course. Odd, that.

"Thank you," she said finally. "Your life is not as bad a place as I expected."

He did not know how the devil to reply to that. Should he be pleased or angry? In the end, he said nothing, and before long, he saw that she slept.

He continued to rub her back for as long as he could keep his eyes open, and the next thing he knew, the light of morning had cast a beam across the bed.

Gideon managed to rise without disturbing his wife and left her to sleep for as long as she was able.

Rather than sit down to breakfast alone, he grabbed the *Morning Post* and retired to his study. He had not read for more than a minute, when he was rising from his chair in fury over an anonymous *on-dit*. "The Duke of S. has married hastily, and of necessity, to a nesting canary . . . with nary a feather to fly with. This author suggests that S. beware upon whose 'perch' his canary next hops."

Gideon vowed that when he got his hands around Veronica's throat, he was going to squeeze.

First he wrote a scathing letter to the newspaper, demanding a retraction. Then he wrote a scathing letter to Veronica.

Feeling better after the exercise, he pondered a diversion of pint-size proportions.

Down in the kitchen, he grabbed so many sweet rolls, Mrs. Chalmer gave him a chiding look, for which he gave her a wink, before going outside to look for Damon.

The sweet rolls were bait.

Gideon searched, but the boy was not to be found, not in the mews, nor the kennel. He had just about given up, when he spotted the lad walking purposefully in his direction.

"Good morning, young man. What have you got there?"

"A weapon. I am going hunting." Damon pointed toward Grosvenor Park across the road in the center of the square. "There, in the jungle."

Gideon nodded. "I see. Care for some company?"

"Sure, do you want to come?"

Since they were going hunting, Gideon thought it a good thing he brought bait. Hand in hand, they crossed to the park. "What kind of animal are we hunting," he asked the boy.

"Cat."

"Panther? Lion?"

"Are panthers and lions noisy?"

"As a matter of fact, I think they sometimes are."

"Then I do not want either of those."

"What kind do you want?"

"I want a quiet cat to keep in the nursery with me. Mama said I can have one."

A nursery denoted a large house, which must be nearby, Gideon surmised, since the boy could usually be found near the mews. "You are hunting for a housecat, then?"

"I s'pose." Damon looked sharply up, his eyes suddenly bright with knowledge. " 'Cause housecats must be the kind you keep in the house, right?"

The boy's grin was deadly, bringing Gideon's own, and he found himself chuckling and ruffling that small head of dark hair.

Be damned, they were hunting for a pussycat.

Gideon regarded the lad's weapon askance—a club, if he ever saw one. "If we are hunting for a housecat, I do not think you want to be hitting it with that."

"Why not?"

"Because you will do some damage."

"You mean I might hurt it? Do animals hurt like people do when they are hit?"

"Afraid so."

The boy paled, as if he knew what being hit was like, making Gideon want to defend him against he knew not what.

Now the boy's bottom lip trembled. "I only want to find a quiet cat to come home with me. I would never hurt it."

"I will help you catch it. You may discard the club."

"Thank you."

The shrill whistle that sent the boy scurrying from the kennel yesterday sounded again, but Damon only slowed, became more alert, and kept walking.

Gideon shrugged and followed. They pursued that illusive creature, cat, without success. As time passed, joy left the boy's face and discouragement loomed heavy.

"There does not seem to be an abundance of cats loose in the jungle this morning," Gideon said. "Perhaps we should go and investigate over in that direction."

If he had had any notion that the boy wanted a cat, he would have acquired a kitten from some kitchen mouser. Perhaps he might still be able to find one, to give himself an excuse to locate and visit the boy's home.

He noticed that Damon was dressed appropriately for the cooler morning. Though his nankeen skeleton suit appeared similar to the outfit he wore the day before, a warmer jacket and knee-length stockings had been added in honor of the brisker day. One of those stockings, Gideon noticed, had a rip in it and drooped a bit, giving the lad that reckless-little-boy look.

"Do you know anyone up at number twenty-three?" Gideon asked nonchalantly. "I have seen you around there several times now."

"Miss Minchip, I know. Not much of anybody else."

"Ah," Gideon said. "Well, shall we see if we can build us a cat trap? You go and find some branches, and I will start putting our trap together."

The boy skipped off, and before long, he was back with an assortment of spindly branches.

Together they fashioned a rather foolish-looking contraption that Gideon was certain would blow over in a light breeze.

Nevertheless, they sat back, man and boy alike, filled with eager anticipation, to await the appearance of a dumb cat.

# Eleven

While Damon and Gideon waited for a jingle-brained cat to collapse their trap—never mind become caught in it—Gideon offered Damon a sweet roll, which the boy accepted with alacrity.

In return, the boy pulled from a leather sack, which Gideon had not previously noticed, an earthen jar, and offered it to him. On its label was marked "pickled cabbage." Gideon hefted the vessel and examined its seal.

"For in case we get hungry," Damon explained sniffling.

Gideon fished out his linen handkerchief and handed it over. "How were you planning to open the jar?"

Instantly, Damon saw the dilemma, and scanned the area with his gaze, looking for an answer. "I know," he said, using the handkerchief. "We can smash it open on that big rock over there."

"Bad idea. You will cut yourself on the shards. Let us just eat the sweet rolls, shall we?"

The boy shrugged and offered the used handkerchief back.

Gideon smothered his chuckle by clearing his

throat. "You may keep it, in case you need it again. Just tuck it into your jacket pocket. There's a boy."

"So," Gideon said, to make conversation and pass the time. "What do you and Miss Minchip find to talk about?" But the boy got an odd, cornered look on his face, one of panic and distress, which did not seem to fit his usually happy mien. Then again, Gideon had not known Damon for that—

"I do not know anybody named Miss Minchip."

"I see," Gideon said after a minute, more than a bit intrigued by the sudden turnabout. "Well, then, tell me about your mama. Why did she send you hunting for a quiet cat?"

"She said we make enough noise by ourselves."

"We?"

"Me 'n— Me. I make lotsa noise all by myself."

Gideon felt disoriented, as if he were speaking to an entirely different child, quite an odd feeling. "Do you have any brothers or sisters?" he asked without knowing why, but he awaited the boy's answer, almost with baited breath, while the rooks in the trees above cawed and squabbled louder than usual.

"Mama is getting me a new brother real soon," he said. "She has a big belly."

"Lot of that going around," Gideon remarked, his thoughts teeming with speculation, his gaze assessing.

This must be Damon. Regard the expressive face, the sable hair, those freckles, the short blue serge jacket, droopy stockings—

Gideon sat straighter. Neither stocking was torn, neither drooped.

He saw only the one small discrepancy, and yet, one was often sufficient.

The lad crawled over to check the cat trap as Gideon watched. "Damon," he called softly but loud enough to be heard, to see whether the child would respond automatically to his name.

Damon did not, which proved nothing, of course.

Gideon rose and tapped him on the shoulder. "I have an idea. Let us go and set up more traps." He stepped quickly from the clearing, hoping to catch some phantom child with drooping socks, he supposed, but no one was there.

When he turned back, however, he saw the lad leave a sweet roll on the boulder before dashing away.

They walked side by side after that, each lost in his own thoughts, until Gideon stopped. "Forgot something," he said. "Wait right here."

Back in the clearing, nothing had changed except that the roll was missing. Gideon walked around to the far side of the boulder, and there sat Damon, eating the roll.

"What?" Gideon asked, hands on hips. "Three rolls were not enough for you?"

"Three?" the boy said, at once indignant and appalled, until he stopped short, as if to reconsider, and shrugged. "Growing boys need lots of good food. Guess I must be growing."

"That will be quite enough, young man. Come on out." He lifted Damon out and sat him on the boulder. "We need to have a talk."

" 'Bout what?"

"Remember the puppy, yesterday?"

The giggle was surely Damon's "He was funny, drizzling on you like that. Too bad cats are quieter."

"Tell me," Gideon said. "What is your brother's name?"

"Hunh?"

"Your twin. At least he *said* he was your twin."

Damon huffed. "Rafe's a squealer. His real name is Rafferty, but he likes to be called Rafe."

"Rafe," Gideon called. "Come see what I found."

The boy came tumbling into the clearing, the ugliest cat on God's green earth in his arms. "Did you catch one too?" he asked, breathless.

"Caught this." Gideon indicated Damon, sitting on the boulder, swinging his legs, finishing his sweet roll.

"Aw, he's not a cat, he's my brother."

"So I noticed." The secret, Gideon perceived, was more than the fact that they were twins, though that must be part of it. A wild notion had been scampering in and out of his brain, but it was just too fantastic to be possible.

One step at a time, Gideon cautioned himself, regarding the two, identically innocent expressions. "Why did you pretend there was only one of you?"

"Two is trouble," Rafe said. "Two is noisier."

"And messier." Damon shrugged. "People see us and they say, 'Oh, no, two of them,' so we pretend, sometimes, like we're just one. It's fun fooling people."

"You never feel as if you are lying?"

"No, only playing."

Damon nodded. "Telling fibs is bad; we know that."

"Unless fibbing is the only way to keep Mama from getting hit," Rafe said.

Damon nodded. "Right."

Once again, Gideon felt as if he had stepped into a world where he was playing a game he must win, except that he did not know the rules. And whatever those rules were, he would not be learning them today, nor would he pursue such sad and revealing statements with children, especially ones he did not know.

Gideon regarded them and ignored the tightening of his chest. "I commend you on your care of your mother."

Then he smiled. "Rafe, my boy, are you certain that is a cat you have there?"

The mangy, three-legged feline, with one and a half ears and half a tail, licked sweet-roll icing off Rafe's fingers as if it had not eaten in a month, precisely how the ghastly creature looked. Pry the burrs from its fur, where fur grew, and Rafe's feline might increase in beauty all the way up to—god-awful.

"O' course this is a cat." Rafe grinned. "He's our cat now."

He was a she, but Gideon did not know if you explained such things to four-year-olds. He would have to ask Sabrina. He had a sneaking suspicion she would know.

He did not know exactly how he felt about any of it.

There was a good possibility that she had lied to him. Oh, all right, she had not lied, she had omitted the truth, as he had omitted his title. As the boys omitted the fact that there were two of them. As she omitted the fact that there were any of them.

Gad, he was making himself dizzy.

But children? Two of them? Gideon groaned inwardly. Two *more*, he should say, if he considered the babe.

No wonder Sabrina was nervous.

Had he not recently thought he might not be ready to become immediately and directly responsible for a child? One child.

Gideon felt almost ill and needed to sit on the boulder while his stomach calmed and his head cleared.

The boys watched him with wide, uneasy eyes. Eyes so closely resembling Sabrina's that—

As it did in the woman he believed was their mother, fear lived inside these two.

Gideon ruffled Rafe's hair, and Damon stepped near for a hair-ruffle of his own.

"How did you manage to catch the cat?"

"He let me pick him up, did you not, pretty boy," Rafe crooned to his purring pet, his expression full of love and admiration.

"What color would you say his fur is?" Gideon asked, thinking that it looked like mud to him.

"It is like when we mix up our paints," Rafe said, "and all the bright colors run together, except for that tan patch around one of his eyes."

Ugly, Gideon thought.

Damon tilted his head to study the scruffy creature in question. "I think he looks exactly the color of the stuff inside a Christmas pie."

"Mincemeat," Rafe said. "We can call him Mincemeat."

Gideon barked a laugh. If a better name for that cat existed anywhere, he could not imagine what it might be. "Shall we head back across the street before someone misses you?"

They walked side by side, Gideon in the middle, Rafe petting nightmare-cat, Damon pensive.

"Do you think Mincemeat is a quiet enough cat for your mother?" Gideon asked. "You know how she worries about noise and everything." He asked the question with nonchalance, hoping to garner information about their mother, but neither boy spoke. Instead, their expressions had become serious.

Together they crossed Grosvenor Square and Gideon stopped by the kissing gate of number twenty-three to bend on his haunches before them. "Your mama is often sad, is she not?"

Unsmiling, Damon nodded, then he brightened. "But not so much since we came here."

Gideon experienced a bittersweet jubilation at that. She was less sad, perhaps, but no more trusting.

"Even when she is sad, she plays games with us," Rafe said. "When she can get away from that man."

"Let me ask you something else," Gideon said. "And I want you to be honest in your answer. Are you afraid of me?"

"No," Damon said as if the question were absurd. "We had fun together with the puppies yesterday, and even hunting today, did we not?"

"We certainly did," Gideon said, that odd, threatening jubilation back. "Do you not wonder why you always see me around here?"

"You take care of the kennel," Damon said. "Miss Minchip told Mama that you are a nice man, so it is all right for us to talk to you."

"Can you keep a secret?"

Both boys nodded, wide-eyed, eager for a scrap of surreptitious knowledge.

"First, tell me your name," Gideon said.

Gideon was glad Rafe could laugh as easily as his twin, because laughter was how they both reacted to his question.

"You know who we are. We're Damon and Rafferty."

"I mean your second names."

"Oh. Whitcomb."

Gideon had known, of course, but still, it came as a dizzying blow.

He would not, after all, be responsible for one child, but for three. Suddenly the irresponsible life of a scapegrace rogue seemed far from reach and excessively appealing. But he shook off regret and turned his attention to the twins. Sabrina's twins. His twins now too. He sighed. "You live in this house, then, do you not, and Miss Minchip takes care of you up in the nursery?"

Twin nods.

"Which one of you went into your mother's bedchamber the other night and almost got caught?"

Rafe fingered a nasty burr in Mincemeat's coat. "That was me," he said, not looking up. "I was thirsty."

"You did not see the man's face very well, did you?"

Now he looked up. "I do not like him."

"But he likes you." Gideon shook his head, unclear as to how to proceed. "Come." He took their hands. "I have an idea, but I will need your help," he said as they made their way toward the kennel. "First, we will get that puppy you like from the kennel, so you can take him up to the nursery with you."

"But Mama said we cannot. That man—"

"Your new father, you mean?" Sweat broke out on Gideon's brow just knowing he was speaking of himself.

Not that he was frightened exactly. He supposed he could raise a boy or . . . three as well as the next man. He just did not know if he could summon up the required . . . love—God help him—that such an immense responsibility required.

"We have a new father?" Damon asked.

And Gideon was affronted, which made him wonder what insanity prompted him to run from fatherhood one minute, then claim it the next. And what would make Sabrina deny her boys a father, whether she did so consciously or not? "Yes, the man you saw, Rafe, is your new father, and he would like very much for you to like him."

"Our *other* father hated noisy boys. We tried to be good, but we got him mad at Mama all the time." The revelation came from Rafe, but both boys lost their spark.

Gideon knew then that as far as fatherhood was concerned, there had never been a choice for him. For good or ill, he had two boys to raise now, and soon, very soon, there would be three.

"Our new father might not like the noise we make either," Damon said. "Mama worries about that."

About them, Gideon thought. Sabrina worried about them, as they worried about her.

"What if our new father hates us too? And he hates the puppy and Mincemeat?"

Damon, Gideon knew, was begging for more than a simple answer to his question.

Facing a pregnant bride seemed, in retrospect, child's play compared to this. Gideon wiped his damp palms on his knees and allowed his breathing to catch up with his pumping heart. He knew panic and fury, but more than that, he felt the boys' pain.

No, he more than felt it, he remembered it vividly from his own boyhood.

Aware of the dangers in confession, but despite them, Gideon was prepared to jump into deep water. He stopped and sat on the garden wall before them, winked at one, and chucked the chin of the other. "Rafe, Damon, you should know that I am not the kennel man." He looked from one to the other of them—and took the plunge. "I am your new father."

Gideon allowed his words to sink in as he watched.

They were so like their mother, these two. Why had he not noticed that before? The dusting of freckles, the hair, the eyes, their giveaway expressions plain as day. Wonder, realization, fear, then wonder again.

Damon sidled a bit closer, and however slight a beginning, the action clogged Gideon's throat and trembled the tentative hand he placed at the boy's back.

Rafe stood unmoving, his expression guarded. Gideon had already suspected that Rafe would be the tougher of the two.

Gideon moved his hand to Damon's shoulder and reached over to play with Mincemeat's paw near Rafe's arm. "I want you to know right off that I like you," he said. "Both of you. I understand that boys make noise when they play. Boys *should* play. Even I make noise sometimes.

"Do not mistake me, I am not saying that I will never ask you to quiet down. I am saying that when

I do ask, I will give you a good reason for my request, so you will understand why I ask."

Rafe took to breathing again. Damon leaned closer in, until his small shoulder touched Gideon's larger one, and Gideon felt almost as if his own shoulders broadened then, with pride and perhaps with the need to carry these amazing new responsibilities.

He led the boys to the puppies, and sure enough, the friendly pup took to squealing and jumping and drizzling and yapping with glee, unlike his six brothers, who were more interested in lunch.

"Will the pup belong to both of us?" Rafe asked, petting Mincemeat.

"So your mama will not be angry, I think the puppy should remain mine. But I want you to take care of him up in the nursery for me. It is clear how much he loves you. He is a special pup, and you two are special boys, which is exactly what he needs." The pup was, in truth, too gentle, and too enamored of people, to make a good hunter anyway.

Gideon scratched the ecstatic canine under an ear. "Do you think you can take care of him?"

Twin, very serious, nods.

"What about Mincemeat?" Rafe asked, hugging ugly-cat protectively.

"I think Mincemeat needs you even more than the pup does. So you may keep her . . . er . . . him too."

"A dog *and* a cat," Damon whispered with reverence.

"Now I need you to help me play a silly game with your mama. Will you?"

\* \* \*

Mr. Chalmer told Gideon that her grace was working in her sitting room and wished to speak with him when he came in, if his grace pleased.

Gideon headed straight there. Part of him wanted to make Sabrina squirm for her mischief, but another part of him understood her motives. He almost wished he did not.

When he entered, he found her bent over her desk in concentration. As he approached, she rose with a smile to greet him. And he wondered if her response meant that she was eager for his company, or if she was accustomed simply to pretence.

If possible, she seemed to grow more beautiful with time. Today, she positively glowed.

"You look ravishing," he said, taking her into his arms to kiss her, lingering, nibbling at her lips for longer than he intended.

"Gideon," she said, breathless, but not averse to his attention if he did not miss his guess. "We need to talk."

"Talking can wait. I brought you a surprise."

"No, really. This is important." She noted his torn cuff, stepped back, and did a hasty scan of his countenance. "What happened to your clothes? You are positively filthy."

Gideon looked down at his unkempt self and shrugged. "I went hunting."

"What?" She placed her hands on her hips. "Gideon—"

"Stay here," he said. "I shall be right back."

He reminded her of a small boy with a fancy sea-shell or a shiny colored rock to show off.

Sabrina lowered herself to the settee to await his schoolboy whim. This was yet another interesting and surprising facet of her complicated new husband, and charming, but . . . She sighed with frustration.

She needed to tell him about the boys and put the momentous confession behind her. Ever since last night, when he had patiently rubbed her back for what seemed like hours, she understood that she might be able to tell him without fear of reprisal.

When she awoke this morning, she knew the time had come, but once she had made the decision, she had become desperate to be done with it.

"Surprise!" Gideon shouted. "Look what followed me home." Like sacks of grain, he carried her sons, slung, one under each arm.

And Sabrina gasped and clasped a hand to her pounding heart.

Gideon raised a brow. "Can we keep them?"

Sabrina did not know if her husband's foolish question, or his sporadic jiggling, tickled her sons' fancies, but their fit of the giggles was something to hear.

And while they laughed, Sabrina regarded Gideon as he regarded her, a thousand serious questions and as many difficult answers hanging between them. But despite the grave implications in her boys' sudden appearance, Sabrina became breathless, and the mist over her eyes had nothing to do with fear and everything to do with joy.

"We hunted us up a cat, Mama. Just like you said we could." Rafe beamed with happiness, and Sabrina realized that whatever Gideon's reaction— and his anger would certainly be justified—he had not taken it out on the boys.

"There he is, Mama," Rafe said. "There is our cat."

"Good God," Sabrina said when she spotted the hideous creature.

Though she knew that before the day ended she would be forced to answer for her deception, she could not help embrace her sons' happiness.

Close behind the cat, and only half its size, waddled a beagle pup, poking and snuffling its way in her direction.

"He is cute, is he not, Mama?" Damon asked.

Hanging there suspended, the boys' rare smiles and rarer laughter transformed their freckled faces, bringing one thought to Sabrina's mind. They rarely, if ever, misjudged people, for they had learned early in life the danger in doing so.

Filled with rioting emotions, Sabrina tried not to cry. "Did you hunt him up too?"

Gideon cleared his throat. "Ah, Drizzle is mine," he said. "But I asked Rafe and Damon to take care of him, upstairs in the nursery, as a favor to me, because Drizzle needs them. If you agree to the plan, that is." Her husband seemed again like a boy, in that moment.

Sabrina hauled the pup into her lap and allowed that he *was* quite cute. "Drizzle is not the same—"

"Hunter who wet my boots?" Gideon shrugged. "He gets excited around people."

Fast as lightning, Sabrina lifted the pup from her lap, but not fast enough.

Drizzle was drizzling on her dress.

# Twelve

For the rest of that day, Sabrina and Gideon sorted life into new and uncharted order—disorder really, for despite their best efforts, chaos reigned, the more so for two happy little boys no longer confined to the nursery.

Sabrina could not believe how well Gideon seemed to be adjusting. But she was so used to working to keep peace in explosive situations, she kept waiting for an explosion to take place. Not knowing what might set Gideon off was exhausting.

"We need to move to the country," he said later over an informal tea in the nursery. "London is no place to raise children. My house in Hertfordshire is perfect. Damon and Rafe can each have their own rooms, off a huge nursery. Plenty of grass and trees outside to romp with Mincemeat and Drizzle. The stables and kennels are larger as well."

"Stables big enough for ponies?" Rafe asked.

"Ponies?" Damon said. "Can we have ponies?"

Sabrina blushed. "Boys, please. Your manners."

The twins ran with the possibilities of life in the country. They talked so quickly of plans and projects, and with such overwhelming excitement, that Damon spilled his milk.

When everybody rose to move out of flood range, or to clean the spill, Mincemeat jumped on the table, lapped some milk, and ate some shortbread. By the time they got the cat down, Drizzle was standing on a chair, tail wagging, eating a scone.

Sabrina saw her frightened boys move out of the way, expecting a reprimand, or worse, until they saw that Gideon was laughing, and released their breaths.

Tears sprang to Sabrina's eyes.

"Bree, what is wrong?" Gideon asked, worried. He went to her, the boys one step behind him.

"Thank you for not being angry," she said. "This is silly. I never cry. It is just that everything is happening so fast."

Rafe rubbed her back, Damon her arm, and Gideon realized they were used to caring for their mother themselves. As she was used to caring for them—without him.

He was still an outsider, likely always would be.

As a child, the knowledge had carved a raw and heavy place in his small chest. Old feelings—very old—of yearning, inferiority, and unworthiness threatened to swamp him, even in memory. Always, it had seemed that he stood to the side, insignificant, desperate for attention, never daring to hope for affection.

He moved to the window. He knew his place now and he was comfortable with it. Even with this new family, he knew where he stood, and he accepted the position. He would watch over them, from afar.

"Perhaps we should slow our pace a bit," he said, turning to face them. "Accept our new situation, become comfortable with it, before we make any significant changes."

Sabrina laughed, almost with hysteria, and Gideon regarded her with concern.

"You might not have noticed," she said, attempting a smile and failing, "but we have undergone several significant changes already, and there are more on the way."

More changes, Gideon wondered, or more babies, plural, as in twins again? He shivered.

Sabrina regarded her belly and then him. "I am in no condition to pack up a household and move it fifty miles to the north."

"I had not noticed," Gideon said, sharing a smile with her, which reminded him of their nights alone in the big bed upstairs, and brought him back from the window into their tenuous family circle. At that moment, he almost felt as if anything could happen.

Could they become something of a family, however patched and disjointed?

This was not a question to be answered in a day, Gideon knew, or asked ever, or even expected. He knew better than that. But he had to try.

If he trod carefully, he might even carve his own special place among them, a place where they wanted, needed him, to be. More, a place where they welcomed him.

And twenty minutes later, as Damon and Rafferty dragged him, each by a hand, toward the stables, so they could show Sabrina the other pups, hope blossomed in Gideon's breast.


Before the amazing day came to an end, beds needed to be fashioned for the animals and arrangements made for Doggett to oversee the boys as they handled Drizzle's walks and Mincemeat's outdoor jaunts.

Mr. Chalmer was pleased to find all his limbs intact after he slipped in a suspicious puddle in the foyer.

Mrs. Chalmer agreed not to turn the cat into its name after she found Mincemeat up on the sideboard, eating her fresh-roasted dinner ham. For a cat with only three legs, that feline could certainly get around.

Miss Minchip, however, went on strike that night, just after Gideon and Sabrina relegated the boys to the nursery for the night. "Two boys are one thing," said she, back ramrod straight, hands trembling with indignation. "But animals? And one of them Satan's own spawn. Well," she huffed. "I am simply too old for such nonsense."

Gideon apologized for his thoughtlessness and offered the sharp old bird a generous stipend to oversee the nursery, animals and all, with two days off weekly to rest and recover. He even allowed that Mr. Waredraper could assist her when sewing did not rank high on his list of priorities. Yes, of course, she would remain in charge of the nursery at all times.

Miss Minchip grew younger before his eyes.

Once she took the boys in hand, Gideon vowed silently that he would create a place for himself in this new family of his. They needed him. Whether they wanted him was another issue, but that would be their choice. It mattered not to him, one way or the other.

As he prepared to retire, finally, he could not seem to locate his wife.

His life, he concluded as he searched, was noisier,

crazier, more alive, and definitely more challenging with Sabrina and her boys in it.

Yes, she had concealed a colossal fragment of information, namely the existence of twin sons, which she should have revealed before the wedding, not days later.

Well, come to that, she had not revealed their presence at all, had she?

Nevertheless, after the boys' revelations, Gideon understood her reasoning all too well. What he did not understand was why she seemed now to be missing. Already he knew her for a worthier and stronger woman than to run away.

On their wedding night, when he wanted his husbandly rights, she had not really run, she had simply needed to come to terms with her new circumstances, and she decided to do so in the library. Nor did she run when he became surly the previous morning; she had simply refused to respond to his orders, putting him in his place, which, he supposed, he deserved.

But her disappearance tonight seemed very much like running.

He found her, finally, at her desk, where he had located her that morning. She paled when she saw him and put her papers away, as she had done then, almost as if she were hiding something.

But no, he was being overly suspicious, after finding the boys, which, he reminded himself, he understood. When she rose to greet him, however, neither her smile nor her color returned to her face. "Gideon, I realize that you must be—"

"Shh," he said, crossing her lips with a finger. "No apologies, no excuses, however worthy, are necessary. I know."

Her face paled to flour paste. "What do you know?"

"That their father did not like noisy boys. You had spent years hiding them from a man you knew. Of course you would protect them from one you did not."

When she made to speak, he shushed her again. "I seek neither affirmation nor denial, nor do I expect you to share any part of your past that you wish to keep to yourself. My intent is not to take advantage of any misplaced guilt you might feel, or to extract the details of your first less-than-good marriage—your words. I simply wish to assure you that you have not entered a similar, disagreeable union with me."

He placed her trembling hand on his arm, covered it with his own, and led her from the sitting room and up the stairs toward their suite. "Hear my promise: I am the son of such a father. I will never be such a one." He stopped before the door to her bedchamber and raised a brow. "However, if there exist any other skeletons you might be hiding, now would be the time to reveal them."

Sabrina thought of the villain who purchased her, and his purpose in doing so. And she knew that no man, no matter his apparent kindness, could turn a blind eye to that sordid a truth.

Not about his own wife.

Not even this man.

So rather than answer, Sabrina turned to her new husband, put her arms around his neck, and kissed him.

Another day, another sale, she thought, even as she slipped, heart and soul, into the kiss . . . into her first-ever seduction. What difference to a body, bartered so many times, that another, more or less, meant nothing. Besides, she owed him for his gentleness and understanding.

"Oh, my dearest Sabrina, do not toy with a drowning man." Gideon opened his mouth over hers and gave himself into her keeping. "Do with me as you will."

Sabrina almost wanted to smile then. Fancy that, a man who could please her even as he purchased her. A man who carried her to her bedchamber like some knight of old.

This man was an enigma, as was she, even unto herself.

For inasmuch as Sabrina was trading herself for her husband's kindness and trust, however misplaced, an amazing streak of anticipation shivered her limbs, tightened her breasts, and throbbed her womb.

At this moment, Sabrina St. Goddard knew herself less than she knew her strange new husband, with his magic hands and his disarming smile.

Her body and mind once again acting independently of each other, Sabrina ached for fulfillment, for the ecstasy she suspected only Gideon St. Goddard could engender.

Wanton. Slut. In her father's words, in her first husband's, the oft-repeated accusations echoed in her mind. But as if Gideon heard them as well, he altered them. "Sweet, innocent Sabrina. My dearest, my wife."

As he sat her on her bed, Gideon did not simply remove her stockings; he peeled them slowly down, kissing every inch of trembling flesh he exposed along the way.

From her thigh to her toes, he nibbled her.

"Twenty-one blasted buttons," he bit out just before he spread her bodice to expose her mended petticoat of washing silk over her equally tattered shift. "No stays," he said. "Thank God."

Sabrina shook her head. She fretted over her shabby underpinnings. He worried about how quickly he could remove them.

Such a twinkle lit his eyes, that she chuckled. "Stays and nine-month babies do not a happy union make."

"No more than stays and randy husbands," said he with a wicked wink.

Her hands seemed to cup his face of their own accord, but once she had touched him in that intimate and wifely way, she liked the gesture as much as he. Emboldened, she brought his kind and handsome face to hers to initiate a second kiss, a third, and when he raised his head, many, many minutes later, she brought him to her breasts.

Through the linen of her shift, Gideon teased the aching nubbin until a sharp and shocking stab of desire shot straight to her center. She arched and slid her hands into the silken hair at his nape, cool and elegant, and for the first time, she thought of him as hers.

Against cruelty she could perhaps be strong. Against gentleness she had no defense.

"More," she said. "Gideon, give me more."

"Madam," he said, pulling away, lighting a candle on the night table. "You shall have all you can take, but I must be allowed to watch as you do."

Then he began to remove his clothes.

And so she watched him as boldly as he had watched her, and he slowed his pace for her delectation. By the time he unfastened his last stud and removed his shirt, Sabrina imagined, with a frisson of anticipation, running her hands over the mat of hair on his firm, muscled chest.

His shoes went next, then his stockings. But he paid such attention to her watching him that he tripped removing them. Sabrina did not know that any part of the sex act could bring laughter, but then Gideon St. Goddard had already taught her more lessons than she could count.

Her wicked-as-sin duke, and so he especially appeared this night, held her gaze as he undid the flap on his pantaloons, first one side and then the next, and lowered them ever so slowly. Pure, undiluted torture.

Need, anticipation, stroked Sabrina in a physical way. So much so that she sat up to watch, openly curious, as the first man she might actually want as her lover began to slip his drawers down his legs.

Male perfection and all hers.

Gideon's sex sprang free, huge and throbbing, and Sabrina wondered how she could have imagined that portion of his anatomy as harmless.

He stripped her of the last vestiges of her own clothing gently, layer by layer, planting more kisses as he went. He last removed her petticoat and shift, until she lay naked, vulnerable, and strangely unembarrassed.

Sabrina raised her chin at his blatant reaction, shot with pride that she could produce it.

Then he joined her on her bed, and he worshipped her.

Kisses, he planted everywhere. Behind her ear, near the pulse at her throat. He stopped only to suckle and learn her body.

Sabrina grew moist, needy, and still he did not touch where she ached.

She wanted to scream, to rant, to strike him.

Why did he not touch her now, when she finally wanted him to?

Her belly, he adored, then he spoke to the child. If Sabrina were not so frustrated, she might giggle, such nonsense did he speak. "Gideon—"

"Shh. This is between me and the child, if you please."

She did laugh then and swatted him, and he caught her finger and suckled it. Even that aroused her.

Just when she thought he might stroke where she most needed him, he shifted her to her side.

She nearly did strike him then, but he had taken to kissing the small of her back, the backs of her knees, and someone whimpered. Was it her?

Then she was on her back again and he knelt between her legs. "Oh, no. Gideon, no, the baby."

"Shh, sweet. I will not hurt the babe, but I will pleasure his mother until she cries for mercy."

"Mercy," Sabrina whispered as he spread her legs and kissed her there, where every nerve clamored and pulsed.

"Mercy," she cried a bit louder when he spread her nether lips and—

"Mercy," she shouted. "Oh, my God. Gideon, do not. Stop. Do not . . . stop. Do not stop."

Gideon grinned and went back to giving her his undivided . . . attention.

Sabrina screamed, and she begged, and she wept with pleasure as her remarkably talented husband created an escalating wonder of magic inside her.

He took her beyond heaven once, and again, and by the third time, she thought she might swoon.

"Gideon. No more. I cannot, not again."

"Ah, but you can," said he, too cocky by half. "Just one more time."

Twice more, she spiraled upward and shattered into starlike pieces, hot and sparkling. And while she floated, he lay down beside her and kissed her, and kissed her, and neither of them could get enough of those kisses, or of each other.

No sooner did she take him into her hand than he spilled his seed against her belly. And such a warmth flooded her at the intimacy that she drifted to sleep, very much afraid that if she were not careful, she might be foolish enough to fall in love with her rogue of a bridegroom.

"What the devil?" Gideon shouted the question. "The bed is wet. Good God," he said, jumping to stand naked and shocked beside it. "Have I married a bed-wetter?"

That was when Sabrina woke enough to understand her discomfort. "The baby," she whispered, as surprised as he. "The baby is coming."

"Oh, good God." Gideon ran somewhat in circles as he attempted and failed to hop, literally, into his pantaloons, not a stitch covering him, his ballocks swinging, as if in the breeze. "But it is too early," he shouted all in a panic. "What have I done?"

"The twins came early, and rather fast," she said, slipping her night rail over her head, trying to reassure him, but wanting so very badly to laugh instead.

"Yes, but there were two of— Oh, good God," he said again.

Sabrina did laugh then, for he looked just too comical to believe.

To her surprise, her door opened and the twins came strolling in, uninvited, unannounced—fortunately without Miss Minchip—Rafe cradling Mincemeat, Damon bouncing Drizzle on his shoulder.

These midnight visits would have to stop, Sabrina thought while the boys watched Gideon perform.

"He gots a long ding-dong," Rafe said.

"Mine is bigger," Damon said.

And Gideon stopped to gape at the both of them.

Sabrina choked as she laughed, and found it terribly difficult to do both while she endured her first honest-to-goodness birthing pain. "No doubt about it. This is it," she said, bracing herself on the bedpost.

Gideon paled to bleached muslin when he perceived her discomfort. "What have I done?" he whispered as if to himself, but she heard. And so did the boys.

"This is not your fault," Sabrina said.

"I am a selfish bastard . . . er, your pardon, boys, Sabrina. What can we do to help?" In pantaloons, bare feet, and open shirt, Gideon placed a hand on each boy's shoulder.

Touched by that sign of fatherly protectiveness— if only it might last—Sabrina felt suddenly like weeping. "If you could take the boys up to Miss Minchip . . . ah, and find the note that Lady something or other sent me with the midwife's direction. It is around someplace." She endured another contraction.

As much shocked as confused by the sudden turn of events, and by Sabrina's flighty directions, Gideon watched her catch her breath, straighten, and begin to strip the wet bed. "Sabrina, do not tax yourself. Get one of the—"

"Moving around will help," she said. "Ease the way. Go now. Take the boys up. And hurry, please."

'Twas thirty minutes before he returned. "I sent for a doctor, but he was not to be found. Now I have sent for the midwife. I finally located the note with her direction in your desk in the sitting room."

Sabrina stilled and Gideon waited for her to say something more, but she simply released a long breath.

By then, he saw, she had made up the bed with an oilcloth beneath the linens, and ropes tied to the bedposts. She had set out basilicum powder and scissors, needle, thread, absorbent cloth, and two basins.

Gideon paled when he saw them.

"I cannot pick you up off the floor," Sabrina said as another pain seemed to suck her into its jaws. "Do not swoon," she screamed.

As if he would.

"I thought that perhaps Miss Minchip could help you," he said, going to her, sponging her brow. "But she became as quick a case of nerves as I. Worse." Gideon shrugged helplessly.

Sabrina reached for him, thank God, and he took her into his arms and held her tight, wishing he could keep her safe from all life's harm.

"Do not leave me," he whispered. "Please, Sabrina."

"I am not going to die, much as I might wish it."

His head snapped up. "You do not mean that."

"Because I might wish death would end the pain, not because I do not want to live," she said. "Of course I want to live. I must. I have children to care for."

Gideon wished she wanted to live because of him, but that was foolishness.

"Where would you prefer me?" he asked soberly. "Here with you or downstairs, waiting for the mid-wife?"

"The midwife," she said, and nearly broke him.

Gideon left, unable to speak for his disappointment.

# Thirteen

Gideon pounced on the midwife the second she breached the door, but the stench of her pickled breath and unwashed body sent him reeling back. "What the devil?"

"Maggs the midwife," said she, curtsying and tottering against the open door. "At cher servich, yer grache."

Gideon barely understood a word, so slurred was her speech. "You are drunk as an emperor," he accused.

"Nah, jusht a bit squiffed is all. Ta brace meeese-self for the ordeal ahead."

"Out," Gideon ordered. "Your services are no longer required."

"Your grace," Chalmer cautioned. "Her grace will need some—"

"Not a souse. She does not need a bloody drunken harlot for midwife. Out," he said again. "Now."

The midwife gasped, cursed, and squinted at her accuser. "Lay-deee Ver-hon-hic-haaa shall hear about thish." Maggs raised her nose, harumphed, turned on her heel, and tumbled her tangle-footed way down the front steps.

"Oh, for heaven's sakes," Gideon said. "Pick her up, give her a guinea, and send her on her bosky way." He shut the door on the sight of his retainers righting the lush, dusting his hands of the grime he imagined must linger in her wake. "There."

"But, your grace. Who will . . . er . . . ?"

Gideon ran his hand through his hair. "Mrs. Chalmer surely has exper—"

"Went to her sister's in Cheapside not three hours ago. Children come down with the spots."

Gideon raised his chin, squared his shoulders, and took the stairs two at a time. He would tell Sabrina that she would have to wait until the doc—

Every candle in the bedchamber blazed.

In the middle of the huge four-poster, her legs bent, her back arched, a feral animal sound issuing from her throat, Sabrina labored alone.

The sight, the sound, her very isolation in struggle, were like to cut Gideon in two.

He would never forget any of it. Neither would he allow her to struggle alone. He tore off his coat and released his cuff studs. "The midwife was disgusting," he said, taking her hand. "Unwashed, reeking of gin, and God knows what else. Disease-ridden as well, no doubt. Did you say that someone recommended the woman?"

The pleading look Sabrina gave him, when she finally lowered her back to the bed and closed her eyes in exhaustion, turned his heart over in his chest and brought it up into his throat. "I sent her away," he confessed. "I had to, Bree."

Her look incredulous, his wife appeared too breathless, too exhausted, to speak.

"Tell me what I must do," he said, dipping a cloth into the warm, soapy water she had prepared.

He sponged her face and her neck. "I want to help, but you must tell me, Sweetheart, what to do. I am sorry. I am so sorry that I did this to you with my selfish lust. I would not blame you if you never forgave me. But let me help you now. Please."

She stopped his ministrations, took and kissed the back of his hand. "He is almost here. Just catch him when he comes." She started to twist again, her stomach to mound. Then she raised herself on her elbows, pulled her legs back, and pushed.

Gideon did not know which of them perspired more, which was more like to scream.

"Now," she shouted. "Catch him now."

Gideon went to the foot of the bed and watched amazed as a bloody, wiggling bundle of screaming humanity slipped into his waiting hands. He looked up at his wife, awed and shaken by what he had just witnessed. "A girl," he said, the lump in his throat making further speech impossible.

At Sabrina's direction, he cut and tied the cord, his knees going to water. Then he bound the baby's belly. And when he made to lift her, the mite waved her arms as if she were losing her balance. So he brought her close against him, and she nuzzled his neck, clutching him with the tiniest little hands he ever saw, as if—she needed him.

And Gideon knew that he would never be the same again. "There's my girl," he crooned. "You are safe. Do not fret, little one, I will keep you safe."

As Sabrina regarded them, her sparkling emerald eyes bright and alive with some heady emotion he could not fathom, she smiled. Sabrina St. Goddard, the most beautiful woman he had ever beheld. Radiant. "This little one must be the second most beautiful sight in the world," he said, gazing into Sabrina's eyes in such a way as to make her understand that she was the first.

With the babe clinging to him, filling his arms, his heart, Gideon had not felt so protective, so needed, or so strong and capable in his entire thirty-four years.

Sincerely loath to relinquish the wiggling bundle, he nevertheless carried her toward the bed, while near his ear the mite squeaked and cooed and made soft, sweet suckling noises.

His grin, of its own volition, grew so wide, he could barely contain it.

"I think you should name her," Sabrina said, still breathing heavily, looking weak but satisfied. "After all, you delivered her."

"*You* delivered her, make no mistake, but I would—Never mind. Here she is."

"Wait," Sabrina said, arching, appearing to be in pain again.

"Oh. Good Lord," Gideon said, placing the babe on the bed and covering her with a corner of the blanket.

"Is there another?" He went back toward the foot of the bed. "Is it twins?

Sabrina groaned and laughed at the same time, quite an odd sound. "No, thank God. It is only the afterbirth. I can feel it coming."

Gideon received the afterbirth in a basin as Sabrina directed, then he called for one of the maids to dispose of it.

"You are certain," he said, his heart still pounding, "that there is not another babe?"

Sabrina shook her head as she took her new daughter and put her to her breast. "I am certain."

"I ask because you are bleeding heavily." The

amount of blood that flowed with the afterbirth had disturbed him greatly. "So much bleeding cannot be good," he said, feeling foolish. "Of course you would bleed, but— What can I— I do apologize, but I do not know what to do for you."

"The babe's nursing will slow the flux," Sabrina said. "Fold one of the cloths for now, will you, and place it between my legs."

After everything, Gideon could not believe she blushed when she asked.

"Later," she said, "after I rest, I will wash."

Placing the padding between her legs, Gideon found himself shocked by the terrifying amount of blood pooled there.

His head swam and his stomach roiled—and the floor rose up to greet him.

No sooner did he land, however, than he heard the baby wailing furiously, and Sabrina calling his name, both sounds coming to him as if through a long and deep tunnel.

The lightheadedness had come upon him so quickly, he had been caught unawares, but now he turned his head toward the sounds and, despite the dip to the floor and the spin in the room, Gideon moved his arms and legs to brace himself and attempt to rise.

Once he was up, he placed one foot in front of the other and made his way around the bed, determined not to go down again.

His wife and his daughter needed him.

Sabrina's concern, he could tell, despite her attempt to hide it, was tempered with a good deal of amusement. He cared not. He had reached her when she most needed him, which was all that mattered.

"Sit there, on the bedside chair," she said. "And lower your head between your knees. That should help."

Gideon slipped rather than sat, in the chair and did as she bid.

Foolish as the position seemed, the ridiculous contortion did help clear his foggy brain considerably. When he felt almost normal again, he raised his head, rested it against the chair back, and closed his eyes.

"Good," Sabrina said. "Rest for a few minutes. You have had a difficult time of it."

"You need not sound so amused," Gideon said, not bothering to open his eyes while the bedchamber continued to waltz about him. "You have quite established your superiority in the birthing department."

"I have had practice. Double practice, when you come down to it. Did you hurt yourself when you fell, though it was more a fold and glide type of swoon you performed. Very neat."

He opened one eye. "If you ever, *ever*, repeat that I swooned at the birth, I will beat you."

Sabrina giggled. "Sorry. I already perceive you will not."

"Thank you," Gideon said. "That is the nicest compliment you have paid me to date. However, lest we lose track of the subject, let me say that you also had more than a few days to prepare for this."

"I did, and for the first time, I did not give birth alone. Thank you. You were magnificent." She had not seen her first husband for two months before the twins' birth, for he considered her useless to him then. Neither did she see him for three months after, praise be, because the tardy and remorseful midwife had frightened him with tales of birth fever spread through a woman's bloody after-flux.

"Are you up to calling a maid to take and bathe the baby," Sabrina asked her husband. "I think she is finished nursing for the moment."

By then, Gideon seemed to have regained enough of his equilibrium to stand and perform the menial task she assigned him.

By the time the maid answered his summons, Gideon seemed more himself. But he appeared loath to let young Alice take the baby away. "Prepare two basins of warm water," he told her. "And bring them here."

Gideon took the fretting babe from Sabrina's arms then, and the mite's squeaky little whimpers calmed the minute he cuddled and crooned to her, almost as if she knew him.

Sabrina caught her trembling lip between her teeth. "I repeat, she is yours to name, as she believes you are hers to command."

Gideon sat on the bed beside her, the babe cradled in his protective embrace. "I would not mind if she . . . thought of me as her papa. The boys too, except that they knew their father, so perhaps they would not care to. At any rate, it might be best to allow them to decide. It matters not to me, of course."

"Of course," Sabrina said, getting for herself a rare glimpse of the true Gideon St. Goddard.

"But how would you feel if they did call me Papa eventually?"

His wife's hesitation eroded the thread of expectation Gideon refused to name.

"You are a good man, Gideon St. Goddard. I

know you are, and yet I feel compelled to remind you that they are but babes, the three of them. I will not have anyone hurt them. Not again. I will not."

Gideon did not know what to say to that. He understood her warning, was humbled that she considered him good at all, especially when he considered all the ways in which he was not. He understood her need to protect her children.

If only she understood that he would protect them as fiercely himself. With his dying breath if need be.

Sabrina covered his hand with her own. "What shall we call her?"

"Juliana, perhaps?" Gideon dared suggest. "I have loved the name since I was a child. It is my grandmother's."

"Oh, I like that."

Gideon wondered how someone who had just endured so much could remain so beautiful.

"I like it very well, indeed. Juliana St. Goddard."

The sound of it gave Gideon a quick and pleasant flood of warmth in the region of his cold rogue's heart. Juliana would carry his name. Of course she would; he was married to her mother. "Thank you," he said, sincerely moved, though he gave his thanks for so much more than her allowing him to name her daughter.

Alice, the maid, brought Gideon's basins of warm, soapy water, and he set himself up to supervise the girl's attempt at bathing the babe. He ignored his wife's raised brow at his high-handed tactics, because, well, this was important.

"Be careful she does not fall," he cautioned Alice. "Hold her head. No, watch her belly, the cord." And finally, he all but elbowed the poor maid out of his way and sent her up to the nursery for his old cradle.

Gideon proceeded to take great care and inordinate pleasure in giving Juliana her first bath. "Did you ever see such tiny fingernails in your life?" he asked Sabrina, earning himself a muffled giggle in reply.

After that, he did not deign to look in the direction from which the uncivil squeak had come, he simply directed his conjecture toward the beautiful and wide-eyed babe herself. "And look at your little toes," he crooned. "And your perfect little button nose, exactly like your amused mama's."

Alice returned with the cradle, placed it on the floor beside Sabrina's bed, and left again, seeming slightly less put out than before she left. Gideon carried the clean and wrapped baby back to the bed, patting her little back, loving the feel of her, warm and soft and sleepy in his arms. "Forgive me," he said, looking down at his tired wife. "For last night."

Sabrina brought the back of his hand to her cheek, and Gideon experienced that odd heart-flood again.

"Nothing to forgive," she said.

"I should be whipped for my determination. My fault she came early."

"Then I must thank you."

Gideon examined Juliana's tiny pink hand waving before his eyes, kissed the exquisite silk of it, and understood, for the first time in his life, the meaning, the enormity, of love. Then he looked into the eyes of her mother and understood the emotion he had not recognized earlier. Love for her daughter.

Amazing, really, that she could radiate such an abundance of that emotion, lying there as she was, drenched in blood and sweat, exhausted.

Though Gideon hated to let go of Juliana, he needed to tend Sabrina, so he bent on his haunches and placed his daughter in her cradle. "Is she all right, do you think?" he asked his wife, not taking his gaze from the babe.

"Beautifully healthy. Big, shiny eyes, a cry to split our ears, and she suckles as hard as you do."

That got her husband's eye-sparkling attention, as she intended. He had seemed melancholy somehow, though Sabrina suspected he would deny as much if she mentioned it.

"You did enjoy my . . . ministrations last night," he said, looking up at her, his obsidian eyes bright, intense. "Five, maybe six times, if I remember correctly."

Sabrina groaned. "I will never mention the swoon again if you never mention the five or six times."

"It was seven, but I will never mention it again."

"Liar," she accused.

"Here," he said, pulling her blanket back. "Let me wash you and get you into a clean, fresh bed, so you can sleep while Juliana does."

"Oh, no, Gideon . . ."

But he did not listen, for which she was immensely embarrassed, but ever so much more grateful.

Disconcerting as his bathing her—though no worse than his sexual attentions the night before, or his help during the delivery—Sabrina gloried in her husband's gentleness and concern.

He washed her tenderly with the warm, soft, soapy cloth, and before she knew it, he was carrying her into his bedchamber and placing her in his bed.

Then, it seemed, hours had passed, and he was slipping into the huge bed beside her with a screaming Juliana in his arms. Sabrina found his kissing her brow deliciously pleasant upon waking.

Her rogue was dressed and shaved, handsomer today than yesterday. "Good morning, sleepyhead," he said. "You have had a good rest, I hope. Alice is already next door, putting your bedchamber to rights, and here is one hungry little girl wanting her mama." He turned to their fretful babe. "Here she is, Sweetpea."

Juliana was frantic, and Sabrina blushed as she untied the bodice of her gown to bare her breast. As Gideon placed her new daughter—their new daughter—in her arms, Juliana latched ravenously onto her nipple.

Lying on her side, Sabrina settled her daughter to suckle, smoothing an amazing thatch of black curls from her tiny brow. And an overwhelming sense of well-being, of rightness, enveloped her. A new experience that, and one she prayed fervently would continue.

Gideon moved her gown aside, away from Juliana's face so he could see her, and as he did, the babe caught and curled her hand around his finger, bringing it tight against Sabrina's breast as she nursed.

"I had better stop trying to decide which of you is more beautiful," Gideon said, his voice raw with emotion. "And tell you that being here with the two of you, like this, is probably the best gift I have ever received."

Sabrina saw love for Juliana, clear as a summer breeze, in her husband's warm, dark eyes, and realized what an error she might have made in warning him away. How, now, to tell him she would be pleased to have her children call him Papa, without bringing her warning to mind?

"Who else but Juliana's papa should be here," she said.

And Gideon understood her offer. She saw the wary gratitude in his eyes and accepted his thanks with his kiss.

The watcher leaned heavily on his cane as he stood across the street from number twenty-three Grosvenor Square. He needed desperately to know what was going on inside Stanthorpe Place.

The tormented man had recently returned from hell only to find that a worse perdition awaited him.

But before he could face his own devils, he had a score to settle here. Except that he needed to know in which direction the settling needed to be done.

This was, in fact, his first visit, but he had come too soon, he realized now. More time would have to pass, more healing would have to take place before he recovered enough to return.

And return he would.

Integrity and honor would be rewarded, and bounders would be made to pay the price.

# Fourteen

When Gideon got to the nursery to fetch the boys to come and see their baby sister for the first time, Damon and Rafe were playing, but when Rafe looked up, he also looked worried.

Gideon sat in the chair indicated by Miss Minchip. He especially wanted to give this more reserved of the twins his full attention. Rafferty would notice and feel keenly any distraction on his part. Unlike the happily playing Damon, who rarely saw the little things because he was so busy flitting from one exciting aspect of life to the next, Rafferty missed nothing.

Gideon lifted Rafe onto his lap. "And what is on your mind, young man?"

"Is Mama sick? She looked sick last night."

"She did not, Beetle-brain."

"Bird-wit!"

"Nodcock!"

Gideon chuckled. "Mama is feeling fine this morning, and she wants you both to come and see the surprise we have for you."

The pronouncement garnered Damon's immediate and wide-eyed attention as it did Rafferty's skeptical reserve.

"What kind of surprise?" Rafe asked

Gideon grinned. "You will have to wait and see."

Damon ran straight to the nursery door. Rafferty shrugged his shoulders and followed cautiously behind.

For once they, neither of them, thought to take their pets.

Walking beside Gideon, Damon raised a seeking hand his way. Gideon was touched and humbled as he took the small hand in his own. The eager child bounced, pulled ahead, swung back and all but stood on his hands, asking questions all the way down the stairs.

Rafe kept to Gideon's exact pace, giving each and every one of his answers to Damon's questions his full attention. Gideon could almost see the workings of Rafe's mind reflected in his expressions as he measured and weighed those answers.

Sabrina was back in her own bed, washed, dressed, hair brushed and smelling of lilacs, and she beamed when she saw them, and held out a tiny bundle, wrapped like a mummy, for their inspection.

"A brother?" Damon asked, excited.

"A sister," Sabrina said. "Juliana."

Rafferty shook his head. "Send it back. I'd really rather have a brother."

"You have a brother," Damon said, affronted. "Me."

"I want one I like."

Damon shrugged. "Too bad." He grinned. "I wanted a dog and I got one, so a sister is fine, I guess. Can we bring her to the nursery to play now?"

Gideon chuckled. "A little soon for that, I think. Juliana will stay with your mama for a while."

Juliana screwed up her face for a moment, then she calmed and blew a bubble and everyone laughed.

Damon regarded his mother. "We should show her to the man watching us from across the street. He seems sad and I think Juliana would make him laugh."

Gideon sobered, but his wife bristled. No, more than that, she shuddered. Her face lost color, her eyes darkened, and, yes, she pulled Juliana just the smallest bit closer.

"What the deuce?" Gideon asked, questioning all of it, not the least of which was Damon's ludicrous tale. "Damon," he warned. "You are frightening your mama."

"Damon," Sabrina said. "You know what I told you about making up stories."

"But the man is real, Mama. He watched the house for a long time this morning, and he is bent and old and leans on his cane. He is ugly like a hideous beast and scary as a ferocious dragon." Damon growled for good measure.

Rafferty laughed. "What a cork-brained whisker."

"Is not, clod-pole. He even reminds me of someone."

"Who?" Rafe scoffed. "The dragon you keep beneath the bed?"

"What do you know, paper-skull?"

"I know I did not see anyone."

"It was early, mutton-breath. You were still sleeping."

"Dragon-brain."

"Boys. Enough," Sabrina said.

At first, Gideon was afraid Veronica had sent someone to harm Sabrina. But while his spiteful former mistress was certainly capable, Damon's dragon put the unlikelihood into perspective.

Gideon lifted Damon onto the edge of the bed to sit beside Sabrina. "Damon, is something bothering you?"

The boy shook his head, changed his mind midway, and nodded. "Sort of."

Gideon regarded Sabrina, and in a bit of silent communication, he understood that she wanted him to continue. "Tell us what is wrong, Damon, and let us help you solve your problem."

Damon sighed. "I just—"

His new sister sneezed, diverting his attention before he looked back at Gideon. "I need to know what you think Juliana should call you. You know, when she is smart enough to talk and all, 'cause she might be worried about that."

"Ah." Gideon lifted Rafe to perch beside his twin.

Again, Gideon sought and received Sabrina's approval before responding. "I have considered the problem myself," he said.

Damon's eyes widened. "Honestly?"

"Honestly. I thought, because Juliana never knew your father, that she can have no problem calling me Papa if she wishes."

He watched their faces. Damon's expression fell as Rafferty's tightened.

"Now, if you asked what you and Rafferty might call me," Gideon went on, skewering Damon's attention, "I would have to say that the decision must be yours. I have many names. You could call me any of them and perhaps use Uncle before your choice, like Uncle Gideon or Uncle Stanthorpe. I suppose Uncle St. Goddard sounds funny. Though some of my friends just call me Saint. Uncle Saint?"

"That's silly," Damon said, tickled.

"It is," Gideon agreed. "How about if you were to use Papa rather than Uncle before any of my names? Papa Gideon; that could work if you wanted."

Rafe shrugged.

Damon shook his head, not quite liking it, giving Gideon hope. "I think you had best choose either Papa Gideon or just plain Papa, then," he said. "Again, whatever you call me will be your choice. You do not need to decide right away. Think about it for a while and decide when it is comfortable for you."

Without a word, Rafferty slipped off the bed and headed for the door.

"Rafe," Sabrina called. "Where are you going?"

The pensive boy turned toward his mother, keeping his hand on the knob. "Mincemeat needs me."

"Let him go," Gideon said.

Sabrina nodded and Rafe left.

Damon scrambled up to his mother's side and kissed her. "I gots to go think." Then he kissed Juliana's tiny cheek and hopped off the bed. As he passed Gideon, he reached up and tugged his hand, holding it for a moment before he ran out.

"That went well," Gideon said.

Sabrina looked concerned. "We shall see."

When Damon had touched his hand, Gideon sensed a kind of connection, one he did not comprehend, as if Damon had pricked his finger but

Gideon felt the pain. Gideon knew only that it made him both uncomfortable and hopeful.

This fathering business was much more demanding than he anticipated, and still he did not know whether he was up to it.

A father was a man whose seed had "taken," a man like his own. A father ignored small beings and took mothers away from same. A father sneered at questions and physically punished dirty hands and childhood transgressions. He beat rebellion out of one to first blood, and taunted weakness to the point iniquity could be misrepresented as strength.

No wonder he was afraid to be a father. No wonder he had wanted at first to turn tail and run.

At this moment, he was feeling very much as if that might still be a good idea. What did a cold-hearted rogue like him know of children anyway, except what kind of father not to be.

When Juliana started fussing, he took her from Sabrina. And when the babe looked up at him as if he had all the answers in her world, Gideon realized that he would change nothing. He had become a father, whether he wanted to or not, and he would do his best to be a good one, or die trying.

After he walked Juliana for a bit and she fell asleep, he kissed her small cheek and placed her in her cradle. "There's my sleepy girl."

Then he bent over Sabrina. "I need to go and see my poor grandmother, who knows only that I have married, not that I have three children."

Sabrina touched his sleeve. "If there *is* a man across the street . . ."

Gideon smiled his reassurance. "If there is, I

shall send him packing, posthaste, and set the Runners on him."

"Thank you," she said, her relief clear.

"If there is neither a phantom watcher nor a hideous dragon, however, I would like to keep previous appointments with my man of affairs and my tailor, if I possibly can. That is, if you feel you can do without me for the morning. In which case, I shall see you again at luncheon."

Pleased that Gideon felt the need to tell his grandmother about her children, and glad he cared whether she needed him or not, Sabrina kissed him with passion when he bent to her.

"Mmm. Rest while I am gone, so you will be up to giving Papa your attention again someday soon."

Sabrina could not rest, she was too busy fretting over Damon's tale of a man across the street. Yes, Damon had an imagination, but he never insisted his stories into blatant lies. Details like the time of day, the fact that Rafe was sleeping, and most important, that the man seemed familiar, worried her. The boys had been only three when, along with her, they had been given by Brian to Lowick, so they might very well find Lowick familiar.

And Lowick might be hideous now. In her defensive assault with the rusty blade she found in his cellar, she could easily have scarred him, though, God help her, she had hoped she killed him.

More than ever, she wanted to tell Gideon about the man she was sold to for the price of her husband's gambling debts. Life was good here at Stanthorpe Place. Safe. Gideon cared for her in his own way. He cared for the children. But how would he feel if he knew about her shameful past?

Whether he knew of it or not, he would protect

her, of that she was certain. So, if she already had his protection, why risk telling him?

There was the problem. The risk. And she was not willing to take it. Decision made.

Not that she did not trust, Gideon, precisely. She trusted him more than she did most men, especially her first husband. Yes, she was hiding money from him, which she kept in her desk, where he had come upon her twice now. But she kept it for a reason. In the event Lowick located her, she would need the money to get away. Except that for the first time in her life, she did not want to leave.

Here, she was safe. Here, her children were safe. Here, even her money was safe, for if Gideon did find it, he would not take it. She simply did not want to explain its existence. She had worked hard for that money for years, sewing, writing letters, washing clothes.

Her first husband used to search out and steal her secreted coins when he could, until she began sewing them, individually, into flat, oilcloth bellybands the twins wore beneath their diapers.

If not for the money she had kept from Brian's greedy hands, she might never have gotten herself and the twins away from Lowick and safely to Hawksworth.

If they were safe.

In weak moments, Sabrina very much feared that Brian's fall into the Thames had not come about by accident, as the Runners thought, that Homer Lowick had pushed Brian, because her flight negated the payment of his gambling debts.

In weak moments, she expected to come face-to-face with Homer Lowick at every turn.

But here they were safe.

Gideon would keep them safe.



Gideon's paternal grandmother, now the Dowager Duchess of Basingstoke, regarded Gideon as if he had grown horns and a tail. "Three of them?"

Gideon nodded. "Two boys and a girl."

His grandmother shook her head. "I said to get yourself a bride and an heir, not someone else's heirs."

"The boys are scamps." Gideon grinned. "Damon has enough energy to power Trevithick's locomotive. As a matter of fact, 'catch-me-who-can' is a good way to describe that one. And his twin, Rafferty, Rafe, is going to be a great thinker someday. They are full of questions and make me dizzy sometimes."

Gideon regarded his grandmother's appalled expression. "I thought I should run when I first saw them, but you will never believe—"

"I begin to think I can believe anything."

"I rather like them," Gideon said. "Sticky fingers, pup puddles, and all."

"That will pass."

"Not before I get some of my own, I hope."

"Are you ill?" His grandmother rose and tested his brow with the back of her frail, gnarled hand. "What have you done with my heartless rogue of a grandson?"

Gideon took her hand, smoothed his thumb over her translucent, parchmentlike skin, and kissed her knuckles. "We named the new babe Juliana."

His grandmother blinked at the welling of tears in her eyes before turning her hand to cup his cheek. "I do not remember ever having felt so honored."

She squared her shoulders and reclaimed her composure. "I was afraid that your selfish parents had put you off marriage for good. I expected to have to bully you into getting yourself an heir."

Gideon chuckled. "Pray do not tell me how you planned to accomplish that," he said. "The picture in my mind is infamous."

"Rude boy." She kissed the top of his head and Gideon made to rise.

"No, sit, sit. That was not a dismissal. I shall call for tea. Eventually, I want to hear about every member of your new family, especially about your bride. But first, let me tell you something I learned about your brother and Veronica Cartwright."


Gideon returned to Stanthorpe Place later than he expected, because he had made a call at Bow street after all, and set the Runners to looking into Lady Veronica Cartwright's dealings and finances.

When he entered his study, he found Chalmer trying to clean an ink stain the size of a dinner plate off the Oriental carpet.

Gideon smiled when he saw it, not because he disliked the carpet, but because of the inky paw prints weaving in and out of the stain in all directions. "Throw it out and purchase a new one," Gideon said. "Or put it somewhere beneath a bed or a sofa."

He went up to the nursery to talk to the boys.

As one, they backed up when he entered.

Gideon shook his head, knowing that nothing he could say would negate their fear, that he must prove to them, over time, that he would not hurt them. "I came to see if you would like to go exploring with me later this afternoon."

"Exploring where?" Damon asked, stepping nearer.

"This house, of course. The wonders in my study are nothing to the marvels in some of the other rooms. I have a display of Stanthorpe armor in the long gallery. Did you know that?"

Rafe's chin went up. "You mean you will show us whatever we want to see?"

"I will not allow you to play with swords or pistols, mind, but yes, within reason, you may examine whatever you wish."

"Ripping," Damon said.

Rafe narrowed his eyes. "Why?"

"So we can spend some time together, get to know each other better. Like when we went hunting. So you will have a chance to examine things that interest you. So I will be able to answer your questions and keep you from breaking your heads, or whatever else on you that might get cracked. If I were there, I could prevent other breakage and spills as well. But most of all, it is your necks I am concerned about."

Rafe actually grinned. "Famous."

When Gideon got to Sabrina's bedchamber, she had just finished feeding Juliana. "How many times a day does she eat? Ten? Twenty?"

"It seems so," she said, wiping Juliana's milk-wet mouth. "How is your grandmother?"

"She is well. Eager to meet her namesake, and the boys, and you. She will be coming to visit soon."

"Your grandmother is coming here?"

"She is." Gideon could not keep from taking

Juliana from her cradle and putting her on his shoulder.

"What day is she coming?" Sabrina asked, rebuttoning her bodice. "Please tell me you were able to hold her off for a little while."

"Oh, I was." Gideon bounced Juliana as he passed her by. "She should not be here for another hour at the least."

# Fifteen

For a week after Juliana's birth, Gideon moved back into his own bedchamber so Sabrina could get some sleep and recover. During those nights, he missed his wife more than he cared to admit.

On the eighth evening, he appeared in her bed-chamber in his dressing gown. She sat at her dressing table, brushing her hair, and he sat beside her and took up the brush. "I miss sleeping with you," he said. "No, it is more than that. I miss laughing with you when you are in my arms. And I miss being alone with you. We are never alone anymore."

When Sabrina leaned against him, he encircled her with his arms and brought her close.

"And you miss playtime," she said.

Gideon cleared his throat. "Yes, well . . . but not only that."

"I am sorry that we are never alone." She regarded him, steadily. "With three children—"

"I am not complaining about the children."

"I keep expecting you to. The twins are acting like pups, following you around as if you had a brisket bone in your pocket." She touched his face, ran her hand over his day's growth of beard. "Why are they not afraid of you, I wonder, with your dark, brooding looks. Wherever you go, whatever you do, they are either watching or following."

"I had noticed, and at first I found it amusing." He cleared his throat, embarrassed. "It is somewhat like hero worship, is it not? But after a while, I did begin to feel a bit . . . crowded. But today, when they seemed to have disappeared. . . ." He shrugged. "Then I was really bothered."

Sabrina rose, removed her dressing gown, and climbed into her bed.

Gideon just stood there and watched, wanting her in his arms so badly, he could taste the want. Not that he needed her. But, frankly, just the wanting was an experience he found almost too uncomfortable for words.

"I saw the boys following you," she said. "So I told them to give you some time to yourself."

"I am sorry you did that. When you see them in the morning, tell them, first thing, to come and see me, will you? I missed them today."

"You mean that you are not feeling suffocated?"

He liked their attention. He liked when they needed him or just wanted to show him something as simple as a garden snail they had found, but for some reason, he was loath to admit it. "I decided that the unknown was worse," he said. "Perhaps it is because when they are following me, I at least know what they are up to." He sighed, unable to see her and long for her any longer. "I will leave you to sleep."

"Are you not going to kiss me good night?"

Gideon raised his chin, determined to be strong, then he caught her smile and it was just a little too—"Wait a minute. Are you teasing me?" He needed no more provocation than that to move toward her.

When she opened arms to him, his heart tripped. "Come to bed, your grace."

Gideon shed his dressing gown in short order and took his bride in his arms as fast. This is home, he thought, and sighed, aware he would have scoffed at the notion a mere month before. Despite the vulnerable implications, Gideon delighted in having Sabrina in his arms again.

"Mmm." She kissed him. "I have worried that after witnessing Juliana's birth you would never want to sleep with me again."

"You want me to sleep with you, then? It is not just our bargain you are fulfilling?"

"You are being precipitate."

Gideon chuckled. "Whatever you may accuse me of, being 'precipitate' is not among my faults. Nevertheless, for now, because you are not ready for more, I want only to hold you and talk with you. I want to wake up with you to feed Juliana in the night. I—"

Sabrina looked back at him when he did not finish. "You . . . ?"

"Sound like a besotted fool."

"Are you?"

"Whatever I am, naked with you is best. Here," he said. "Let us remove your gown." After they did, Gideon sighed in contentment and began to relearn his wife's body. "Good God, half of you is missing."

Sabrina giggled. "Not missing, sleeping in her cradle, praise be."

"Oh, this is nice," Gideon said. "When you are

not 'with child' you are a fine figure of a woman, I see."

"You see nothing, this room is as dark as your eyes."

"I see in this way," he said, running his hands everywhere now. "No, do not tense up," he said. "I know my limits. You still have healing to do and I promise to be on my best behavior in bed."

Sabrina barked a laugh. "That will be the day. Gideon?"

"Yes, Sabrina."

"I might like being naked in bed with you too."

It was a beginning, he thought.

Damon and Rafferty knocked on Gideon's bed-chamber door during his morning grooming.

Bilbury answered and started to send them away.

"No, Bilbury," Gideon said. "Damon, Rafe, come in," he called. "I missed you yesterday. How are Mincemeat and Drizzle?"

Damon sighed. "Drizzle sprinkled Miss Min-chip."

"Oops," Gideon said.

Rafe grinned. "She was not happy. And she says that Mincemeat is getting too fat."

"Of course he is getting fat. He is always stealing food." Gideon thought the boys seemed intimidated by Bilbury's ferocious presence. "Would you like to sit down while Bilbury shaves me?" he asked them. "We can have a 'man-to-man chat' while he does."

The boys sat on the straight chairs Bilbury brought over, side by side, their small legs out straight. "What do men talk about during man-to-man chats?" Damon wanted to know.

"Man things," Gideon explained. "You know. Horses, racing, carriages, wom—er cats and dogs."

"We never saw a man shaved," Damon said, standing and stepping closer. "Do you ever worry that he will cut your nose off?"

Rafferty snickered.

"No," Gideon said. "But I thought he was going to cut my ear off, once."

Bilbury bristled. "Your grace. I hope you know I am a better valet than to do that."

Rafe stepped very close. "Are valets always starched and bristly?" he asked beneath his breath but loud enough to make Bilbury stiffen.

"Always." Gideon winked at the boy. "And bossy too. But you will never look finer than when your valet has turned you out."

"Thank you, your grace."


The following morning, to Bilbury's dismay, the boys returned at shaving time, as they did the next day, and the next, and the next.

The morning Gideon wanted an early start, he sent Bilbury to fetch them before allowing the man to begin.

That night in bed, Sabrina rolled into her husband's arms. "What do you find to talk about with the boys while you are shaving? They have been raving about your man-to-man chats."

"We talk about man things." Gideon kissed his wife's nose. "Mostly about how to please the ladies."

The day his estate manager, James Warren, came

down from Hertfordshire to meet with Gideon, the boys showed up in Gideon's study during the meeting, so he invited them to stay.

An hour later, Sabrina opened the door in a panic. "I cannot find—"

Damon was sitting on Gideon's lap, Rafe on Jim Warren's. They all four waved at her standing there, dumbstruck.

"We are discussing crop rotation and horse breeding, Mama," Rafe said. "Because one day I shall have an estate of my own." Gideon thought Rafferty looked happier than he had ever seen him.

"I am listening too," Damon said. "Because I am going to raise race horses."

Temporarily, however, the only race horse Damon rode was Gideon himself, daily and with enthusiasm.

Gideon thought the boy a "bruising" rider, literally.


To stop the vicious gossip Veronica had started, Grandmama was going to give a Christmas ball in Sabrina's honor, it was decided after a week of discussion.

"Once everyone gets to know you, my dear," Grandmama said, patting her hand, "they will realize what a liar that woman is."

She regarded her grandson with a raised brow, and Sabrina saw from whence he inherited his habit of doing so. "They will also realize that my grandson's taste in women has finally, vastly, improved."

Gideon, in turn, looked insulted, sheepish, and proud.

Grandmama wanted to introduce her grand-daughter-in-law to Society and show one and all the refined beauty who had won Stanthorpe. "The minute they meet you, Sabrina," she declared. "They will love you as we do. And they will know exactly why Gideon married you."

"Heaven help us all," Sabrina said.

"But everyone who is anyone is off to the country for Christmas," Gideon pointed out.

"Nonsense. I am here," Grandmama snapped. "Yes, I know that town is quiet and thin of company at this time of year, but there are enough of the 'right' people staying through Christmas to make for a comfortable enough squeeze. Soon enough after, the word will spread to the rest."

The day Grandmama came to pick Sabrina up for the final fitting of her ball gown, the poor old woman came upon her tough-as-nails grandson racing through the foyer, whinnying, Rafe on his back, charging him to go faster, Damon running behind.

"I shall need a month in the country, at least, to recover from that sight," she said.

Juliana was nearly four weeks old by then, and Sabrina was glad Gideon worked off his excess energy playing with the boys. Fast approaching was the day she would be well enough to consummate their marriage, and she was more skittish over that than she was at the thought of being introduced to the cream of London Society.

Two days before Christmas, Gideon, Sabrina, and the children climbed into two carriages for the move across town to Grandmama's luxurious town house on St. James's Square. Sabrina's ball would take place there that night.

"You must all move to my house," Grandmama had said several days earlier, beginning her argument. "Sabrina, you would be able to feed Juliana before the ball and return upstairs midway through, if needs be." That pretty much won Sabrina over, Gideon thought. Damn, the old bird was good.

"If the boys were there, I would allow them to peek into the ballroom from the musicians gallery, early in the evening," she said. "They would be able to see you both in your finery, dancing together at a great ball." Gideon knew that second argument won Rafe and Damon's approval.

"And since the day after the ball is Christmas Eve," she added. "We can all settle in for our first family Christmas together." This won him over, though he thought Sabrina and the boys looked less certain by then.

"It all sounded so easy, so reasonable, when Grandmama suggested all of this," Sabrina all but wailed in the carriage on their way to Basingstoke. "But I am nervous as a cat."

"Mincemeat is not nervous, are you, fellow?" Rafe asked the cat purring in his lap.

"Which reminds me," Gideon said to Damon. "You did take Drizzle for his walk, as I asked, right before we left?"

Damon petted his pup's exposed belly. "He drizzled like he was s'pose to, didn't you, boy?"

The boys had not taken to calling him Papa, Gideon mused, regarding them across the carriage with their pets. Neither did they call him Papa Gideon. Damon had, the day after their talk, called him Uncle Papa—for effect, Gideon suspected, then he had rolled on the floor giggling. But nothing more had come of the conversation.

Not that it mattered.

At Basingstoke, the children, including Juliana, were settled into the nursery. Sabrina and Gideon took the master suite that Grandmama had vacated the day she lost husband number two.

The rest of the evening was devoted to dressing for the ball. Because it never took Gideon as long to dress as Sabrina, he bided his time, while Sabrina prepared for the ball. No more black, he thought with a smile.

Suddenly he wondered what he was doing pacing, waiting to see Sabrina in her gown, when he had much rather see her out of it.

By the time the thought was finished, he had crossed his dressing room to hers, where he found her soaking in a slipper bath before the fire, hair piled atop her head in glorious disarray, alabaster skin gleaming from the fire's glow. "A dream come true," he said.

Sabrina squeaked and dropped her soap. "Goodness. You startled me."

"Why have I not caught you in your bath before?" Gideon shut the door between their dressing rooms, lest Bilbury enter on his side. "Forgive me. I could wait no longer to see you."

"You can never wait," she said. "You are the kind of man who would want to see the bride before the wedding."

"Excuse me, but in our case I wanted to *bed* the bride before the wedding."

"You want to bed the bride every day."

"Every hour." He knelt beside the tub, rolled up his sleeves, and went on a search for the soap, except that he found all manner of interesting diversions. "How old is Juliana now?"

"Not old enough. Gideon!" She slapped the water as she went for his hands, splashing them both.

Gideon touched his forehead to hers. "I am going to expire for wanting you."

"You have me."

"Do I?" he asked, sober of a sudden. "Sometimes I am not so sure."

Her maid came in then, and it was all Sabrina could do not to send poor Alice packing.

Gideon rose and left without another word, leaving Sabrina deflated and hurt by his words, despite the truth in them.

Her husband was a powerfully sexual being, she must remember. Even without consummation, she had experienced more fulfillment in her short time with him than she had in her four-year marriage to Brian.

Then again, she could never compare the two men.

Brian felt compelled toward brutality, in and out of bed.

Gideon was a gentle man, in the true sense of the word. Yet the thought of full surrender to him still scared Sabrina witless. Not that he would hurt her. He never would. He would always put her first, whether his aim was her welfare, her well-being, or her sexual fulfillment.

No, it was that she would be giving up the last vestige of herself left to her. But she simply did not know whether she could continue to withhold her heart from a man who demanded everything, in all ways, and who gave her as much, though he, too, seemed to guard his heart much of the time.

She was beginning to fear, however, that she no longer wanted to withhold hers, not from Gideon, and that was the most frightening notion of all.

Sabrina swallowed against tears of confusion and turned her attention to dressing.

In his bedchamber, Gideon ached as he paced, frustration, anger, and determination coursing through him in turn.

All he wanted was to seduce his own damned stubborn wife, by God. He ran a hand through his thick waves. How could he blame Sabrina for shying away from so final a commitment to a worthless rogue like him?

In that moment, he felt somewhat the way he used to as he watched his parents' absorption in each other, wishing that a place existed in their circle for him.

Not much in life had changed for him, except that, perhaps now, to a degree, Damon must see something . . . some worth, in him. Else, why the boy's continued attention, his ease and comfort in his presence? Even Rafe sought him out more often than not.

And Juliana, well, to her, he seemed to be . . . everything. Heady notion. Too bad she was too small to know what she was about.

Still, the children, the "others," they all seemed to look up to him. "So where the bloody devil am I going wrong with my own damned, stubborn wife?" he shouted.

"I am sure I do not know, your grace," Bilbury said, coming into the room.

* * *

Ten minutes before the receiving line was due to form, Bilbury checked Gideon's appearance one last time. That his meticulous valet regarded him as if he were a work of art encouraged Gideon. Bilbury removed a speck from his black tailed frock coat here, straightened its stand-fall collar there.

At the last, his fastidious valet whisked a brush down Gideon's silver satin knee breeches, smoothed his white silk stockings, and quick-buffed his black patent pumps. Within the pocket of Gideon's white-embroidered satin waistcoat, his valet tucked his watch and fob, and last but not least, he tied Gideon's cravat in a perfect Oriental.

"Shall I do, Bilbury?"

His man held up a finger as if all that was required was one last touch, then he slipped Gideon's diamond and ruby stickpin into his neckcloth and beamed. "Splendid, your grace."

Gideon nodded. "Thank you, Bilbury." He grabbed a flat square velvet box and crossed the dressing rooms into his wife's bedchamber. There he stopped—moving and breathing.

The clock struck before he could speak, and even then he could think of only one word. "Stunning."

"But there is too little dress." In panic, Sabrina turned before her cheval glass. "Grandmama insisted it would suit."

"It suits," Gideon said, calming her. "The dress and the goddess within it suit *me* very well. Gad, I am lucky you are mine."

"Oh, Gideon." Tears sprang to her eyes as she stepped into Gideon's arms and he closed them hard around her. They held each other for a time, then they kissed before stepping apart. "Thank you," she said. "I feel better now."

"So do I." He regarded her dress again. "What do you call the style? It is very different, yet very much de rigueur."

"Madame Suzette calls it a 'pseudo-Greek classical Empire-style gown, over a slip of taffeta.' I call it 'amaranthus gown with scandalous décolletage.'"

"I always enjoy anything scandalous, and I applaud the décolletage." He stroked her breast along the edge of it until her eyes seemed as warm as he felt. Dangerous. He lowered his hands to his sides. "I also like that train attached at the back, the way it sweeps the ground behind you as you walk."

"The color is so bright after wearing black for so long."

Too long, Gideon thought, for the likes of Brian Whitcomb. "It is a pinkish sort of purple, so you could, perhaps, think of it as half-mourning, if you must. The dress does suit you, Sabrina. You look a positive confection with your breasts pushed up by the gown's high waist in that way." Gideon grinned and lifted her breasts in his hands, just to test his theory, winning himself a sample of his wife's tinkling laughter.

"You, Sabrina St. Goddard, are every inch the confection I would most like to feast upon, but before I do, there is the small matter of Grandmama's ball."

He offered her the flat velvet box. "For my duchess. Open it."

"What is it?" Sabrina asked as if she were afraid to accept it.

"Something to complement your gown, not that you do not enhance it gloriously without jewels, but. . . ." He pulled the box's lid back for her viewing pleasure.

Gideon feared for a moment that she would faint, so pale did she become when she saw the triple-strand necklace of diamonds and rubies. "It matches your stickpin," she said.

"They are both St. Goddard family heirlooms. This necklace was to be passed to my bride. Later, our eldest son—providing we ever consummate our marriage. . . ." Gideon softened his comment with a wink. "And we will. Our son will someday present this very necklace to his duchess, as I am now presenting it to mine. Turn around, so I may fasten it."

Sabrina's hands were shaking a minute later when she touched the ornate circlet, as if she could not believe it rested there, against her very own skin. "Oh, Gideon, I am afraid I will lose it."

"You will not." He fished in his pocket, opened her hand, and placed something more inside. "Matching ear bobs," he said, watching her in her mirror as she fastened them.

"I will be the envy of every man present," he said, coming to stand behind her.

Their eyes met in the full-length mirror.

"And you, my dragon rogue, will flutter all female hearts. If you were not mine, every unmarried lady at the ball would pursue you."

Gideon raised an arrogant brow.

Sabrina raised her own. "And every married one as well, I suppose?"

Gideon grinned. "Naturally."

# Sixteen

"I feel as if we will grow roots if we stand in this receiving line much longer," Sabrina whispered an hour later. "I have met so many lords and ladies that I will never keep them all straight."

"So many boring lords and ladies, you mean," Gideon said. "And I do feel the distinct sprouting of a taproot."

"That will be enough, you two." Gideon's grandmother tapped his shoulder with her fan. "Behave yourselves."

"Grandmama, if we were not behaving ourselves, we would be in b— Good evening Lady Digby, Lord Digby. May I present my duchess?"

When the receiving line broke up, Gideon led Sabrina behind Grandmama to the top of the stairs. As the announcer intoned "The Duke and Duchess of Stanthorpe," Gideon covered Sabrina's hand on his arm and squeezed it. "Chin up, Beautiful," he said as they descended the long, graceful stairway into the ballroom.

The entire assemblage—hundreds—stopped talking. Some even appeared to stop breathing, simply to watch them descend. Sabrina's heart quickened. "Everyone is staring."

"They are savoring the sight of the most exqui-site woman in England," Gideon replied. "Flash them your smile, Sabrina, and a dozen men will swoon as their ladies turn green. Gad, I am proud to have you on my arm."

They stopped at the bottom of the stairs, until the orchestra struck up the waltz Gideon requested for the first dance.

He bowed. "May I have the honor, your grace?"

Sabrina curtsied. "I would be delighted."

Gideon swept his bride into his arms and waltzed her onto the floor, the two of them dancing alone in the huge gilt-and-crystal ballroom.

Captive to her husband's hot obsidian gaze, Sabrina felt as if they waltzed alone in the center of the universe.

Her bubble burst, however, when the highest echelon of London Society, along the periphery of the ballroom, broke into spontaneous applause.

A few minutes later, Sabrina gazed about her. "Why is no one else dancing? I expected everyone to join us."

"They are affording us the honor of the first dance."

"I feel conspicuous."

"That's what comes of being a duchess."

"Why did you ask Lady Jersey, when she came through the receiving line, if I could waltz? Should you not have asked me?"

"There are rules in London Society, which I will teach you in time, though none are quite as strict for a married woman. In this case, however, be-cause of Veronica's venomous rumors, I thought it prudent to stroke Society's haughtiest feathers, be-ginning at the top. Sally Jersey, you will soon discover, is as close to the top as you can get without tripping over Prinny."

"Prinny?"

"The Prince Regent, someday to become King George the Fourth?"

"I see."

"If we can position ourselves on Sally Jersey's good side," Gideon said, "we are on our way to full acceptance."

"If you care so much to be on Society's good side, why did you marry me?"

"I have often wondered that myself," her husband dared reply.

Indignation stiffened Sabrina's spine, until Gideon leaned near, stroking her ear with his warm breath. "Perhaps because the moment I saw you, I knew that I wanted you in my bed."

Sabrina raised her chin. "I am certain you have wanted to bed any number of women at first sight."

"I have. But they were, none of them, in a delicate condition at the time, believe me. Neither did I consider marriage, even for a minute, to any of them."

"Do not mock my intelligence. You married me to honor your promise to Hawksworth."

"I could have honored it as well, I believe, by buying you a house and settling a more-than-comfortable competence on you. I considered it before I met you. Of course, back then, I did not know that settlements would be required for each of the boys, as would a dowry for Sweetpea."

His words lightened her heart. "We gave our daughter a beautiful name. Why do you call her Sweetpea?"

"Well, she is sweet and she is always p—"

"Gideon."

The outrageous twinkle in his eye made Sabrina laugh outright.

"Do not look now," he said, "but you have just earned the adoration of another score of admirers."

Sabrina scanned the crowd watching them and scoffed.

"Believe it or not, in stroking Society's plumes, I am thinking ahead to the eventual acceptance of Damon, Rafferty, and . . . Sweetpea."

"Why do you not have pet names for the boys?"

"First she chides me about one pet name and now she requires more. But I can think of none that suit our boys better than their own names."

"Hawksworth used to call them Demon and Rapscallion."

Gideon barked a laugh. "That sounds like him, but I do not believe either boy deserves so negative a monogram."

For better or worse, another piece of Sabrina's heart fell to her husband.

She barely made peace with the fact before she noticed, on the sidelines, the figure of a squat little man she could not place being introduced to Lady Veronica. Much as he reminded her of Lowick, she knew that one such as he would never be accepted in this exalted company.

Something in the scene dimmed Sabrina's joy, but since she could not seem to wrap her mind around the reason for her inner tremor, she relegated the odd fancy to the back of her mind.

"We are being watched again," she said, more to make conversation and turn her thoughts than anything.

Gideon chuckled. "I daresay. Like me, none of them can keep their gazes from you."

"Are the jewels too much, do you think?"

"For the Duchess of Stanthorpe, the most breathtaking woman in the room? I think not. Besides, you are not conspicuous in your jewels, Sabrina, but in the beauty you radiate."

"Oh, Gideon."

"Ah," Gideon said. "I see Lady Veronica and her escort are rudely joining us on the dance floor."

Gideon raised a particularly mischievous brow. "The rogue my grandmother names me prompts me to teach the 'Lady,' and I use the term 'loosely,' a lesson." He laughed at his double entendre, slowed, and skewered his wife with a heated gaze. "Shall we?"

"Gideon . . ." But her warning came too late. Her husband swooped in for a kiss, there, before the cream of Society, until she became his slave, fell in with his plan, and gave herself up to his sensual assault.

Applause began, swelled, deafened, and brought them back to earth.

Then, as if an ax had fallen, the roar of approval ended and silence fell.

A man, almost pear-shaped in figure, imperfect, yet magnificent in dress and bearing, crossed the near-empty dance floor, making straight for them.

When the commanding man stopped, Gideon made him an elegant bow.

Heart hammering of a sudden, Sabrina could think only to award him the deep curtsy Grandmama had had her practicing for weeks, in the unlikely event that—

Oh, no, could this be the man for whom she had prepared?

"Shame on you, Stanthorpe," the man said before Sabrina found his bright blue gaze trained on her in a way that suggested he could see beneath her petticoats. And she recognized him.

With one silent, majestic look, the Prince Regent relegated her husband to the sidelines.

Then the prince regarded the other dancing couple and made a shooing motion with his hand, sending Veronica and her escort scurrying off like mice from the scullery.

Sabrina wished she had not again seen the retreating figure of Veronica's escort. She might have enjoyed the moment more.

"My dear?" the prince said. "You look as if you have taken a fright."

"I . . . fear that the honor you do me weakens my knees to the point that I will swoon at your royal feet."

The heir to the throne of England laughed, full-bodied, head thrown back, and swept Sabrina into his arms to complete the dance—thereby bestowing upon her Society's coveted seal of approval.

Sabrina forgot her worry over Veronica's escort and gave herself up to the amazing moment. And as they swept past Gideon, she caught his beaming pride and approval.

Sabrina was more pleased with her husband's approval than she was with her future monarch's lusty regard. She gave her full attention to her royal partner, however, flashing him the smile Gideon earlier praised.

* * *

To all and sundry, the ball was considered a great success, perfect in every way. To everyone, that was, except Sabrina herself.

Yes, she had made a conquest of the Prince of Wales.

Yes, Lady Veronica had scuttled away, tail between her legs, but then, so had the woman's nameless partner, a situation Sabrina still found disquieting. She tried to quiz Gideon on the identity of the man, but apparently her husband had never seen him before either.

She knew she must soon consider telling Gideon of her concerns, and she would—consider it—after the first of the year.

For now, she decided, she would concentrate on getting through Christmas with Gideon and his grandmother.

Grandmama had a Yule log cut, which sat drying outside near the mews. In half an hour's time, they were all to go in carriages to Epping Forest, near Wanstead, on the outskirts of town, to trudge the woods for holly and mistletoe, which they would use later to decorate the house together.

Everyone was going except Juliana, who would remain here at Grandmama's with the nurse Grandmama hired. But Juliana chose this very morning to dawdle over her breakfast. Sabrina was trying to be patient with her, when Gideon arrived to see where his wife had gotten to.

"Juliana does not seem to want to stop nursing," she said. "Though I cannot believe she is still hungry after so long a time."

Gideon bent over to regard the babe. "Good morning, Sweetpea. Mama says you are dawdling and holding up our gay Christmas parade through the woods. I cannot say as I blame you. I tend to dawdle myself over your delicious mama."

"Gideon!"

Juliana cooed and waved her hands in a great show of excitement when he spoke, and she lost her grip on her meal with the smile she gave him.

"Good Lord, she has bestowed upon you her first smile," Sabrina said, straightening her bodice. "Not that I am surprised. She became your slave, or you became hers, at her birth."

"Are you my girl?" Gideon asked, taking the happy baby into his arms. "Are you my Sweetpea? I bet you would like to come with us, would you not? After all," Gideon said, regarding Sabrina. "This is Christmas."

"If we take her, she will require carrying, and we are not certain that the boys will not also require it."

"Nonsense, if Grandmama is coming, the terrain cannot be so bad as that. Come, let us put our Julie in her woolens and take her with us. It is not so very cold today."

"If you keep this up, by the time she is ten, she will have you jumping to her every wish."

"And what else are papas for than to jump through the hoops their little girls set up for them?" Gideon asked his adoring daughter.

To make a merry party, they decided they should all travel in the same carriage—Gideon, Sabrina, the twins, the baby, and Grandmama. Problem was, Damon and Juliana both insisted, rather loudly, that they required the exact same spot on Gideon's lap.

Everyone took turns trying to hold Juliana, but she would quiet only when Gideon took her.

Grandmama crowed and took Rafferty onto her lap. "I shall have my favorite with me," she said, earning Rafe's adoration.

"And I shall take Damon," Sabrina said. "As we can insist that he keep quiet, and save all our ears."

"Done," Gideon said, trading a whining four-year-old for a screaming baby, and when silence descended, everyone breathed a sigh of relief, though to soothe Damon's pout, Gideon gave him a wink.

The trudge through heath and grass, toward groves of hornbeam, beech, and oak, turned out to be wet and chill but brisk and invigorating. It was Christmas after all. Their footsteps in turn crunched and squished, as the layer of snow from the day before had already begun to melt in places. But everyone persisted, the boys chattering and running in turn, except when they were rewarded with deer sightings, and they turned still as statues to watch.

Finally they came to a coppice edged by a huge holly, bright with berries in its upper branches.

"The berries are too high up in the tree," Sabrina said.

"Nonsense, Gideon can reach them," Grandmama said. "Can you not, my boy?"

"Of course, but someone else will have to take Juliana."

"I will take her," Sabrina said. "She looks sleepy enough not to care who holds her."

Juliana, it turned out, did care, but everyone ignored her wailing. They were too busy watching, with bated breath, as Gideon climbed an oak near the holly bush, chosen for the mistletoe clinging to its upper branches. When he reached up and caught the thick-leafed parasite lush with waxy-white berries high above him, water rained down on him in torrents.

Gideon shouted with the cold shower but discovered that, rather than garner sympathy, he had become a laughingstock. Between Sabrina and his grandmama, he could not tell which of them was more highly entertained, but he suspected that it might be Sabrina.

Standing high above them, Gideon tossed the great bunch of mistletoe he had won, and got back a bit of his own as it sprinkled the lot of them. Then he placed his hands on his hips and looked down his nose at them with haughty disdain. "Take care, Sabrina, if you please, not to laugh yourself so silly that you drop the baby." Which speech somehow managed to tickle her and his grandmama the more.

Even the boys laughed, especially Rafferty. A good sight that, Gideon thought. "Well, young Rafferty," he said. "I suppose you think you can do better?"

Smiling, Rafe nodded up at him, so Gideon climbed down and put the boy up in the tree, climbing up behind him.

"Gideon, what do you think you are doing?" Sabrina shouted. "Bring that boy down here at once."

Gideon laughed. "This boy is going to reach us some holly."

Sabrina gasped but Gideon held Rafe tight at his waist, while the boy climbed onto an oak branch less sturdy than would hold a man's weight. And Rafe managed to become the hero of the day, earning hugs and a slap on his back, even, from Damon.

One more climb, so Damon could have his turn, and they had enough holly and mistletoe to decorate Basingstoke Manor and then some.

After they returned, changed into dry clothes, and partook of hot chocolate and iced gingerbread men, Sabrina made a kissing bough with the mistletoe, and Grandmama fashioned wreaths and garlands with the holly.

Rafe and Damon were set to cutting and painting gold and silver stars and bells with which to decorate the garlands, while Juliana's cradle, in the center of the holiday bustle, sat empty.

With Juliana on his shoulder, Gideon happily supervised. But he could not help consider past Christmases, and a question that had often nagged him as a child, plagued him again now.

Gideon set Juliana in her cradle and went to his grandmother. He kissed her cheek and placed an arm about her shoulders. "Why did you not take me when I was the twins' age?"

Her eyes filled on the instant. "I tried, but they would not let me have you," she whispered. "I am so sorry."

Gideon brought her close. "Shh. I did not mean to make you cry. I have always wondered. You were my ray of sunshine during those years, my one source of hope, did you know that? You will never know how much you meant to me then, and how much more you mean to me now."

Damon snorted. "I think you are supposed to be kissing Mama under that kissing bow, not Grandmama."

Gideon gave his grandmother a smacking kiss. "No, young man. You are wrong. I am supposed to kiss *'all the girls'* under the kissing bow." He left his grandmother, went for his wife, and waltzed her, laughing, toward the mistletoe.

The kiss he gave Sabrina lasted longer and ended with applause from their audience.

Then he went for Juliana and danced with her on his shoulder until he held her up beneath the mistletoe and kissed her on her bubbly little heart-shaped mouth.

That entertained the devil out of the boys, until Gideon made each of them kiss their baby sister under the mistletoe and then their great-grand-mama, then their mother.

The Yule log was brought into the great hall a short while later, and the servants gathered round.

Veering slightly from tradition, Gideon chose *two* sturdy brands, out of several saved from last year's log, and handed one each to Rafe and Damon.

One on each side of the giant log, the boys set tinder to flame with the burning brands, and every-one cheered.

Gideon placed his arm around Sabrina's shoul-ders. "Best of luck in the year to come, and Happy Christmas to all."

After long afternoon naps, even the boys were allowed to stay up late, to take the holly-festooned carriage to St. George's, Hanover Square, for the midnight service.

Rafe fell asleep at about the same moment the vicar began his sermon, and so Gideon took him on his lap, smoothing the hair from his eyes as he cradled this stubborn, contemplative twin against his chest.

In Gideon's heart, aloneness and unworthiness vanished. In their place stood life, celebration, fam-ily. Instinct told him to run, that this heady sentiment could not last, that he would end the worse for having grasped and lost it.

That was when he knew that he would never be sorry for taking on Sabrina and her children, nor for caring about them, no matter what the future held.

# Seventeen

For once in his life, Gideon did not care how long the sermon lasted. Instead, he opened himself up to the Christmas message, drawing strength from Rafe, asleep on his lap, and Damon and Sabrina beside him.

These were moments to savor, family moments that might keep the wonder of Christmas alive throughout the year.

He had already received so many new and amazing gifts, Gideon could not keep his joy inside and found it emerging as a smile.

He caught Sabrina watching him then, her expression reflecting the emotion inside him, and something warm and uplifting, even spiritual, passed between them. And Gideon experienced the holiness of Christmas, and understood its true meaning for the first time.

Rather than awaiting the completion of the final Christmas carol in impatient silence, he sang "Joy to the World," and he meant every word.

Back at Basingstoke, after everyone was tucked into bed, neither Gideon nor Sabrina spoke of Christmas morning, which made Gideon think he must have a treat in store. They merely climbed into bed and reached for each other, embracing, as if they had become personal anchors for each other.

"This was the best Christmas ever," Sabrina said as she drifted off. Wait until tomorrow, Gideon thought, smiling.

In the morning, however, everything seemed different. The boys were cranky and furtive, holding their pets close, as if someone might jump out and take them away. And when Gideon spoke to them, the boys acted as if he should not notice them skulking about the house, looking miserable.

He remembered feeling just so as a child on Christmas, always a particularly lonely day for him, with his parents either away partying, or partying at home, without him.

Occasionally, he saw them exchange gifts with the servants, with friends, with each other, but never with him. He always received the oranges and sugar plums Cook sent up with eagerness, and he was grateful, but he had also known that there must be something more.

To his mother and her new husband, wrapped up in each other as they were, he did not seem to exist, a situation he came to accept, eventually, though he always did resent it.

This year, he could barely wait to give everyone the gifts he had purchased for them. Except that Sabrina needed to finish feeding Juliana first. He had only come downstairs at all to help Grandmama pass out gifts to her staff.

When that was done, however, he searched out the boys and marched their mulish-faced selves up the stairs to the master suite.

Sabrina was just putting Juliana into her cradle,

when he knocked and they entered her bedchamber.

"I thought we could have a quiet Christmas celebration of our own up here," he said. "Before we give Grandmama her gifts."

But no reaction did Gideon receive from Sabrina or the boys.

"You do exchange gifts, do you not?" He was becoming suspicious.

They, all three, looked at him as if he had grown horns and turned blue.

"Do you object philosophically to gift giving, then, Sabrina?"

"Do *I*?"

"That is my question. You all seem so—I do not know—rigid or frightened." And then he thought that, perhaps, no gifts had been allowed them previous to this, or they could not afford any.

"Sit," he said. "Everybody up on Mama's bed." He lifted Damon onto the bed and Rafe scrambled up on his own. "There you go. I have surprises. Wait here."

Before he entered his own bedchamber, Gideon caught Sabrina shrugging at the boys, as if perhaps he had grown horns after all, or gone daft.

When he took his stash of gifts from the bottom of his cupboard, Gideon feared that perhaps he had not purchased enough. He had assumed that Sabrina would also have gifts for the boys. But if that were not the case, then his would have to suffice as a little something with which to celebrate the day.

Both boys had moved up close to Sabrina by the time he looked in on them from his room. She held them in a protective embrace, one on each side of her, as if she would defend them to the death.

"I am not going to ask what is wrong," Gideon said, standing in the doorway. "But I must say, I am puzzled. Nevertheless, Happy Christmas, Damon and Rafferty." He carried from his bedchamber, with great flourish, two large, gaily painted wooden rocking horses, one for each boy.

No one on Sabrina's bed moved. No one seemed capable.

Gideon stood alone between the two rocking horses, feeling foolishly deflated.

"One of you will please say something," he begged. "I feel rather stupid and . . . conspicuous . . . at the moment," which speech seemed to open some invisible floodgate.

They were suddenly all three crying. Sabrina wept quietly, but the boys cried in great racking sobs.

Gideon abandoned the horses and went to sit beside everyone on the bed. He took them, all three, inasmuch as he could, into his arms. Runny noses abounded. He tried to pass them his handkerchief, but they were so overcome, he had to wipe their noses himself, even Sabrina's.

She laughed when he did, then she cried the more.

All he could do was soothe his wife, squeeze the boys' shoulders, and ruffle their small, dark heads. He hugged and tried to calm each one in turn, but to no avail. And none seemed able to explain.

"I wanted to make our first Christmas special," he said when tears finally slowed. "I did not intend to ruin the day. To tell you the truth, I do not even know where I went wrong, but I am sorry. So very sorry."

"Mama?" Damon asked, a new and brighter glint to his eye.

Sabrina regarded Gideon, and she cupped his cheek in her hand, which he loved, so he turned his face to kiss her palm.

"Boys," she said without taking her gaze from him. "I believe it is safe for you to go and play with your rocking horses."

"Safe?" Gideon watched Rafe and Damon approach the horses for all the world as if the steeds might rear up and crush them beneath their hooves.

To Gideon's silent inquiry, Sabrina shrugged. "I attempted for several Christmases to sneak gifts to the boys," she said. "But, last year, I did not even try. It was too painful a day to repeat, so we did not celebrate at all."

"You will not hurt Mama for giving us gifts," Damon said, and Gideon was surprised to find the boy back beside them, leaning on the bed. He was also speechless at Damon's comment.

"And you will not smack us for playing with them." Damon spoke with surety.

Gideon turned to Sabrina. "I knew he struck all of you at one time or another, but at Christmas for the giving of gifts?"

Sabrina raised her chin. "One of many reasons I ran to Hawksworth."

"So you left while your husband was still living?"

"He died shortly thereafter."

For a moment, Gideon wondered if the man had died at her hand. If so, he could not blame her, but even the possibility made him regard his wife in a whole new way.

"I see," he said. "You never celebrated Christmas with Hawksworth, then, I take it?" Surely his friend would have celebrated as Gideon had always believed most people did.

"Wellington got Hawksworth first," Sabrina said.

"So we got you," Damon said.

Hawksworth was their first choice, Damon did not quite say. Gideon was the man they ended up with because Hawksworth died.

Feeling very much unwanted, a mistake, in the way, too familiar an experience to be borne, Gideon rose from the bed. "Enjoy your horses, boys. Sabrina, I will not burden y—"

Damon threw his arms around Gideon's legs, stopping him beside the door. "Papa?"

Heart thumping, limbs prickling—in triumph, if he heard correctly, in dismay, if he did not—Gideon regarded Damon, standing there, attached to his legs, looking up at him with—"Thank you, Papa," he said.

Gideon hauled the boy into his arms and held him tight.

After a minute, Damon leaned back and toyed with the knot in Gideon's neckcloth. "I do not have a present for *you.*"

Kissing Damon's small cheek, Gideon closed his eyes. "I have my Christmas present," he said, his voice hoarse. "Having you call me Papa is everything I ever wanted."

Sabrina began sniffling and searching again for his handkerchief.

Gideon pulled it from his pocket and tossed it her way.

She laughed as she caught it.

"Papa," when you least expected it, he thought. He was proud and humbled. But something uncomfortable and vague also filled him, because Damon caught him by surprise, he supposed. A lump of . . . inadequacy, perhaps, or incompetence clogged his throat and blurred his vision.

Then all-out fear gripped him. He did not feel qualified to fulfill the awesome duties required of a "papa."

A lifetime of responsibility, times three.

Once again, running, fast and far, seemed a wise choice, yet the trusting, hopeful eyes of a small lad rooted him to the spot.

Gideon was not certain he was up to the task, but felt in that moment, with Damon's faith, almost as if he could do anything.

Someday, he might even make Rafe believe in him.

Rafe, his reticent son, who, Gideon noticed, rode his rocking horse with energy, smiled at them. "Lucky is a prime goer," he said.

Gideon carried Damon over to place him on his own horse, then he went back into his room, returning this time to give Juliana a doll twice her size, and the boys each a map puzzle.

Then he brought out a German-made marquetry Noah's ark, complete with two of every species. "This is to be shared by all our children, present and future." He regarded the mother of said children, until she blushed.

Then he brought out a stack of boxes for her. The boys came to watch her remove from the first a red velvet Empire-style gown, vandyked around the petticoat. "That one is for today," Gideon said.

From the second box, she removed a green velvet riding habit complete with a top hat trimmed in blonde lace. "That is for Hyde Park at five in the afternoon, so I may show you off."

From another, she removed a pale pink walking dress of jaconet muslin embroidered up the front. The same box held a matching cottage mantel of gray, lined with pale pink silk.

Sabrina exclaimed and gasped in delight, thanking him over and over, but despite her smiles, tears swam in her eyes, overflowing more often than not.

Gideon went to his bedchamber and came back with a stack of handkerchiefs. "I should have done better to buy you six dozen of your own," he said, to make her laugh, as he handed them to her.

"You did not choose all these clothes yourself?" she said.

"You must know that Grandmama picked them out for me. I purchased them from Madame Suzette, the dressmaker who created your ball gown. She had all your measurements after all."

"The red velvet is perfect for today, but I cannot wear it, for I will need—"

"In my bedchamber," Gideon said stopping her. "I thought it best not to . . . you know . . . reveal every layer, though I do not hold to that rule where I am concerned and when we are alone."

Sabrina threw her arms around his neck. "You are the best Christmas gift any of us has ever received." She kissed him. Then she ran into his room and shut the door to change.

And her words, Gideon thought, ranked right up there as part and parcel of his best Christmas, right alongside Damon's choosing today to call him Papa for the first time.

Much as he would have liked to help Sabrina dress, he sat on the floor and helped the boys put together their map puzzle of India, telling them stories of his experiences there during his visit to a friend in the East India Company.

By the time Grandmama sent for them, Sabrina was dressed and looking exquisite in red velvet. Before they went upstairs, Gideon handed the boys the perfume and handkerchiefs he had purchased for them to give their great-grandmother. From him and Sabrina, Gideon had purchased a ruby brooch in the shape of a heart.

"I am ashamed that I have nothing for her myself," Sabrina said.

"Nonsense." Gideon kissed her brow. "It is a wonder you do not become hysterical at the very notion of Christmas."

"I do."

In answer, Gideon could do nothing but hold his wife close, until the boys became so rowdy, they had no choice but to make their way upstairs to his grandmother's private suite.

Grandmama gave the boys each a tray of tin soldiers, one painted the bright red and white of the Life Guards, Gideon's own regiment, and the other the deep blue of the Royal Horse Guards.

To Sabrina she gave a pair of exquisite carved ivory combs to dress her beautiful, long hair, with a fan of painted silk and carved ivory to match.

Juliana received a bright red shaker rattle that entertained the babe enormously.

And to Gideon, her grandson, she presented his grandfather's prized watch, and a copy of her will, with her love and pride.

Later, the entire family and their guests, Miss

Minchip, Mr. Waredraper, and Doggett, sat down to partake of a sumptuous Christmas goose, with sliced beef, roasted parsnips and potatoes, and plum pudding for dessert.

Two days later, Gideon, Sabrina and the children stepped into the foyer of Stanthorpe Place. "Lord, it is good to be home," Sabrina said.

*Home?* She stopped and looked about her, arrested by the sentiment. Yes, she had come to think of Stanthorpe Place as home, a gift of itself, a precious one that must be appreciated, and worked at, all year long.

"I need to check my correspondence," Gideon said, handing Juliana to Sabrina. "Five days is a long time to neglect the business of my estates. Give me an hour to read and catch up and I will see you upstairs."

He aimed for her cheek, but she turned and gave him her mouth. He accepted with enthusiasm, for several long beats. "You do know how to tempt a man," he whispered with bright eyes as they pulled apart and he turned toward his study.

"Do you need us to help you with your business, Papa?" Rafe asked.

Gideon stopped dead and turned to regard the boy. His wonder, he knew, must be written plainly on his features. Wonder, yes, and humility as well, filled Gideon. He even waited for that uncomfortable and vague discomfort that he had felt when Damon first called him Papa.

But that unworthy feeling did not clog his throat or blur his vision this time. And Gideon felt a modicum of self-worth reflected in the wide eyes of the two little boys waiting for his answer.

A lifetime of responsibility, times three, no longer seemed so awesomely impossible. And running far and fast did not even rank as a choice.

Gideon got down on his haunches and opened his arms, and Rafe launched himself into that circle for the first time.

With a single breathtaking word, this boy had given him hope for the future, as his twin had done just a few days before.

Gideon opened his arms for Damon to step in as well. Two boys who called him Papa. It was almost too much to take in.

Gideon rose, clearing his throat, and took the boys' hands. "Sabrina," he said, his voice rusty and telling. "I need the boys to help with estate business for a while. I think we can dispense with naps for this afternoon."

Eyes bright, Sabrina nodded. "Of course."

As he made his way to the study, holding the boys hands, contentment enveloped Gideon. Then he opened the study door and found Doggett, unconscious. Dried blood caked his temple. In his hand he clutched a handful of brown hair shot with silver.

Gideon sent the boys for Sabrina and told them to stay with Miss Minchip.

Sabrina came down the minute she was informed and set the servants to getting Doggett back up to his bedchamber. Gideon sent for the doctor, who brought their friend around in good order.

"Happened early this morning, your grace," Doggett said.

"Anybody you recognized?"

"Didn't see his face. Small frame. Wiry. Rifling through your papers. The fellows of my . . . er . . . acquaintance would be looking for shiny baubles to turn into quick brass. Nothing big or easy to spot. Never papers. The likes of them don't read."

Frustration heavy on his shoulders, Gideon returned to the master suite.

"Did you find that anything important had gone missing?" Sabrina asked.

"A few papers," Gideon said. "Nothing for which to worry overmuch." His new will, in fact, the one leaving his unentailed wealth and property to Sabrina and the children. The Hertfordshire estate to Rafe, the stud farm in Sussex to Damon, the equivalent—fifty thousand pounds—to Juliana, and two hundred thousand to their mother. The rest was entailed, and would go to his heir, as should be, that inheritance considerably larger than the rest put together.

Gideon was not happy to have such information "out there," where anyone could learn of it. He bristled particularly at the notion that Veronica might. She was dangerous enough without such powerful motivation. Worse, he feared *she* had hired someone to steal the will.

He did not know whether he should go again to speak with the Runners, and then pay Veronica a visit, or whether visiting her should be attempted at all.

Sabrina carried her own set of concerns. She suspected Lowick as the villain who broke in, that he would use the missing papers against Gideon in some way.

"The papers that were taken?" she asked as she

walked Juliana. "They worry you, do they not? They were of some value. Much more than you let on."

"What makes you so clever?"

"I have worried about money all my life," she said. "Of course I will recognize the concern in others."

Gideon sighed and rose from the bed, an admirable male beast, all sinew and strength, the fire's glow bronzing his skin and carving his face to hawklike angles.

Magnificent, alluring.

"Always money," he said, his attraction replaced of a sudden by an aura of danger. "No need to worry on that score, Sabrina. I still have the wherewithall to keep you in excellent style. But thank you for reminding me that you are here merely because I purchased you. My forgetting such an important fact could become tedious for the both of us."

When he shut the door between their rooms, Sabrina wept.

After she put Juliana down for the night, she remained alone in her bed, awake, waiting, worrying that Gideon must finally be wrong.

God help her; she was very much afraid that she was here because she wanted to be.

If so, her greatest strength had deserted her—the ability to run and never look back.

# Eighteen

In his study, Gideon paced. He was a selfish bastard. But, damn all money to hell, he wanted Sabrina to be his, free of charge, and he did not know how to bring such a fool's fancy about.

He could set her up with ten thousand pounds, now, today, make her independent, see if she made a final choice to stay. Except that he was afraid she would not. Though they were married after all, why would she go?

Fear. That was why. Sabrina was afraid of something . . . likely only of being poor. It all came back to the fact that making her independent was a risk he was not willing to take.

If he were poor, however, and she decided to stay— In a rush of recognized madness, Gideon sat at his desk and began to write. By the time he was finished, he had forged a reasonably authentic-looking document attesting to the fact that he had lost all his funds on the 'Change.

His hand shook as he folded the forgery and placed it in a small hidden drawer at the back of his desk.

Bold move, he thought. Too bad he was too much the coward to use it. Yet.

Back upstairs, outside Sabrina's bedchamber door, despite the frustration raging inside him, Gideon wanted nothing more than to slip into bed beside her, place his arms around her, and close his eyes.

Even in sleep, she soothed him. Giving in to his desire, he entered her bedchamber and returned to her bed.

It seemed as if he had no sooner settled against her, than Damon was tugging his arm. "Papa, Rafferty is afraid of the storm and I cannot—I mean Rafe cannot wake Miss Minchip."

"I am coming, Sweet," Sabrina said, sitting up, all but talking in her sleep.

"Stay," Gideon told her, urging her back down. "Go back to sleep. I am still awake. I will see to 'Rafe's' fears."

"Mmm, thank—" That fast, Sabrina slipped back into the waiting arms of Morpheus.

Gideon rose, slipped into his pantaloons and dressing gown without lighting a candle, and lifted Damon into his arms to take him back up to the nursery.

His head on Gideon's shoulder, the winsome lad sighed. "Can I have a pony ride back?"

Gideon chuckled. "Not up the stairs, you cannot. Despite indications to the contrary, I am not so mighty a steed as you suppose."

Some time later, Sabrina awoke to her daughter's demands for nourishment and remembered Damon coming to them afraid of the storm.

"Your brother must have come down an hour or more ago," she told Juliana as she nursed. "I wonder what happened to your papa?"

"Papa," Sabrina thought, remembering Gideon's face just this morning when Rafe had called him that for the first time. How like a rogue, *her* rogue, to charm her children and claim them for himself, one by one.

When he had returned earlier, after their quarrel of sorts, though they had not spoken, he had seemed his roguish self again. He had sighed as if in contentment and had become aroused just holding her in his arms, as if nothing had happened.

And so it had not. Quite. An argument, but not. Only with Gideon could she imagine the like. Only with him could she emerge physically unscathed, yet emotionally bereft, mourning the loss of something she could not seem to wrap her mind around. "Even now I cannot say what it is," she told Juliana.

When the babe finished nursing, Sabrina changed her and carried her upstairs to the nursery to check on the men in their lives.

And there she found them, all in one bed, Gideon on his back in the center, snoring and snorting like the famous "Puffing Billy" Locomotive, his long, graceful bare feet hanging off the bed's edge, a boy clutched in each arm.

Drizzle slept between Gideon's legs, and Mincemeat was draped across his chest. Animals always knew who was safe and who was not, Sabrina thought. Like her boys.

"Papa is protecting us from the thunder," Damon said softly when she got close.

"I think his snores must be scaring the thunder away," Rafe added.

Sabrina chuckled. "Do you want me to stay too?"

"No," her twins said in unison.

"Sleep well, then," she whispered, kissing all three foreheads, not certain how she felt about not being needed by her sons. But she did know of a sudden how she felt about this remarkable new papa of theirs.

She cared. And the knowledge frightened her.

She cared a great deal more than she wanted to.

Somewhere along the way, while she worried about Lowick and protected her children, had she become so distracted that she had forgotten to protect her heart?

Had she already lost her heart to her husband without even realizing it?

God help her if she did. God help them all.

As the storm howled without, and Sabrina fretted within, and everyone else at Stanthorpe Place slept, a man with a gold hoop in his ear, and another with a mustache, broke into Gideon's study.

"Lookee here, I found me a silver flask. Ah, and an ivory letter opener." While one thief hid his baubles on his person, his crony dragged out a drawer and dropped it on the floor. Then he pulled out another. "That Doggett is a smart one, getting himself perched in this fancy nest."

"Not smart enough. Are Chinese snuff bottles worth anything?"

"Some, take it anyway."

Elsewhere in the room, they discovered and took a venetian glass inkwell, a mother-of-pearl card case, and a tortoiseshell snuff box in the shape of a shoe.


For the first time in weeks, the watcher stood across the street from number twenty-three Grosvenor Square.

He was strong again, nearly as strong as he used

to be, though not nearly so fine. He was up to learning what he must, and setting everything to rights.

So far, he had learned nothing but the fact that Stanthorpe had too many people coming and going at odd hours of the night.

Right now, if he were capable of walking normally, he would go right up to the door and knock. To the devil with the consequences.

If he were capable.

Images of the reason he was not filled the watcher's head with ugliness and horror, with the things men are forced to do, terrible things that changed their lives forever. Acts that ruin them, and often through no fault of their own, the innocents those men touch, and corrupt, in the doing.

Nevertheless, someone always had to pay.

Sometimes men were forced to act. To take matters into their own hands. More often than not, the women suffered.

Some women were forced to suffer. He knew that too.

They were bystanders, pawns, or playthings.

And some women just needed to be taught a lesson.

One in particular came to his mind as he stood there.


Sabrina had lain awake in turmoil half the night, sleeping only near dawn, and then, deeply and dreamlessly. The following morning, in the event Gideon had returned to his rooms and dressed before she woke, she went to his study to find him.

He was not there, but he surely had been. Sabrina shook her head at the mess he left behind.

For the first time since she had known him, Gideon must actually have lost his temper. He certainly seemed angry the night before, close to fury when he left her. Now the results lay scattered undeniably before her. A tantrum of formidable proportions, by the looks of it.

In the process of straightening the disorder, Sabrina found, beneath a small, upended, unvarnished inner drawer, a scrap of paper that intrigued her. Folded numerous times into very small squares, the scrap fit the small drawer perfectly.

She located the inner drawer's resting place, behind a visible outer drawer, and recognized the small compartment for what it was, a secret drawer. This document had been secreted away and was never meant to be seen.

So of course Sabrina unfolded the document and spread it out before her.

Even after reading it twice, she did not know what to make of it.

The official-looking certificate almost appeared—

If she did not know better—

Sabrina sat. Had Gideon lost his fortune on the stock exchange? The puzzling record before her certainly made the possibility appear fact. If so, he must be frantic with worry.

Could this be the prize Lowick sought? If, indeed, it had been Lowick who broke in and struck poor Doggett before they returned from Christmas at Grandmama's house.

Homer Lowick devoured the vulnerable, and losing one's fortune certainly made a man vulnerable. Poverty could turn Gideon into prey, rather than protector. It could at least make him appear weak, rather than strong.

"Poor Gideon."

Yet Sabrina found it difficult to imagine Gideon St. Goddard, Duke of Stanthorpe, radiating anything less than absolute strength, control, and power. Weakness simply did not suit his nature, yet the document clearly revealed . . .

No wonder his ire, nay his frustration, of the night before. No wonder—

Poor Gideon, did she say?

What was wrong with her? She should be worried about his inability to support her and the children, not about his feelings.

Rogues, she must remember, experienced nothing so mundane as feelings. For the sake of her children, she should leave Stanthorpe Place and seek more able protection. But as long as her children had a roof over their heads and food in their bellies, how could she leave Gideon, when he must need . . . someone, more than ever?

Besides, he had become everything to the children.

Sabrina went back upstairs, her mind filled with her husband's problems. She was pacing his bedchamber considering those problems when he returned.

In nothing but his breeches and open dressing gown, her sleep-mussed husband looked as if he had run all the way down the stairs. His brow was furrowed with . . . embarrassment? And chagrin was written clearly there.

Sabrina's imagination painted a picture of what might have taken place upstairs in the nursery, and she grinned. "Such a lecherous rogue you look.

Do not say that you faced Miss Minchip in your morning dishabille and frightened her witless."

"Faced her? Frightened her? I was sound asleep, thank you very much, my dressing gown open, if you please. 'Twas she who frightened me with her foolish screams." He ran a hand through his sleep-tossed locks. "I woke and scurried away like a thief in my own house."

"My poor, cross bear," Sabrina said, talking baby talk, stroking the night's growth of beard on his cheek. "Did the nasty old nanny scare you?"

For half a minute, the frown on Gideon's brow became more pronounced. And just when his eyes lit, and he became focused on the fact that she was playing, and he reached for her, his valet stepped into the bedchamber, and made to back out as fast.

"His grace will not need you today, Bilbury," Sabrina said, turning to the valet. "I will handle his morning ablutions myself. Will you just see that a tub of hot water is readied in his dressing room?"

"Very good, your grace."

"Thank you, Bilbury."

Gideon's grin appeared. *"You* will see to my morning ablutions? This becomes intriguing. To what do I owe the pleasure of your undivided attention."

Gideon began to advance, and Sabrina allowed him to catch her.

When he had her in his clutches, she slipped his dressing gown from his shoulders. "I simply want to thank you for protecting the boys from the storm last night."

"I should, perhaps, point out that I was given little choice in the matter. You were like to sleep-walk your way out the front door."

Sabrina grimaced. "Well, I know that you did not." She ran her hands over his chest, allowing herself to absorb and enjoy the feel of his skin against her palms, of his chest hair, silky, not coarse, as she used to think, enticing and strangely arousing as it slid between her eager fingers.

She found a hidden nubbin, teased it with her finger, then her tongue, as he often did to her, and a low growl emerged from Gideon's throat. By the time she looked up, he was opening his mouth over hers, bending her backward in his arms.

Afraid she would fall, Sabrina grasped him tighter, but he arranged to have them land on his bed, him on top, smiling victoriously down at her.

They had never come together in broad daylight. She had never wanted, in the true sense, to experience "almost everything" with him when she was alert and awake, and accountable to herself for her actions.

Perhaps her boldness stemmed from the fact that she had it in her mind that she could help him for a change. She was acting from a position of strength for once, a feeling she embraced.

She knew not what, exactly, drove her to seduce her husband amidst her worry over his losses, but she did feel driven.

They heard the servants filling the slipper bath in his dressing room and pulled somewhat apart, lest one of the retainers enter, but they did not.

"You said you would care for me yourself," Gideon said, his voice butter smooth, enticing. "Does that mean you will help me with my bath?"

"I will." She raised her chin but lowered her lashes, aware she was flirting. Flirting. With her own husband.

Gideon hardened the more against her. She would never stop thrilling to the knowledge that she aroused him. "I missed you last night," she said. "I went looking for you."

"Did you? We were all asleep?"

"*You* were. The boys were awake. Rafferty said you were frightening the thunder away with your snores."

"The bounder. Much good it did me to protect him."

"He was smiling when he said it."

"I suppose that must count for something."

"With our Rafe, it must. Do you care for your bath now, your grace?"

"Have I any other choice?"

Sabrina sighed. "I wish."

"Do you?" Gideon pulled back so he could see her better. "Honestly?"

Sabrina blushed, which apparently became answer enough, for his grin reminded her of the undeniable rogue who drove so sensual a bargain on their wedding night.

"Away to my bath, then, milady, and scrub your lord and master's back, and whatever else comes to . . . hand."

# Nineteen

"How can I bathe you with 'that' getting in my way?" Sabrina asked not five minutes later as she leaned over Gideon's bathtub, washcloth in hand.

"How can you blame me? Since Juliana's birth, we have abstained for, what, six months?"

"Four and a half weeks."

"Is that all, by damn?" Gideon threw his head back in a caricature of martyrdom. "Yea, how I have suffered."

Sabrina smiled at his play, enjoyed it even, so much so that she dared reach into the water to grasp his poor neglected . . . self. "Let me make it better."

Like Neptune rising from the sea, Gideon stood, stepped from the tub, and lifted his wife in his arms, all in one shocking move.

He carried her to his bed and they went down as one, dripping, soaking the covers, and kissing as if they had not kissed in months.

"Touch me now," Gideon said, "the way you just did in—ah, yes." He set his jaw and closed his eyes in an ecstasy of sweet suffering. Then he touched her in return, more gently than ever, so lightly and beautifully that together they found the release denied them.

They remained entwined for a long, splendid eternity of kisses, until Juliana in the next room began to make her presence known.

While Gideon took his bath, Sabrina changed her clothes and fed the baby, and just when she got to the point of beginning his shave, the boys trooped in.

Sabrina gaped at them, and then she gaped at Gideon. "I assumed that your door had a l-o-c-k."

"N-o." He grinned, looking jocular beneath his shaving cream. "I never needed one before."

"Well, you need one now. I mean, I knew that my door did not, but I assumed that the duke's . . . Good God. We . . . They . . ."

Sabrina gave up raving and shaved her husband.

"Do not cut off anything important," Damon said.

"What do you mean by important?" Sabrina asked.

Damon rolled his eyes. "His nose, of course, and his ears."

"And take care to shave his chin dimple well," Rafe said. "Old Mr. Bundy, the farmer—do you remember him, Mama?—he always had pig whiskers bristling from his chin dimple."

Sabrina had to stop, because Gideon had broken into a fit of laughter. When he caught his breath, he regarded Rafe seriously. "How do you know they were pig whiskers?"

"Well, they were his own whiskers, of course, but one day his porker came up to him as he spoke to me and I saw that their whiskers were exactly like."

"Will you stop laughing," Sabrina ordered her

husband. "It is not easy to shave you while you do. I *shall* snip something important if you do not calm yourself."

Gideon cleared his throat and relaxed, though his shoulders shook at regular intervals after that.

"There," Sabrina said when she was done. "Everything still attached, and, Rafferty, you will note that I did a good job on the chin dimple. Not a single pig whisker bristles from it."

"It is time to go back upstairs and do ciphers with Miss Minchip, is it not?" Gideon asked the boys while Sabrina wiped the excess froth of shaving soap from his face.

They groaned in unison, but they went.

When they were gone, Sabrina broached the subject preying on her mind. "I am a bang-up rider, Gideon, did you know that?"

Gideon started in surprise at the question. "I did not. When we go down to Sussex, I shall have to let you ride one of my Arabians."

"I am better than a simple rider, I mean. I once jockeyed in a race where a certain gamester lacked the funds to pay a real jockey."

"Your husband lacked the funds, you mean?"

"I won a fat purse."

"Congratulations. I did not know I had married a horse jockey."

"There is a race at the St. Eustace Winter Fair in three weeks' time. I have seen your Arabian. Deviltry is a prime goer. I could ride him at the fair race and win you the purse. I imagine five thousand pounds would help."

"What?" Gideon took the towel from her hand and wiped his face more thoroughly. "What are you talking about?" he asked, rising. "You want to play jockey in a race? Whyever would you want to do that? And, of course, you will *not*."

"I want to help you recover some of your fortune."

"I am sorry, Bree, but you make absolutely no sense."

Sabrina took from her pocket the folded paper she had found beneath the upended drawer and handed it to him.

Gideon barely needed to read the document she gave him. He had only forged and hidden it last night. He rubbed his freshly shaved face and considered this unexpected turn of events. "Where did you find this?"

On the floor in your study with everything else you tossed about in your rage last night. Shame on you. But do not worry, I cleaned everything up so no one else would realize that you gave in to a tantrum. I know you do not usually lose your temper in that unruly way."

Sabrina paced to the window and back. "I knew, of course, when you left me last night that you were upset about money, but I never dreamed—until I saw this. Then I understood."

"I see."

Gideon's brain and his heart ran a rioting gamut of emotions. At first he was taken aback, then chagrined. Then he moved to bewildered, and finally to hopeful.

He had purchased this woman. She had made it clear to him that money meant everything to her. And now she supposed him penniless and rather than releasing her rage or threatening to find a rich protector, she was offering to help him recover his losses.

It made no sense, but, Lord, it made him hope as he had never dared.

As he slipped into a fresh shirt, Gideon wondered how long Sabrina would remain with him if he allowed her to continue to believe him destitute.

Ignoring the anguish engendered by the very possibility of losing her, he regarded her levelly. "You saw this and realized I needed funds."

His wife nodded. "I would like to show you how well I ride, so I will need you to help me dress like a man. Then I will need help walking and talking like a man as well, because it has been a long time since I raced, before even the twins were born."

"Let us be clear, here. You want me to help you dress, ride, walk, and talk like a man?"

Sabrina nodded.

"Now, there is a scheme I can sink my teeth into." Aware he was ignoring any and all possible repercussions, he also knew that if he did not snatch at this opportunity to become closer to his wife, he might never be allowed another. "When shall we begin?"

"This evening, after the children are asleep?"

Gideon stepped up to her, took her into his arms, and kissed her as if she were his lover in fact. "This evening. I can barely wait." He gave her a look heavy with promise before he went downstairs to his study to see what might have gone wrong.

By the time he was finished examining his study, he was not certain what to think. It left him with new questions, when already too many had been left unanswered, not the least of which was the nagging question of whether he could be so foolish as to be falling in love with his wife.

A query with no answer, one to be saved for another day.

For today, he needed to confront Doggett, because several—what had he called them? Oh, yes, baubles. Several baubles were missing.

By the time evening arrived, and the children were finally all asleep, the phrase "I can barely wait" had become Gideon's mantra. He placed on his bed all the clothing Sabrina would need, as she regarded the assortment with a critical eye.

"Drawers?" She held up a pair for a thorough examination. "Why do I need drawers? They will bunch, I think."

"Because you have nothing with which to fill them."

"The better for you," said she.

"Saucy wench. What did you wear under your pantaloons the last time you raced?"

"Nothing."

"Even better." He went for her.

She sidestepped his reach. "Gideon, now, stop that. We seek to arrive at a particular destination, do not forget. We are undressing me to redress me."

"But there can be nothing wrong with a little side journey, now and again, before we reach our destination, can there?"

"Hmm. A journey to where?"

Her rogue raised a speaking brow. "Heaven."

Sabrina laughed and danced from his reach once more. Under cover of her dress, she attempted to pull on the pantaloons he had set out for her.

"Oh, no fair. You have to take the dress off first."

"We will never reach our desired destination if I go about dressing in that way."

"Will we not?"

But Sabrina's opinion held sway. And after she successfully pulled on and fastened his pantaloons, she did remove her dress.

Gideon decided that she filled his breeches out in remarkable ways. Come to think of it, he was filling his own out quite well at the moment. His palms itched to touch, his mouth watered to sample. "I must be the luckiest man on earth."

"Mama, Damon is sick."

Sabrina turned her back and slipped into her wrapper, tugged off her riding boots, checked to be certain Juliana slept, and followed Rafferty and Gideon up the stairs.

Miss Minchip was holding Damon's head over a bucket when they arrived.

"Oh, baby," Sabrina said. "Did you eat something that upset your stomach?"

He shook his head, his face red. Very red. Sabrina examined his neck and his chest as well.

"Spots," Miss Minchip said. "T'other one will get it too, him sleeping in the same bed last night."

All heads turned to Gideon.

He raised both hands and backed away. "Oh, no. I do not do spots, thank you very much. I do not have any now. I will not have any later. End of discussion." He turned and left the nursery.

Sabrina grinned at the boys, who were grinning back. "If Papa gets the spots, he will be cross as a bear."

Gideon was waiting for Sabrina when she returned to her bedchamber. "Can we go back to where we were?" he asked, already churlish.

"First, let me check you for spots."

He crossed his arms before him stubbornly. "I refuse to be checked, and I refuse to have spots."

"I would have to check you everywhere. You would have to take off—"

He relaxed his stance. "That could be agreeable."

"You did sleep with the boys, so you must allow me to check you. Come here so I can—"

The minute he got close enough, Gideon removed her wrapper and grinned when he saw that she was still wearing his pantaloons but nothing much else, except her chemise. "I had forgotten where we were up to."

"I remember where you were up to," she said, unbuttoning his shirt, watching him react to her standing there as she was, half dressed.

"Gideon," she said, stepping into his arms. "What we have together is not so bad, is it? Even children and dogs and cats and spots? You do not have any, by the way. Spots, that is."

He kissed her. "I feel much the same, Sabrina. Not about the spots, but that this is good, our life." He carried her to his bed. "I have also been thinking that it is about time Papa had another turn."

And though it was still too soon for consummation, they did not do much talking before they slept the sleep of the sated.


The watcher wondered if any stranger would invade Stanthorpe Place this night. There were so many intrusions, it was a wonder Stanthorpe did not just leave the front door open.

Once upon a time he might have been welcome at that door himself.

Back then he stood tall, taller than most, and strong. Used to be, he stood handsomer than most as well. A heartbreaker women had once called him.

A rogue, a lady-killer. He scoffed. Not anymore, not unless the women he gazed upon died of fright.

The only heart he broke now was his own, every time he looked into a mirror.

Every time he regarded the scar slashing his cheek, he recalled everything ugly in his life. They told him, of the knife wound to his face, that it sat "close enough to his eye so that only a miracle could save his sight."

Only a miracle could have saved his life as well.

Yes, he got his miracles, both of them, much good they did him. He had paid a high price.

But he supposed someone had to pay.

Someone always did.

That evening, when Gideon came into her bedchamber, Sabrina was already wearing his pantaloons and trying to button his shirt. "I cannot fit my breasts into your shirt," she said in greeting.

"That is not the only problem," Gideon said, regarding her, hands on hips, his look warm and assessing.

"What could be worse than this tight thing?"

"Those two wet spots at the front."

"Oh, Lord, I am leaking. I will expel all Juliana's dinner if I am not careful. I told you it was too tight."

"That, my sweet, I can see for myself."

"Help me out of this, will you?"

"I have never been more eager to assist."

"Oh, you. Will you never pay attention to anything more than the desires of the flesh?"

"I did not hear you complaining last evening. As a matter of fact, I seem to recall someone asking for more. Was that me? I did not think it was me."

Sabrina kissed him and danced from his reach. "That will be enough. Deviltry is to be saddled in two days' time at dawn, so we can go for an early ride in Hyde Park and I can demonstrate my riding skills. I will set Waredraper to making me a larger shirt tomorrow."

"And what do you plan to wear for a coat?"

"He found an old one of his and is fixing that for me. I knew the coat would be a problem, but I did not consider the shirt. Now you must teach me to walk like a man."

Teaching his seductive wife to walk like a man became an exercise in futility. When she tried to walk straight, Gideon found the swivel in her hips truly amazing.

When they got down to business, they decided she must at least learn to swagger like a man. This she tried with Gideon behind her, his hands at her hips, to keep them from swiveling, but it was no use.

Sabrina could not walk like a man for anything.

All the exercise served to do was arouse Gideon, which was fine with him. He had rather be the rider, where his wife was concerned. He certainly had no intention of letting her jockey in a race. He was simply having as good a time with her foolish notion as he could while it lasted.

\* \* \*

Both the coat and the shirt turned out well, and on the day of their early morning ride, Sabrina woke Juliana to feed her early. Then they were off.

In Hyde Park at five o'clock in the afternoon, all the fashionables paraded through the gates, in open carriages, on horseback, or even arm in arm, some of them even in winter. But at five o'clock in the morning, summer or winter, none but a robust and dedicated few riders could be found there.

Since Gideon kept several good stallions in the mews behind his Grosvenor Square house, he gave his blood bay to Sabrina for the ride there and he rode Deviltry himself. "When we arrive," he told Sabrina. "We can trade mounts."

Truth to tell, he wanted to be certain that she did, indeed, ride well, and that she had a good seat, before he took a chance either with her neck or Deviltry's.

As good as her word, Sabrina proved to Gideon that she could handle and sit a horse as well as any member of the Jockey Club, so they switched mounts.

Once she was up and settled on Deviltry's back, they chose a course for a short race between them. Gideon was so cocksure that he would win, even on Ransom, simply because of his superior male riding skills, that when the race began, he did not even try. But when he saw what an exceptional race jockey Sabrina proved to be, he bent low over his horse and gave it his best.

Still, Sabrina won, hands down.

"Where did you learn to ride like that?" Gideon asked. They turned their horses back toward Grosvenor Square, she still on Deviltry, he on Ransom.

Sabrina petted Deviltry's neck. "I rode every day when I was a child on my father's estate in Exeter."

"You said you were not of the gentry." Gideon slowed and allowed her to take the lead on the left turn toward his stable in the Grosvenor mews.

"I said I was not a member of the fashionable set, not that I was never a member of the gentry," Sabrina said, dismounting.

She waited for him to dismount and join her. "My father lost our estate ages ago," she continued as they approached the house. "Therefore, as an adult, I was not fashionable."

"Who are your parents?" he asked as they crossed the kitchen and took the stairs toward their bedchambers.

"My father was a country squire who gambled away the money and property his father left him. And I do not see that it makes any difference," she said, preceding him into her bedchamber. She turned to face him, for once allowing her self-confidence to show. "What matters is that I ride well, do I not?"

"*Very* well."

She threw herself into his arms. "Then you will allow me to race at the St. Eustace Winter Fair, to win you the purse?"

Gideon pulled her close and tried to distract her with kisses.

She pulled away. "You will, will you not?"

Gideon sighed. "I will not."

To his shock, she shoved away from him so quickly, and with such force, she left him off balance, literally.

"Why did you let me race you this morning?" she cried. "Why dress me and—"

"Undress you?" Gideon raised one, speaking brow. "Why, indeed."

"The race, everything, it was all a hum? A big fat Banbury tale?"

"This morning's race between us was a lark, Sabrina. Nothing more. Of course you will not ride in a public race."

"You bounder, you reprobate, you . . . you—"

"Husband."

"But—"

"No. You cannot. Absolutely not. Over my dead body. Next question."

Sabrina marched across the room tapping her hand with her riding crop, arguing beneath her breath at a ripping pace.

Gideon could just imagine her working up her best argument, while he fortified himself against same, by going off to his club and not returning until long after she slept.

Unfortunately, he had discovered that spending time at his club did not hold the appeal it used to.


Before he opened his eyes the following morning, Gideon knew that the bedchamber spun about him. He even suspected that someone had set the bed afire.

He wished he had gotten drunk the night before, so there would be a good reason for this misery. As it was, he had done nothing but play cards and win.

"Oh, oh," he heard Damon say from somewhere beside him.

Loath to open his painful eyes, Gideon hoped, for once, that the exclamation meant Drizzle had desecrated a carpet.

"What is it, Sweetheart?" Sabrina asked, stirring as she woke beside Gideon. "What is wrong?"

"Papa has—"

"Do not say it," Gideon begged, keeping his eyes closed against the room's gyration.

"Spots," the boy said anyway.

"Damn."

# Twenty

"You are the worst patient I have ever come across," Sabrina said on the evening of the fourth day of Gideon's confinement.

"Of course I am," he snapped. "I am hungry, but food does not stay with me. I am dizzy, and the room will not settle. I itch where one should never scratch, and that usually happens while Grandmama is reading to me."

Sabrina giggled. "But you are better today. I see that your spots are fading."

"Thank God for that. Except that I am fading, too, and it is barely dark outside."

"Sleep, then," she said, kissing him and rubbing his back as he turned on his side to sleep. "Come to bed," he said as he drifted. "I will sleep better if you do."

Gideon awoke late the following morning, feeling worlds better. After his breakfast was delivered, he ate, and was pleased to discover his food stayed where it ought.

When Bilbury returned for the tray, Gideon asked him to fetch Sabrina.

"I am sorry, your grace," he said nearly an hour later. "But we cannot seem to locate the duchess."

"Did you look in the nursery?"

"Of course, your grace."

"In the kitchen?"

"We looked everywhere, your grace. Your wife is nowhere on the premises."

"Nowhere?" Gideon said. "She cannot be nowhere. Wait. What day is this?"

"It is the third of February, your grace, in the year of our Lord, eighteen hundred and sixt—"

"Stuff it." Gideon jumped from the bed. "And fetch my clothes."

Bilbury offered the pantaloons he had already brought in. "But, your grace—"

"The St. Eustace Winter Fair begins today, does it not?" Gideon tugged his pantaloons from his disapproving valet's reluctant grasp.

"Er . . . yes, your grace. It does begin today."

"Have my carriage brought around. Hurry, man."

By the time Gideon's carriage arrived in Chelsea, it was early afternoon and obvious from the cheering crowd that the race had already begun.

Gideon jumped from the conveyance, blocked on all sides by farm animals, farmers, and other assorted fair fanciers. He fought his way amid the throng, weaving through a score of gaily decorated booths and tents selling every item from silk gloves to baby pigs.

He rejected an opportunity to buy a manure spreader and bypassed a miracle elixir, advertising a cure for ailments ranging from apoplexy to temper tantrums. "Too bad they do not have one for headstrong wives," he muttered.

He almost cut through an abandoned cockfight ring, until he saw that it was littered with the carcasses of birds that looked to have exploded.

In a huge open ale tent, a table full of red-faced merrymakers, back teeth awash, invited him in for a nip. He damned near joined them.

At a Far Eastern pavilion, a bearded lady propositioned him, stopping him in his tracks. Gideon apologized and told her that he had enough problems, thank you very much, with the woman he already had.

By the time he made it to the front of the race crowd, he saw Deviltry pass by, clear as day, a length ahead of the rest.

Gideon could not moderate his grin, no matter how angry he tried to be.

"Two more times around the bell course," he heard the announcer say.

His palms sweat and his knees knocked. Gideon had never been so worried. If Sabrina got out of this alive, he was going to have to beat her, after he assured himself she had not broken anything but his trust.

The runners passed again. Only one more time around—he just might make it.

A rider was down. Damn.

Gideon charged onto the course, nearly getting himself trampled, but he fell and rolled, just in time, and neither horse nor rider was forced to break stride.

When he reached the felled rider, the injured man was cursing a blue streak, accusing the race commissioners of allowing a professional jockey on the course with a blasted Arabian.

Sabrina. They thought Sabrina was a professional. "I'll be—"

The race was over, the spectators were cheering and crowding around the winner.

Gideon elbowed his way through. Sabrina sat atop a snorting Deviltry, grinning with pride, laughing, congratulating Deviltry, until she saw him.

When he grabbed her by the waist and hauled her to the ground, she yelped. Then he crushed her in his embrace and kissed her dizzy.

The crowd went dead silent. The Duke of Stanthorpe had just kissed his boy jockey before the entire "world and his brother."

Someone tapped Sabrina on the back, stealing her attention from the fiery exhibition she and Gideon had just presented. She turned to accept the five-thousand-pound purse and caught sight of Homer Lowick, grinning, not ten feet away.

Amidst the chaos of happy congratulations, the horrible little man tipped his hat and made a cutting motion with a finger across his neck.

Sabrina tried not to faint or to run. She turned away, but stood her ground, glad now that Gideon had come, glad to have his supporting arm around her.

In addition to the race purse, she received an additional thirty-five hundred pounds from the bet she had Doggett place. When Doggett brought her the second purse, Gideon all but growled at the man, likely for abetting her in this jaunt. Then her husband had the gall to ask Doggett to bring Deviltry home for them.

Through it all, Sabrina felt sick, she was so worried. There remained no doubt in her mind any longer. Homer Lowick knew where to find her and whom to find her with. He was closing in and she would be forced to run again or she would have no choice but to stand and face her enemy.

After the race crowd finally thinned, they began to make their silent way back toward Gideon's carriage. But it was getting late, so Gideon stopped to purchase tup'ney pies and found a bench where they could sit and eat them.

"Tell me," he said, breaking the tense silence. "Did our daughter receive any sustenance today?"

"I expressed my milk so Miss Minchip could bottle-feed her. If I was not back by now, she was going to feed her pap. Do not worry. Juliana is not at home starving."

"I am pleased to hear it."

And that was the end of their dinner conversation.

By the time Gideon's driver was able to move the carriage from its location amid the merrymakers, dusk had just begun to paint the horizon with wild streaks of pinks and grays.

They rode home in silence as well, on opposite seats in the closed carriage, facing each other, but not.

Gideon was furious. Sabrina knew that. She could still see the tic working in his cheek. Yet, he had kissed her. Why?

She could not bear his silence, because guilt rode her. She could not bear her own silence, because she kept seeing Lowick's threatening action in her mind's eye.

"When it was clear that you wanted to beat me, why did you kiss me instead?"

"To keep from beating you."

"Oh."

He turned from his absorption in the passing scenery to regard her. "I thought at first that *you* had fallen and broken your neck, but by the time I saw you, I had already discovered the injured to be a different rider. I was grateful enough that you were spared to need to kiss you."

Thunderclouds formed on his brow and his voice rose an octave. "But I need to beat you as well, because you *could have been* the rider who was injured. Damn it, Sabrina, you could have been killed!"

"Is the fallen rider badly hurt?"

"Not as badly as you will be when I am finished with you."

"Oh."

"Your vocabulary seems to have deserted you."

"I believe I dropped it somewhere near the finish line . . . when I saw your face."

"And trampled it underfoot, like the years you took from my life with that stunt." Gideon lay his head against the squabs and closed his eyes. "God, Sabrina, I would never have forgiven myself if something had happened to you."

"Why? I made the choice. Why would you blame yourself?"

He regarded her as if she had grown an extra head. "Because I told Hawksworth I would care for and protect you. And if you were injured, I would have failed to honor that promise."

"Oh. I thought, perhaps, you might have had . . . a different reason."

"Like?"

"Me."

Gideon reached for her and hauled her across the carriage to his lap. "I had many very good reasons," he said as he opened his mouth over hers and kissed her in such a way as to leave her with no doubt of his feelings on the matter.

"Because you like me?" she asked with a satisfied smile when he allowed her up for air.

"Hoyden," he said, kissing her again. "Vixen." Another kiss. "Enfant terrible."

"I am not a child," she snapped, pulling away and crossing her arms.

He stroked her breast, and she moved to accommodate his possession, sliding back into his embrace.

"Point taken. You are not a child."

In an unprecedented move, Sabrina slipped her hand inside the flap on his tightening pantaloons, garnering an oath from her husband that seemed less a curse and more an exclamation of appreciation.

The carriage came to a sudden stop.

Gideon swore as the door opened, nearly on the instant.

Grandmama stood on the walk, tapping her foot, her annoyed countenance still visible in the smoky light of full dusk. "Where the devil have you two been? The house is all in an uproar."

Having turned to present her back to the open door, not that anyone could see much in the dark interior, Sabrina tried to slip her hand from the very full front of her husband's breeches.

"Better stay behind a minute," she whispered before stepping down and chuckling at the growl he returned.

She walked Grandmama to the steps to give her husband a chance to gather his wits about him and emerge from the carriage without embarrassing himself. "To what do we owe the pleasure of this unexpected visit?" she asked his grandmother.

"To my granddaughter riding in a race in Chelsea and going missing for all of a day. I did not think you had windmills in your head, girl. What was this racing nonsense all about?"

"Just a lark, says Gideon. He thinks I am an enfant terrible hoping my husband will take some notice of me."

"Take notice of you?" Grandmama said. "That will not wash. That boy fairly trips over himself every time you walk into a room."

"Does he?"

"Lovesick fool."

"Gideon? Oh, I do not think so."

"Same as you. Calf-eyed, the two of you, and everybody knows it but you. Need to face the facts, my girl."

Grandmama kissed her cheek. "Minchip sent for me a while ago, all in a dither. But now that you two are back, I will be on my way, so you may finish what you started in the carriage."

Sabrina opened her mouth . . . and closed it again.

Grandmama left chuckling, and when she passed by her grandson, she thwhacked him with her cane.

"Ow." He rubbed his arm. "What did you do that for?"

"Good measure." She shook her head. "Beef-witted looby."

"A looby? Me?" Gideon was still watching his grandmother climb into her carriage when he reached his wife at the door. "What got into her?"

Sabrina sighed. "I suppose wisdom would be too much to hope for."

"What? Why was she here? Why is she leaving?"

"So we can finish what we started in the carriage."

"The devil you say?"

"Meet you in your bedchamber in five minutes."

When they met upstairs half an hour later, after having checked on all their sleeping offspring, Sabrina found herself picturing the looks on the faces of the fair crowd when Gideon hauled her off her horse and kissed her.

Well, one face she tried not to recall.

"Do you realize that you kissed a boy before all and sundry right out in the open. Soon the world will believe that Gideon St. Goddard, Duke of Stanthorpe, prefers boys."

Gideon barked a laugh as he approached her. "I kissed Sabrina St. Goddard, my wife, and I do not care who knows it. Besides, the world will laugh at such a foolish rumor about any St. Goddard. Any who know me will not doubt me."

'Twas she who doubted, Sabrina thought. In the same way that she did *not* doubt her husband's dedication to the pleasures of the flesh, she doubted herself capable of arousing any of the more tender emotions in him.

Grandmama must be wrong.

Lowick was at the core of her doubts, of course, her fears, her anxiety over the future. But she refused to speak or even think of him for the rest of the night.

She wanted Gideon to erase from her mind the memory of Lowick's evil smile, the unspeakable future that might very well be in store for her, for all of them.

She could think of only one way to do that, and she felt certain, if she went about her seduction in the proper fashion, that her rogue of a husband would cooperate.

As a beginning, Sabrina allowed him to unbutton each and every one of the buttons down the front of her racing shirt.

After he removed it, she began to undo the binding around her breasts, until he took over and walked around her, unwinding her as he went, revealing her in her beauty, until he had worked his way down to her shift, where two wet stains gave evidence to the fact that she had not given Juliana her evening meal as yet.

Gideon slipped one of her shift's straps off her shoulder, exposing a breast. "I will not steal Julie's dinner, but I have yearned to taste . . . fantasized doing do."

Her husband awaited her approval.

Sabrina nodded, the shock of his suggestion touching her physically. But the actuality shot a fiery pleasure through her every fiber. He grew hard and heavy against her belly, the swiftness of his arousal matching hers.

Just as her legs began to tremble, as if they might give out, Gideon raised his head and licked his lips. "Sweet." And he opened his mouth over hers.

Sabrina tasted her own milk on her husband's tongue.

Mating. This was the prelude to mating at its most primal. Her seduction was working, Sabrina thought absurdly.

"More later," Gideon said, replacing her strap against her shoulder. Then he began to slip the pins from her hair. He massaged her nape, kissed the back of her ear, nibbled her lobe.

That she was willing to consummate their marriage did not mean that she was ready to give up the last vestiges of self left to her, Sabrina told herself. Her decision simply meant that consummation, at this time, would serve her "self" well.

Awake on all counts, as far as this final, pivotal step in her marriage was concerned, she simply would not allow herself to emerge from the experience so attached to Gideon that she could not separate her life from his.

She would not.

From behind her, he slipped his hands beneath her shift and cupped her breasts. "Mine," he said.

Sabrina smiled and allowed pleasure to wash over her.

She admitted to herself one undeniable truth, a fact she had suspected since marrying this man: Against brutality she could erect the strongest of barriers. Against gentleness, she could mount no defense.

Her gentle rogue took remarkable care of everyone placed into his keeping by her. She honestly believed that, if ever there was a man who would care for her individual "self," Gideon was that man.

That they seemed doomed not to spend their future together, she would not allow herself to contemplate at this moment.

"These clothes have to go, beginning with your boots," he said. "Sorry." He was not. He was glad. He led his wife to a chair and pushed her into it. Then he straddled her legs, his back to her, grasped her boot, and tried to tug it off her foot.

Sabrina planted her other foot against his backside and pushed him forward, during which process the boot came off and he went flying.

Her laughter soothed his injured dignity.

When he attempted to remove the second boot in the same way as the first, Sabrina tried some fancy footwork, teasing him by running her bare foot up his leg, along the inside of his thighs, and, incredibly, between his legs, before she actually aided in the second boot's removal.

Having landed halfway across the bedchamber, Gideon put the boot down and turned to her, more than ready to move forward. "I fear I will never be able to have my boots removed again without becoming aroused," he said. "Bilbury will quit, I tell you, and I will not blame him. Gad, what made you think to do that?"

Sabrina shrugged. "Instinct?"

"Yes, well, now you shall see how my instincts take over, wife, and then you will be . . . delighted." He grinned a wicked promise, then he began to advance, exactly in the way she wanted him to, with lust in his eyes and determination in his step.

In a token show of resistance and to heighten her seduction, Sabrina jumped from the chair and began to back away from his advance. But all the while she wanted him to assume she was trying to get away from him, she was leading him to her ultimate destination, his bed.

Lord, she was a smart one, she mused, inordinately pleased with herself.

Then he lunged, unexpectedly, surprising and frightening her, and she screamed and jumped on the bed, in an instinctual move of self-preservation. As much to put space between them as anything, she scrambled up the bed to stand at its head, her back against the wall.

Gideon stood on the floor, at the bed's foot, his hands on his hips, his grin deadly and so filled with promise, Sabrina forgot almost to breathe.

"Now I have you," he said. "There can be no further escape for you."

Sabrina looked to the left, and he stepped in that direction. The right, and he stepped there.

She laughed, her heart pounding with excited anticipation, but she had never even gotten near *her* goal. She had thought she had him where she wanted him. Foolish girl.

"Do you think you are fooling me?" he asked.

Did he mean that he knew she had led him there? "I did think I was fooling you, but now I realize that I was fooling only myself."

"In what way?"

Sabrina cocked her head. "In what way do you suppose I thought I was fooling you?"

Gideon grinned. "In every way."

"Oh." Sabrina bit her lip in concentration. "I thought I was ready for you physically, but even though I had the mistaken impression that I was seducing you, you taught me that you have the stronger power to seduce."

"Do I?" Gideon's grin formed even as he pulled off and threw down his own boots. "What other power do I hold over you?"

"I would be a fool to tell you."

He unbuttoned the front placket on his breeches. "You would be a fool not to tell me."

Sabrina raised a brow and undid the placket on her own pantaloons in the same slow manner. "Is that a threat?" she asked coyly. She stepped out of the pantaloons and threw off her shift. "I dare you to be more specific."

"Is that my wife daring me?" Gideon undid the buttons on his shirt, and given her current state, ran out of patience and tore the uncooperative garment open. Buttons flew even as he tossed it off.

But when he made to join her on the bed, she stopped him with an imperious hand, halfway there.

"Naked, if you please," she intoned like a majesty on her throne. Except that she stood on his bed in glorious nakedness, like Godiva on her steed, her hair her only cover.

# Twenty-one

Standing on the floor at the foot of his bed, Gideon slipped his drawers down his legs, almost awed by the fact that Sabrina awaited his touch, begged for it even. Was she ready, finally, for the consummation of their marriage?

He watched her atop the bed, her back to the wall, watching him, her eyes wide, eager, and assessing. Her smile began in their verdant depths first, until the invitation in that smile transformed her entire face. "I want us to become as close as two human beings can," she said, her voice a rusty rasp, shivering his spine and thrumming his taut nerves. "Hurry," she added. "I want to feel every inch of you along every inch of me."

And there was his answer.

Gideon shed the last of his clothes and made his way toward her, across the bed, on his knees, rather than on all fours. Damn, she had him at a disadvantage, and she knew it.

Still, he could not help his cocksure grin, like some crowing rooster who has just captured his prize. "Any chance you might be willing to lie down when we match inches?"

Sabrina turned serious. In her smoldering eyes,

in her lips gone dry, and in her sweet, moistening tongue, Gideon saw exactly when arousal overtook her. "Standing would be . . . different," she said, her voice nothing more than a shiver of promise.

She was a goddess and he was her disciple, kneeling before her, adoring her. "Standing up would be . . . difficult . . . for the first time, at least." He slid his hands up from her ankles, along her calves, and all the way to the insides of her thighs, where he kissed her softly, near yet too far from his ultimate destination.

When her legs began to tremble, she clasped his head to keep from falling, and he knew then that he had her exactly where he wanted her.

"You must come down here with me," he said, learning the contours of her bottom with his palms, breathing warmth against her core.

And like a quivering bowl of cool mint jelly, his wife did a folding slide into his eager embrace.

Sabrina loved the way Gideon opened his mouth over hers and took heated possession of her pulsing self, as if he were starving and she, manna from heaven. She felt the same desperate longing for him, and their mutually frantic need thrilled her.

He took to suckling her again, and the blaze he stoked warmed her to her core.

Home, Sabrina thought, was not a place, home was a state of being and a matching of minds and hearts.

Home was the one's strength balancing the other's weakness.

Home was the instinctive knowledge of when and where to listen or speak, to hug or hold, to stroke or kiss.

Home was the person who completed you in the way only heaven could ordain.

Gideon was her home. Why had she not realized that sooner?

Earlier, she might have been able to run away.

Now she could only run toward.

As if Gideon sensed her surrender, he stretched out on his back and took her atop him, skin to skin, every inch of her matching every inch of him. "Glory," she whispered.

"Alleluia," he replied.

Every dip and rise in her seemed to match, perfectly, every rise and dip in him, so that they meshed and melded into one, almost.

"Soon," he said. "It must be soon." He turned them and lay facing her, pulling all their contours into blatant focus.

Gideon touched Sabrina then, to prepare her. "I want to make this good for you," he whispered, kissing her brow, her eyes. "I want this to be the best experience ever for you. When I am inside you, you must have no doubt that there is where I belong."

He touched her and Sabrina opened and moaned, arched and begged, in a silent frenzy of need.

Gideon made of her a new-rising star, coaxing her to soar, encouraging her to sparkle, then allowing her to float glistening to rest.

Then he rekindled her spark till she blazed and reached heaven once more.

He plied her with sweet, soft touches, with tantalizing tongue-licking kisses, stopping to stroke and suckle.

As he feasted on her, he gloried in her expressions, from impatient need to overwhelming amazement, to satisfaction and contentment.

She trusted him and he rewarded her trust. She allowed him to weave a spell along her every hollow and curve, and with her generous blessing he made magic within her.

At a point where Sabrina thought she must stop or swoon, her rogue denied her request and flew her past bearing to a place so high, they fractured the sun.

Stars rained a sparkling cascade all about them. And he sustained the sunburst with practiced hands until he, too, thought she might expire, then he lowered her slowly back to earth and the realization of his arms encircling her.

Gideon rose above her only then, and he watched her as he made to enter her. "You are mine," he shouted as he slipped inside her.

"Mine," he said as she closed about him, milking him with her pulsing need.

"Mine," he whispered, moving within her, arching her, riding her, until she wept with her release.

"Mine," she whispered on a sob.

Then the rogue carried his wife to heaven again, and when she reached it, and the stars singed them with their sparkling tips, Gideon gave her his seed, shouting at the last, "Mine," as did she.

They kissed, and kissed again, more ravenous than even in the melding. Touching, confirming, settling arms and legs, bodies, to meet and touch, unable to get close enough.

Never enough.

Hours or minutes later, Sabrina awoke to a crying babe and aching, milk-full breasts. She rose to feed Juliana, and Gideon never woke.

When she returned, a staff of moonlight crossed the bed. She slipped into her husband's possessive embrace and remembered that she had not given him her prize.

"Gideon," she whispered. "Gideon, wake up."

He moaned and turned into her embrace, hard on the instant. She could feel his grin grow against her breast. "Again, my greedy wife?"

She laughed. "Not quite."

He moaned. "Oh, do not burst my fantasy."

"I want to give you something first."

"As I want to give you something . . . more."

Sabrina chuckled at the promise in his voice, at his playfulness, as she rose from their bed and sought the purse she had dropped upon entering the bedchamber.

When she returned to the bed, she sat, looking down at him, prone, half asleep, one wide-awake portion of his anatomy tenting the bedclothes. With a finger, she stroked his erection through the sheet and he lunged and wrapped himself around her, making her scream in surprise.

"Shh," he said. "You will bring the house down around us."

Sabrina sought and found the purse, then she lifted it and placed it on his chest.

"Oomph. What is that?"

"The race purse, plus my winnings from a wager. Eighty-five hundred pounds. All yours."

Gideon pulled away from her, and she heard the purse thunk when it hit the floor as he rose.

Rising herself to a kneeling position on the bed, she watched her rankled husband light candles, one by one, his movements severe, until the bedchamber was bathed in light and nearly as bright as day.

Fury shadowed his brow and chiseled his hawk-like features to harder angles, until he stood before her, an arrogant rogue once more, handsome and wicked, and all but threatening in stance.

"Gideon?"

"What do you take me for? Do you think I am the kind of man would send my wife out to make my fortune. Damn you if you do. Damn you for a fool."

"I do not understand."

"Money is nothing to your safety. Nothing, do you hear?"

"But you need—"

"I need you safe. What would I— What would the children do if something happened to you?"

That was when Sabrina knew that there would be no flight this time for her. Because if she ran now, she would leave her heart, her very "self" behind.

She was his and he was hers.

She loved him. God help her, she did. With a love the likes of which she never imagined could be hers. Pray God, such a vulnerable love would not destroy them both.

Sabrina rose from the bed, took the purse, and threw it in the corner. Neither of them turned, even when the cloth bag split and coins scattered and rolled to every corner.

He cared for her, Gideon thought.

He cared for her, but all she cared about was that he have enough money to keep her.

That broke him. Always for the money with her. He had almost forgotten that everything she did was for money. He wanted to ask if she had finally taken his seed for the money as well. But he could not, for he could not bear her answer.

It might destroy his last thread of hope.

It almost did destroy his pride, because, God help him, in that moment, he did not even care. He wanted her any way he could have her, as he had from the first.

He cared only that she was safe, and here, and his.

His.

He took in the picture of her then, almost defeated as she moved to the chiffonier, where he had left her hairpins. She bent to the side, to cascade her hair in that direction, her profile perfect. She took the fall of hair, twined it, and set it atop her head, slipping hairpins into it before turning to regard him.

In the full glow of candlelight, her breasts were high and heavy, proud and free. Sabrina. His wife, the woman he loved, the most beautiful—

The candle's flame flickered and brightened in the breeze he stirred as he moved toward her. Light danced off . . . a scar, clarifying it, bringing it into stark relief.

The closer he got, the more such imperfections did he notice. Another and another, too many of a sudden. Scars slashed her shoulders, a breast.

Gideon grasped those fine shoulders and turned her so he could examine each horrid desecration marking her porcelain skin.

Her scars, Gideon thought absurdly, were all on the outside.

Other scars marked the nape of her neck, the back of an arm.

Rage, and an abounding tenderness, filled him to the point that he feared he must crush her in his embrace, beat on her tormentor, or smash something.

Taking his hands from her, lest he leave bruises of his own, Gideon fingered one particularly thick white blemish along the back of a shoulder. "Tell me about this one."

"I . . . fell against a hot poker."

"He attacked you with a hot poker."

Sabrina regarded the floor.

"And this one?" He kissed the circular scar at her nape.

"A nail."

"A bloody, huge nail," he snapped.

"Sticking out of the wall . . . and I got . . . pushed . . . more than once . . . against it."

She had been pinned, literally, to the wall. Gideon's stomach churned, his throat closed. Something constricted his chest. "I want to kill him."

"You cannot. Someone else already did."

"Would that I could end his despicable life a second time."

"You would have to wait your turn. He was much despised." Sabrina wanted to tell Gideon then that she feared she knew Brian's murderer, that Lowick must even now be looking for her. But she could not.

"Why, Sabrina? Why did you marry him?"

"I was seventeen when my father sold me to Brian. I believed Brian must be an improvement over my father. In such cases, one always assumes that the unknown must be better."

She shrugged. "As it turned out, they were two of a kind."

Dear God, Gideon thought. How many men had she been wronged by, passed to? Her father gave her to her first husband, whom she must have fled to go to Hawksworth, who passed her to Gideon. Lord, this could end badly.

Or had it already done so?

"Did you kill your husband?"

"No."

"More's the pity."

"I am a coward."

"You have more strength than ten of the best men who fought Boney beside me."

"I endured."

"You survived."

"I did not remove my children soon enough from danger."

"You got your children to safety."

She had not. Oh, she had not. "I got them to you, which is as close to safety as they can get."

"But not complete safety."

Long moments of silence passed, during which time Gideon became more and more agitated. "I had thought that we were beyond secrets, you and I."

She shivered. "I am afraid."

He grabbed a blanket from the bed and wrapped it around her. "Of me?"

"Not so much anymore."

"The day you become certain that I will not hurt you is the day I pray for and will celebrate."

"Celebrate now. I am certain you will not hurt me."

"Then why are you afraid?"

"I am not even certain why. Not quite."

"You do not think me strong enough, or yours enough, to stand with you?"

"I think you the most wonderful man it has ever been my privilege to know. I thank God daily for your presence in our lives."

"But . . . ?"

"You are human, and only a man after all."

"After all." Frustration ate at Gideon, fury, but over what, precisely, he did not know. "The danger you fear is from an outside source?"

"Yes, and no."

"Damn it, Sabrina!" Gideon turned away in anger, and came back as fast. "Damn, damn. Damn! You *must* trust me enough to tell me."

"If I did, I would place you in danger."

"To hell with your lack of faith in me. Tell me, damn it!"

She turned away from him instead. "I cannot."

Crushed, almost broken, Gideon regarded her steadily. "Tell me, at least, if I must set the Runners to watching the house day *and* night."

"You must."

"Can you give me a description of your enemy?"

"Satan's worst nightmare."

Gideon ran both hands through his hair. "Veronica must be one you see as your enemy?"

"Yes, but not only her."

"A man, too, you see as dangerous?"

Sabrina nodded.

"He is tall with a beard. Confirm or deny."

"Short and clean-shaven."

"A skinny man."

"Sturdy, barrel-chested, and thick-limbed."

Gideon saw that Sabrina was breaking under the

weight of his questioning, but he needed to know more. "His eyes, they—"

She sobbed. "No more, please."

Gideon lifted her into his arms and carried her to his bed.

# Twenty-two

Gideon had left Sabrina alone in his bed almost as soon as she fell asleep.

From the moment he extracted from her something of a description of her tormentor—though he still had no understanding of her torment, which worried the hell out of him—and from the degree of her fear, he knew he must do something immediately to set her mind at rest and protect her and the children.

He *must* act quickly.

For his own peace of mind, he went first into Sabrina's bedchamber to look in on Juliana in her cradle and assure himself that all was fine with her. She slept on her stomach, and he could not see much more of her than her tiny hand covering her pink little face, but she was there, safe, and sleeping well. Then he dressed and went up to check on the boys. He covered Damon's shoulders and tucked one of Rafe's feet beneath his blanket.

Everyone in his world was tucked into their beds, safe.

Drizzle gave a squeaky yip as Gideon was leaving, and he stooped down to scratch behind a small ear, and even the pup went back to sleep.

On the second floor, Gideon woke Doggett, then Waredraper. Doggett had not patrolled since his accident, but it was time again.

After the men dressed, they met him in his study. "I need your help," Gideon said. "Sabrina is afraid of someone, and though I do not have a name, I need you to begin patrolling again, both of you. Day and night. Keep an eye out for anyone who looks suspicious."

Gideon took to pacing. "You once said that you would do anything for Sabrina. Well, do this. Prove to her that she and the children are safe at all times, beginning now."

"Can you give us a description of the fellow?" Waredraper asked.

"Only that he is robust, thick-limbed, and barrel-chested."

"That will have to do," their "seamstress" said, rising.

"Thank you." Before he left, Gideon made for Sabrina's sitting room to see if he could find something that might give him, or Bow Street, a clue as to her tormentor's identity.

She might not appreciate him going through her things, but he remembered her scars, and for that reason felt justified in trying to help her despite her reluctance to trust.

Other than her writing things, he found a canister containing a hundred pounds sterling, a small fortune to someone for whom money had always been a problem, he supposed. What he did not understand was her reason for secreting it away from him, when he gave her a more-than-generous allowance.

The canister was, as far as he could see, the only

item of value in her desk. Before he left the house, he took the container of money to his study and locked it in the safe.

After he did that, Gideon went straight to the mews, behind the house, to saddle Deviltry, for it was unlikely that even the stable lad was awake at this early hour.

Unfortunately, Grandmama would soon be, because Gideon was going to awaken her himself and persuade her to pack up her household and move back to Kent today. He wanted her to take Sabrina and the children with her, for he believed they would be safer away from London.

On his way to Grandmama's he would stop at Bow Street. If it was not too early, he would request round-the-clock protection for his family. If it was too early, he would go back after he left Grandmama's.

Last would be a very quick stop at his solicitor's, to have the man set up an account in Sabrina's name with the eighty-five hundred pounds she had won at the St. Eustace Winter Fair. It was hers. She had earned it, every penny.

Not only had she stayed when she thought he was poor, she had tried to help him by winning the race purse and giving it to him.

Lord, if he had not already loved her— The realization stopped him in his tracks. Did he?

Yes, he loved her. He had not even realized it. Perhaps it had taken root only sometime last night. Perhaps when she stood on his bed and ordered him not to come to her unless he was "naked, if you please." Or when she helped him remove that second boot. Perhaps when he had seen her scars and wished they were his, wished that he could take on all her pain.

He supposed his love for her had been sneaking up on him for some time. Perhaps, since she threw flour in his face . . . or made a conquest of England's prince.

*When* he loved her mattered not; he wished only that she loved him in return. Though life would probably go easier on them both if she simply trusted him.

Ah, but he wanted her love.

He needed her love.

He needed her.

When Sabrina awoke alone, she realized that within the ultimate tenderness of their second loving, Gideon had made their first encounter, earlier in the night, seem almost brutal.

She thought then that he might have attempted that second time to make love to her.

If that was his intent, he had succeeded.

He had cherished her into forgetting the ugliness that marked her. He had carried her all the way to heaven and promised her eternity.

Then why, when she slept, did he leave her?

Had he taken a disgust of her when he awoke and realized the horror she had brought to their marriage?

Like him, the scattered coins were gone, and Sabrina did not know whether to be pleased or saddened by the fact.

Foolishly afraid that she would never see him again, Sabrina rose to a more-than-frantic wail from her daughter.

\* \* \*

Not fifteen minutes after Gideon left by way of the mews behind the house, Damon woke and went to his favorite spot on the window seat, with its view to the street out front. What he saw made him run for his brother.

"Rafe, wake up."

Rafferty sat up and rubbed the sleep from his eyes. "What? What is wrong?"

"He is there, across the street again. The man who watches us. Come."

Rafe fell backward in the bed, moaning. "It is still nighttime."

Damon pulled his twin's covers off. "Wake up. Come and see."

"No." Rafe pulled them back up. "Leave me be."

"But there is something about him. He reminds me of—" Damon tugged on Rafe's arm. "Just come and look. Now."

"In a while," Rafe said, turning over. "I just need one more sleep."

"No. You will not sleep when I need you to see that man. Rafe, he reminds me of—of Uncle Bryceson."

"That is not funny," Rafe said, yawning hugely and hugging his pillow tighter, fighting suddenly to stay asleep, though he opened one eye. "Uncle Bryceson died at Waterloo. Mama would scold you for your faradiddle."

"Suppose he is not dead after all, and is watching over us? Suppose that, hunh?"

Rafe sighed and sat up, allowing himself to be tugged from his bed, dragging his feet on principle, when he was curious enough to run to the window and see Damon's ghost. He even threw in a complaint about sisters being quieter than brothers.

"Look, there," Damon said. "Does that man not look like Uncle Bryceson if he were not bent and used a cane and had scars and longish hair like a lion?"

"I think you are having another bad dream, and what happened to your dragon?" Rafe picked up the purring Mincemeat, sliding against his leg. "All I see is a lonely old man."

"Then why does he watch us all the time? Answer me that."

"All the time?" Rafe snorted. "Have you seen him more than twice, then? And what makes you think he can see us? It is almost still dark out, and he looks so old and broken, he might also be blind."

"He is not blind."

"Is."

"Is not."

"Wave at him, then. Go ahead. Wave."

Rafferty waved and laughed, until the watcher shrugged his shoulders and waved back. But before Rafe could react, he turned to a scraping sound behind him, then something covered his face, making it difficult to breathe. Panic clawed at his middle. "Damon!" he shouted, kicking out with instinct. "Damon, you stop this right now."

"Help," Damon yelled. "I am caught."

Mincemeat was torn from Rafe's arms.

Rafe screamed, heard his brother screaming, until a blow silenced him, as the next did for Damon.

Below, in the hazy gray of awakening dawn, the

watcher straightened despite the pain in the action. "Damon! Rafe!" he shouted.

Neither boy returned to the window.

The scarred man was not even certain what he had seen. Perhaps Demon and Rapscallion were only playing a trick on him, except that it was a bit early in the day, even for those two.

Then the watcher saw, just down the road, two ruffians, each with a thick rolled rug over his shoulder, emerging from the mews road, several houses down from Stanthorpe Place. Side by side, the rug-toting rotters made their scurrying way toward Henrietta Street and disappeared from sight.

The watcher made to charge forward, as if he would run after them, but he was thwarted by his bad leg. He tripped and dropped his cane, cursed and glanced down the street, but he saw nothing save the smoky fog of London's dawn. "Hello the watch!" he shouted, hoping to catch the attention of a retiring night watchman. "Hello the watch!"

"Damn." The kidnappers were getting away, if they were kidnappers. Except that he had seen no one in the nursery window since that scuffle of a sort was played out before his eyes. One minute both boys were there, waving, then something cut his view of them, giving him the absurd notion that curtains, or bags, had come down over them, as if the boys were butterflies caught in nets. Except that all had been darkness inside the nursery, making it difficult for him to discern much of anything beyond the window.

As hobbled as he was, he would follow the route the men with the rugs had taken, he decided, until he came upon someone who would help. If only he could reach his cane, far below him on the ground, and get back up again, after he did.

But before he could attempt that feat, a beefy arm hooked him around the neck, and something hard—a knee, perhaps—wedged itself in the small of his back.

"Never you mind shouting for your thieving cronies, mate, you got Stanthorpe's own guard dogs, at cher service. We saw you watching the house."

Another man stepped before the watcher, wielding a kitchen knife in a parody of swordsmanship, for all the world as if he were stitching a sampler in the air. "Waredraper and Doggett, sentinels, guardians, and protectors of the righteous," said the knife-wielder.

"Thank God," the watcher said, tongue in cheek, wishing Doggy, or Dogwart—or whatever the devil the oaf behind him called himself—would loosen his bully hold. "Enough of your burlesque performance," the watcher snapped. "The Whitcomb lads have been kidnapped."

The sham sentinels laughed. "Kidnapped? By who?" the prissy one facing him asked. "Those two would bruise an abductor bloody."

That was true, the watcher thought. "Look, if it is all the same to you, the men I believe to be their kidnappers scurried toward Henrietta Street, likely heading for Oxford Street. You had better go after them."

"Sure we will, just as soon as we get you settled, won't we, mate?" Dogwart asked his prissy, grinning friend.

"If you do not believe me," the watcher tried. "Then take me to Sabr—to her grace. She will tell you who I am and she will listen to me, by God, which is what you should be doing. You will rue this morning's work. Her boys are taken, I tell you."

"What do you say, Doggett? Think we should take the scoundrel inside to see if her grace knows him?"

"We can't go scaring her ladyship, now, can we? But we can put 'im in the cellar, truss him up right 'n' tight, and wait till himself comes back."

"You are making a terrible mistake," the watcher said as he was dragged along, tripping over his accursed leg. "Do you have any idea who I am?"

"The king of England?" Prissy-man suggested.

"Nah." Doggy-breath cackled. " 'E's the bloody queen."

"I happen to be—"

"Not so bloody sturdy and thick-limbed as you're s'posed to be, I can tell you that," Dogwart said, shoving him forward again, forcing the watcher to center his concentration on remaining upright.

If he fell and cracked his senseless skull, he would be no use to Sabrina or the boys, he thought. And this time he must be. God, he must. "At least go and see if the boys are in the nursery," he said.

And the fools laughed again.


More than an hour later, Gideon dismounted, threw his reins to his stable lad, and made for the house.

Grandmama had been more than willing to pack up on the instant and take her "sweet daughter-in-law and dear grandbabies," into Kent with her to protect them. A situation for which Gideon was incredibly grateful.

Though his wife did not yet know it, she would

soon be safe away and in possession of an account with money enough to keep her comfortable. At this point, all he cared about was keeping her and the children safe and cared for. Nothing else mattered.

He had barely made it into the kitchen, when Waredraper and Doggett came racketing down the backstairs, attacking him with frantic, meaningless prattle before he could draw breath.

"The lads," Doggett said.

" 'Twas a half-hour before we even looked." Waredraper groaned. "And only then because of that yapping pup. We just don't know."

Gideon raised both brows. "What are you talking about?"

"*Could* have rolled 'em up in the carpet."

Doggett shook his head. "Bloke's a blackguard. He didn't know for sure."

"Then where are the missing carpets?"

"Stop!" Gideon shouted, a sick feeling churning in his gut. "Tell me first that 'the lads' are *not* Rafe and Damon."

Doggett and Waredraper glanced at each other. Doggett swallowed. "But they are."

"What about them?" Gideon snapped.

Doggett backed up a step. "Gone."

"Are you saying you lost my children?" Gideon's voice rose. "How could that be, when they were in their beds even as I put you on watch?"

Gideon saw his guard-dogs cower, forced himself into a pretense of calm, and took a deep breath. "You will excuse my outburst. Where do the boys usually hide?"

"If they are hiding, it is not in this house."

"Are you certain?" Gideon asked. "Did you look

in the park, across the street, where we hunted
cat?"

"Hunted what?"

"Across the street, man. Did you look across the
street?"

Doggett nodded. "We looked."

"Everywhere," Waredraper added.

Gideon named a dozen places the boys might
hide, but his men insisted the boys were in none
of them.

"I will find them myself, by damn."

Waredraper grabbed Gideon's arm to stop him
as he stepped determinedly forward. "Wasting
time. Signs of a struggle."

That was Gideon's undoing. A struggle. He could
barely breathe. Fear grew in his belly like a canker.
Who would do such a thing?

Veronica was the first person who came to his
mind. "What have you told her grace?"

"Nothing." Doggett shook his head. "Didn't
want to give her a fright."

Gideon released his breath. "Do not. Not yet.
Veronica is trying to draw me out. I am certain of
it." Except that he had learned, only that morning
on Bow Street, that Veronica was likely more dangerous than any of them suspected.

"What if her grace looks for them?" Waredraper
asked.

The question stopped Gideon's scrambling
thoughts. "Wait a minute. It is past nine. Why has
Sabrina not discovered the boys missing for herself? Are you certain they are not with her?"

"The babe's fussing up a storm," Doggett said.
"Spots. Her grace doesn't want the boys catching
it again. Told Minchip to keep—"

"Minchip!"

"Hysterical. Knows nothing. They were gone when she woke."

Gideon's heart raced, and guilt snapped at his heels. He would have served the boys better if he had stayed rather than gone. His fault they were missing. His doing. "Have my horse saddled at once."

"Where are you going?" Doggett asked Gideon, as Waredraper left to tend the horse.

"Lady Veronica Cartwright's. Keep this . . . situation quiet until I return." He turned to Alice, standing on the far side of the kitchen, her mouth pursed as if she had sucked a hothouse lemon. "Say nothing to your mistress," Gideon told her. "That is an order."

He waited for the maid's nod before regarding Doggett. "Come with me while I get my pistols. If I am lucky, I will have the boys back before Sabrina ever realizes they went missing."

Gideon loaded his pistols as efficiently as if he were the second in a duel. "After I leave, go for the Runners and hurry them up," he told Doggett. "I went to Bow Street this morning and left a request. They will help when you tell them the situation has worsened."

From atop his horse, five minutes later, Gideon regarded his watchdogs. "If you do not hear from me in half an hour, then you must tell her grace. If it comes to that, keep her here at all costs. Do you understand me? I know who is behind this, and I believe the boys are safe. I must believe it." He nodded before turning his horse. "I will have them back in a trice." Please God.

Doggett and Waredraper watched Gideon ride from sight.

"Blast it," Doggett said. "You forgot to tell him about the bloke in the cellar."

"*I* forgot?" Waredraper shouted. "Me? I was supposed to tell him?"

"No matter. You'll be forgiven. Says he has everything under control."

Minutes later, Gideon stormed Veronica's house without resistance. Obviously, she had neglected to inform her servants that he would no longer be paying their wages. So much for the better, under the circumstances.

He cut through her dressing room, and when her maid both curtseyed and crossed herself upon seeing him, he knew what he was like to find.

He did not even try the knob on the bedchamber door, but kicked that portal open.

The bed's copulating occupants separated in shock, the both of them cursing like guttersnipes. Veronica's nameless partner jumped to his feet, then the puny fellow had the audacity to bow. No small insult, given his nude state.

"I daresay, he is smaller, Ronnie, than you used to prefer." Realizing the man must be a rookery acquaintance, Gideon was bedeviled into insulting his height, but as a result, all of them regarded his limp little wick instead.

God help him, despite all panic and good sense, Gideon laughed.

The man growled and demanded satisfaction.

Gideon ignored him. "Give me the boys, Ronnie. If you give them to me now, your perfidy will go no further." He wanted to tell her what he learned of her treachery this morning, but this was no time to anger her. "Kidnapping is too cruel, even for you."

Her lover straightened. "Kidnapped, you say? Well, in that case, I shall let your insult pass . . . due to the overabundance of anxiety you must be feeling." The little man pulled on his trousers with haste and turned to the bed. "Good-bye, my dear." He seemed almost to grin, except that his lips remained a slash of firmness. "Thank you. It has been . . . interesting." As quick as that, the curious little man was gone.

Veronica waved him away, even as she regarded Gideon with narrowed eyes. And like a black widow spider still hungry for a mate, she threw back her covers, for all the world as if she were inviting him into her bed.

"I want my boys," Gideon said, more disgusted than ever, but determined not to reveal it. "Just give them to me, so I may go."

"If you are referring to the children of that slut you married, does this mean that you have misplaced them already? By accident, or by design? I knew you could not stomach raising another man's get."

Gideon wondered when she had become so destructive a woman. His brother had gotten his throat cut in a bordello, the Runners recently discovered, an establishment Veronica owned.

She rose from her bed now, employing all the wiles of a temptress, though she fell so far short of the mark as she stalked toward him, it was all Gideon could do not to reveal how ill her ploy, their very association, made him. He understood now the difference between making love and the physical act itself.

"You loved me once," she said. "Surely you could do so again."

"For a time, I bedded you, to our mutual physical gratification. That time has now passed."

Shedding her cunning like a snake sheds its skin, Veronica Cartwright looked every inch a strumpet, screeching in mortified fury.

Fists raised to do damage, she rushed him.

Gideon stepped from her path.

She turned and rounded on him. "You are a fool, Gideon St. Goddard. Do you mean to say that you think you care about that whore you married?"

"She is not a subject I will profane by discussing her with you."

The woman who was nothing more to him now than a caricature of depravity laughed. "The more fool you." She took up her dressing gown and slipped into it. "I am sorry to be the one to break the news, *darling,* but you had best resign yourself to having me. Because your harlot of a wife is on her way to save her precious brats even now."

Gideon grasped her shoulders. "What do you know?"

"That *he* will never let her go once he has her. And that by the time he is finished with her, you will not want her anymore."

# Twenty-three

"Your grace," Alice said, entering Sabrina's bedchamber and holding forward a sealed note. "This has just arrived for you."

Sabrina tore open the missive and was trembling before she finished the first line. "Dear God," she whispered. "He says he has the boys. Alice, go upstairs and fetch the twins . . . or stay with Julie while I—"

"They are not there, your grace."

Sabrina stepped around her maid. "I will go for them myself then—"

"The boys are missing."

"No," Sabrina wailed. "Please no," but she could tell from the look on her maid's face that it was true.

Sabrina wanted to rant, to scream, to blame someone, but she knew she must calm herself or be useless to them. She also knew that the fault was hers.

She read the note again. It said she must go to Seven Dials, else Damon and Rafferty would be harmed. Worse, he promised, if she did not go alone, they would die. Sabrina sobbed at the very words. She did not need the undisclosed address or signature to know who had taken them or where in the Dials she must go to save them. She did not need his signature to know that the fiend meant every word.

He, Homer Lowick, had stolen her boys. Dear God; they must be so frightened.

Sabrina began to search her bedchamber for anything she could fit in her reticule that might serve as a weapon. Then she came to a dead stop, realization dawning. "You knew? Why did no one tell me? Who else knows?"

Alice hesitated. "Everyone is out looking for them, your grace, even the Runners now."

"Does his grace know too? And kept it from me? Is he searching for them as well?"

Alice bit her lip. "He is out looking for them, yes."

Sabrina moved from panic to fury, then to relief, all in a flash. Perhaps it was best that Gideon was away, else he would try to prevent her from going, or try to go with her, or in her stead, and place the boys in mortal danger. "Will you care for Juliana, Alice, while I go out?"

"But where—"

"Do not ask."

"Of course, your grace."

"Thank you, Alice." Sabrina picked up Juliana to kiss and snuggle her one last time, then she all but ran down the stairs. She dared not give voice to how long she might be gone—or that she might never return.

Sick over leaving, afraid she would never see her daughter or her husband again, Sabrina made her surreptitious way toward Oxford Street, avoiding the main roads whenever she could. On Oxford, she gave in to her anxiety and hailed a hack. People were too busy there going about their own business to notice her.

Inside the hack, head back, eyes closed, she could think of nothing but the danger to her boys. The man in whose hands their fate rested had already committed murder, of that she was certain. She had placed her children in danger by not doing something about Lowick sooner.

She would never forgive herself.

At St. Giles High Street, she had to argue with the hack driver before he would set her down. But despite his dire warnings, Sabrina planned to lose herself among the motley mix of close-set buildings. She did not intend to be followed.

As the hack drove off, she stood unmoving, alone, and afraid, for perhaps the first time since she came to know Gideon. She had never consciously placed her trust in him. Yet, she did trust him, she came to realize as she made her way through a nefarious aggregate of humanity, most in need of a wash.

On Monmouth, near Seven Dials, a grimy urchin, twelve at the most, in stovepipe hat but no shoes, accosted her, demanding her purse or her virtue.

Sabrina laughed somewhat hysterically at the ultimatum. "I have neither," she said, throwing him off his guard. "And Lowick will not want me to be late."

As she expected, her assailant stepped back and looked about as if the demon might jump from the shadows, and Sabrina continued on her way.

Perhaps she should have told Gideon about Lowick. Except that her husband might now be dead if she had, for he would surely have tried to rid the world of such a one. At least this way, if something happened to her, Gideon could raise Juliana, the boys too, if she could manage it, please God.

In Seven Dials, a dingy neighborhood of costermongers, bird fanciers, and sellers of old clothes and shoes, a body could go missing just walking down the street. There, heart hammering against her ribs, bold on the outside, shaking on the inside, Sabrina approached a battered front door and stepped gingerly into the house.

Having fled this place some seven months before, Sabrina knew something of the extravagant layout. Her only hope for Damon and Rafferty was that they, too, remembered, so that when she distracted Lowick in whatever way she could manage, the boys could get away.

She hoped she would have a chance to tell them how to get to Gideon from the crypt in the St. Giles churchyard, where the old priest-tunnel exited.

She had only ever told one person about the underground passage, and that man was dead. She should have told Gideon about Lowick, if only so he would know about the tunnel. Except that she did not want Gideon following, Sabrina reminded herself.

If he came, her husband would die, just as her time here would no longer matter by the time he arrived, for it was entirely possible that when she and Lowick were finished with each other, either Lowick would be dead, or she would.

Upstairs, Lowick rubbed his hands together, smiled, and studied his bait. Huddled together on a single attic cot, identical twin boys, in nightshirts and bare feet, sniveled like two peas adrift in a leaky pod.

Taking them had been too easy to be fun, his men had complained. Lowick was sorry for their lack of sport, though they had had sport enough later, what with that bloody Runner breaking down the front door. Served the idiots right, walking down the street with stolen rugs, bold as you please, for all the world to see.

Lowick was only sorry that he would now have to replace the men, and he was furious over the cost of disposing of the bodies. He hoped no one came looking for the missing Runner anytime soon.

Nevertheless, he had Whitcomb's brats, no matter the nuisance. Besides, he would keep them around only long enough to get him the prize, then he would dispose of them.

Brian Whitcomb's woman was all he cared about. That she was now St. Goddard's would only make his mounting of her that much the sweeter.

First, he was going to work the money Whitcomb owed him out of her, every shilling, then he was going to make her pay double for the insult St. Goddard had paid him. It was just too bad he would not be able to keep her around for a bit of fun later, but she would be just too hot a property if St. Goddard lived.

One of the boys took to sniveling again, and Lowick snickered. "Be good and you can make me some brass," he said. "If St. Goddard won't pay to have you back—as he can well afford to do—you'll make a fine pair of chimney sweeps. Might even get me a guinea for a matched set." Lowick laughed. "Give me trouble and I'll set you adrift in fact, and there'll be no boat beneath you, leaky or otherwise."

They remembered him, he thought. He could tell from the way their eyes had widened when he'd walked into the room and from the way they clutched each other now. He wondered what else they remembered.

"How did your slut of a mother get you out of here the last time?" he asked. "Tell me and I'll let your baby sister go."

Rafferty charged him for his groundless taunt, throwing his whole body into the action, but Lowick boxed the cheeky boy's ears and sent him sprawling to the floor.

"Papa is going to find you," Damon spat. "He will find you and—*beat* you."

Lowick laughed. "Too late," he said. "Your papa hasn't got it in him anymore."

"Uncle Bryce does."

"There's a new name," Lowick said. "And who is this fine uncle of yours?"

"He is the Duke of Hawksworth," Damon said. "And *very* powerful."

"Hawksworth. Hawksworth? Didn't he come to a bad end at Waterloo? Blimey, if you two keep depending on people from the netherworld, you're going to find yourselves joining 'em real soon."

Lowick leaned in close. "In this life, best you remember who can help you and who cannot." He pointed to himself. "Me," Lowick said, "I am the only man who can help you now." Then he screamed in rage and twisted around as if to grab something.

"Mama, Mama," the boys shouted when they saw her.

Lowick choked her with an arm, and while her boys beat against him, he forced her hand into the air, the hand with the bloody scissors she had stabbed into his shoulder. When he bent her wrist back, Sabrina screamed in pain and frustration, and dropped them.

With a curse, Lowick kicked the sharp-edged cutters under a chest of drawers, then he picked her up and carried her, kicking, toward the staircase.

Remaining silent, so as not to terrify her boys any more than they already were, Sabrina managed to drop her reticule before Lowick carried her down the stairs.

At Stanthorpe Place, Gideon called Sabrina's name as he ran up the stairs and into her bedchamber, all the while praying that Veronica's insane tale was false. When he failed to find Sabrina in either bedchamber, he went up to the nursery.

There, he found Alice walking Juliana, the babe red-faced and screaming. "Sabrina?" he asked, but his heartbeat had already trebled, for he knew that Sabrina would not leave her sick baby unless she had a compelling reason to do so.

Gideon felt as if he had stepped off the edge of the world and dropped into hell. Veronica's tale could very well be true.

Fighting a knot of emotion stronger than any he had ever encountered, scared enough to break under the weight of his fear, Gideon regarded the maid. "Where is your mistress?"

"I read her note," Alice wailed as if she expected him to cuff her for her impertinence.

"What?" Still breathing hard, Gideon searched

the nursery with his gaze, for a clue, something to lead him to the boys, while he also tried to make sense of the maid's words above the din of his daughter's fretting.

Alice bounced Julie. "I sent Doggett to see if he could find her," she said. "It is so bad a place after all, and I hoped he could tell you, but he is not back. And the man in the cellar has been making ever so much noise, I am afraid he will break free and murder us all."

Frustrated and anxious as Gideon was to set off and make everything right again, he needed to hear what Alice knew, so he took Juliana to quiet her. "Tell me now, Alice."

When the maid's discourse became disjointed, Gideon set her gently back on the simple path, until she began to make sense. Then he perceived that Veronica had been correct. Panic set in and he gave her the baby back.

When Alice pulled a note from her apron pocket and offered it, Gideon gaped at her for not presenting it sooner, but he said nothing and read it. Then he cursed as he crumpled it, tossed it to the floor, and was on his way out the door again.

Alice placed the baby in a cradle. Then she bent down to pick up the crushed note, and as she regarded it, she remembered the man Waredraper was guarding. "Wait!" she called. "What about the man in the cellar?" But when she got to the top of the stairs, Gideon was long gone, and the very man she feared was on his way up.

"Where is Sabrina?" he shouted, his cane smacking each step as he climbed. "Where is your mistress?"

Alice backed up a step.

"It is all right," Waredraper said, coming up behind him. "I am convinced he is a friend."

Alice extended her trembling hand to reveal the crumpled note.

The man who had been locked in the cellar snatched it from her, and Alice screamed and ran back to the nursery to lock herself and the baby inside.


Gideon found Doggett hurrying down Oxford Street, halfway between Stanthorpe Place and one of the worst sections of London.

Gideon hauled the man up on his horse. "Did you find her?"

"Seven Dials. I know the house. I was just—"

They rode hell for leather toward Seven Dials.

Down the street from the house Doggett indicated, Gideon pulled his pistols from his greatcoat. "Take my horse and go for the Runners. Where the bloody devil have they been anyway?"

"Out searching for the boys, but I'll bring them here," Doggett said. "You be careful, your grace. That Lowick's a bad one."

"Describe him to me."

"Like you said, short, sturdy, and barrel-chested, but I never made the connection. Not till I came here."

Gideon cursed and moved forward.

Getting inside the house was easy, almost too easy, Gideon thought as he stepped into a setting that became eerie for its contradiction of lavishness amid London's squalor.

The sound of weeping led Gideon down a set of dank stone stairs and into a dim milled-stone cellar.

There, huddled together beside a massive door, closed against them, sat his barefoot boys in their nightclothes, Rafe clutching Sabrina's reticule.

Pistol in hand, Gideon held a finger to his lips, so that when he advanced and they looked up and saw him, they did not announce his presence. Nevertheless, they shouted "Papa" when they saw him, though not as loudly as they might have, as they launched themselves into his arms.

"Where is Mama?" Gideon whispered, accepting hugs, kissing heads, wishing he could hug them back, except that he must keep his pistols at the ready and clear of the boys at the same time.

"The little man is hurting her," Rafe said. "And I want to hurt him back, Papa."

Rafe's words fired Gideon's hunger for vengeance. "I shall deal with him for you, son, but first, I want you to go upstairs and wait just inside the front door for the runners. And when they arrive, I want you to direct them down here. Go ahead now, so I can get your mama and bring her safe up to you."

Gideon's attention focused suddenly on what he could not see, on the opposite side of the massive door, the more-frantic tone of Sabrina's weeping, and the heightened fervor of the man's cursing.

He tried the knob while he watched the boys climb the stairs, but he did not aim his pistols or try to force the door until they were out of sight. When he did try, the blasted portal would not budge. Gideon swore, looked about him, and unearthed a downed beam which he used as a battering ram.

On the second try, the door gave with a splintering crack and flew open to smack the stone wall.

Across the room, the struggling heap on the bed separated into a man launching himself up and off—Sabrina.

The bastard was still dressed, praise be, his face and arms were raked bloody, and blood soaked his shoulder. Gideon cocked his pistols, aimed one at Lowick's heart, the other much lower.

Gideon's gaze strayed to Sabrina, pushing down her skirts, shivering to the point of teeth-chattering, looking at him as if she could not bear the sight of him. "Sabrina?"

His distraction allowed for another pistol to be cocked. Lowick's.

"Go ahead," Gideon said, refocusing, facing down Lowick's gun. "But I will send you to hell before me."

Lowick grinned and shifted his aim toward Sabrina.

Gideon lowered his pistols.

A knife sliced the air, buried itself in Lowick's thigh, and as the fiend roared his rage, he redirected his aim toward Rafe, coming up beside Gideon.

"He was going to shoot Mama!"

Gideon knocked Rafe down, covered him, and caught Lowick's shot.

Sabrina screamed. Rafe's name. Gideon's. A good sign, Gideon thought as he rolled off the boy, ignoring the pain, thinking he needed to look for his pistols.

He shook off a sudden dizziness to focus on Sabrina, holding Rafe. His wife. His. So close, yet too far away to touch. She knelt over him then, one minute regarding his bloody side with anguish, the next fixated on the doorway.

Damon stood framed there. Veronica stood behind him, her hands on his shoulders, narrowing her gaze on Sabrina. "This could have been avoided, my dear, and your boys might have survived you if you had just stepped into my carriage that morning or even accepted the services of the midwife I took the trouble to send."

Gideon called himself a hundred times a fool. "Ronnie," he said. "Let Sabrina and the children go. Let my man take them home."

"I care less than nothing for the brats. I want only to remove the harlot you were coerced into marrying." She gave him a fanatical smile. "So you may come back to me."

"I saved your life once," Gideon said to her now. "Give me my family's lives in return, and you may have mine to end, or to keep."

"No," Lowick said, holding Gideon's pistols.

Sabrina began to weep even as a thundering filled the chamber, vibrating the floor beneath them, as if the end of the world had come.

One of the cut stones in the floor shuddered until it disappeared, leaving a hole through which a strange man rose, abetted by a second—Waredraper.

Fast as the first man appeared, he dropped and rolled, knocking Lowick off his feet.

Waredraper tackled Veronica, freeing Damon.

Ignoring the burning in his side, Gideon sought his pistols, but they were caught in the fight between Waredraper and Veronica, a near thing, until Waredraper ended on top, Veronica screaming and kicking beneath him. From his perch, the old man grinned. "Ain't as old or as stupid as I thought I was. Good thing I let my friend, here, talk me into this."

"Who put the knife in this one?" the friend asked, his familiar voice catching Gideon's attention, Sabrina's.

"I did," Rafe said. "Found it in Mama's reticule."

The man yanked the knife from Lowick's thigh to hold at his throat, ignoring his string of curses. "That's my Rapscallion."

Sabrina gasped.

"Hawksworth?" Gideon asked. If not for the voice, he would not have thought it possible, the stranger was so different, yet he had used Hawk's pet name for Rafe. "Hawksworth?" he asked again, with more hope.

"I told you to protect her, damn it," Hawksworth shouted in fury. "How the devil could you let this happen, Stanthorpe?"

Fury eclipsed hope. "I thought I was protecting her from indigence," Gideon snapped. "Neither of you bothered to tell me that I was supposed to be protecting her from Satan himself."

Gideon and Hawksworth looked at Sabrina, clutching her boys, being clutched by them, and weeping into their arms. And neither had the heart to hold her accountable for her foolhardy omission.

Silently, they bound Lowick and Veronica.

When they were done, Gideon regarded his wife. "Sabrina, are you all right?" But she would not look at him, and Gideon was cut to the quick by her aversion and rejection.

Lowick sneered. "You are agreeable with having my leftovers, then, your grace? Oh, I forgot, you already have had them, for I had the slattern before you. As I had her again today, make no mistake."

Despite the ache in his side, Gideon took great pleasure in cutting his knuckles on the man's jaw.

Hawksworth sat back against the wall with a half-smile on his face and closed his eyes.

Gideon thought his old friend looked as if all the fight had left him. He was pale, and the scars on his face only now registered. But Gideon could not keep his attention from Sabrina, there, beside him, bending over him, binding the wound in his side.

Safe. Sabrina was safe. The boys were safe.

Inhaling her fresh lilac scent, Gideon touched her hair as she tended him. He stroked her cheek with his fingertip, all the while begging silently for her to look at him. But she did not, and in the end he was forced to close his eyes against the pain of having the wound bound.

When Sabrina finished and pain subsided, Gideon opened his eyes, only to find her in Hawksworth's arms.

All the blood seemed to drain from him.

The event he wanted to rejoice over, his good friend's return from the dead, now made him ill, for it meant the loss of all Gideon had come to care for.

Hawksworth was alive. Alive and holding Sabrina as if he would never let her go. As she held Hawksworth, the man she loved, running her hands over the scars on his "poor, beautiful face" and weeping in his arms, thanking God that he did not die after all.

# Twenty-four

As Gideon watched Hawksworth and Sabrina together, he knew that he had lost her to the only man she had ever loved. Even Damon and Rafferty, the boys he had come to think of as his, were being crushed in Hawksworth's embrace. They called him Uncle Bryce and said they had recognized him watching the house, that they knew he would save them.

Soon, even Juliana, Gideon's bright little star, would be lost to him as well.

Like a man in a trance, Gideon watched Doggett arrive with the Runners and pull Lowick and Veronica to their feet. Before they got Lowick out the door, the bastard turned to Sabrina. "You ruined me with your whoring ways. This is your doing."

And on his wife's face, Gideon saw only an unbearable and haunted sadness as she turned from his silent entreaty and leaned into her lover's waiting arms.

Gideon's eyes met Veronica's, and she read his anguish, and started to laugh. He could hear her demented laughter all the way up the stairs.

At that moment, Gideon wanted more than ever to commit murder. Lowick and Veronica first, just for the satisfaction of it. Then, if only he could, Sabrina's first husband, and perhaps her father.

And last, Gideon would do in Hawksworth, the friend who had given him heaven and taken it away again.

He watched Sabrina stand and show concern, not for him, but for Hawksworth. She helped his old friend to rise, offering herself as his crutch, and they made to leave together.

Almost as an afterthought, she turned to him, but rather than look at him, she regarded the bloody bandage against his side. "Thank you for saving Rafe," she said as if she were speaking to a stranger. "It is a flesh wound, but wait for the doctor. We will have him sent to you." With that, she turned and walked from his life.

Gideon saw the boys hesitate and look from him to their mother and back.

Sabrina called them sharply, and they sent a last anguished look in his direction.

Gideon smiled and nodded. "Listen to your mother," he said. And they did.

It was over then.

*We* will have the doctor sent, she had said. Already, in his wife's mind, she and Hawksworth were together again.

When Sabrina, Hawksworth, and the boys arrived back at Stanthorpe Place, she ordered refreshment for Hawksworth and went up to the nursery to comfort and settle the boys.

They were tired and cranky. They did not understand why they had left their papa behind.

Once she took them away from Stanthorpe Place

for good, which she must do, Sabrina realized that her own sons might never speak to her again. But what choice did she have? She would not remain to wait for her husband's disgust, his eventual hate, to destroy them all.

Sabrina found Alice and Miss Minchip in the nursery with Juliana, so she fed and cuddled her baby girl, and thanked Alice, before she went back downstairs to say good-bye to Hawksworth.

She needed to pack herself and the children up and leave Stanthorpe Place as quickly as she could.

If she were lucky, they could be gone before Gideon returned.

A sob escaped her at the thought.

"My bachelor accommodation at Stephen's Hotel on Bond Street is not fit for you and the boys," Hawksworth said when she revealed her plan to leave. "But you can go to my town house. It is for sale, I have learned, but still mine, I believe. Alexandra is not there, I understand, though she would welcome you if she were. *If* you truly wish to leave Stanthorpe," Hawksworth qualified. "Which is not what I have been hearing."

"What do you perceive you have been hearing?"

"That you have no choice but to leave, except that you look as if you would just as soon stay." He smiled grimly. "Not to mention the way Stanthorpe looked when we left him. Why did we abandon him like that, by the way? And after he saved Rafe's life?"

"What do you mean about the way Gideon looked?"

"Broken, is the way he appeared to me, as if he had lost his best friend . . . or his only love."

Another sob escaped her, and Sabrina turned away. "Ah, Hawk, what did you do to me, giving me to him of all men?"

"Why? What do you find so bad in Stanthorpe?" Hawksworth turned Sabrina's gaze back toward him with a finger to her chin. "Can you not bear to look at my scars, Sabrina? Or can you not look me in the eye and say you do not love your husband?"

Sabrina raised her chin. "It is your scars," she lied, and then she wept in earnest, because he had winked even as she said it. But despite his attempt at levity, she had had a glimpse of the agony deep inside him. She took to crying in earnest then, and Hawksworth held her in his arms as she did. If she could not bear the destruction of her dearest friend's legendary perfection, how then could he?

Sabrina wept for them both, and for her children's loss of a father, and for Gideon himself. And for her, because she would love and mourn Gideon forever. Hawksworth, she suspected, wept as well, and they consoled each other.

Gideon stepped into the foyer, with Doggett and Waredraper, and found his wife and her lover thus, clutching each other as if they would never let go. They were so wrapped up in their quiet embrace, Gideon brooded, that they did not even notice her invalid husband's tardy return.

Gideon slapped Hawksworth briskly on the back as he passed. "Hello, old friend. Make yourself at home. Anything I can get for you? Ah, yes. I almost forgot. 'Tis my wife, you want . . . and have."

Waredraper and Doggett went directly upstairs.

Gideon stepped into his study but remained inside the door watching Sabrina and Hawk. "I am fine," he said. "Thank you for asking. As you said, it is only a flesh wound." He shut the door with a decided slam.

Sabrina shed a new bout of tears before she stepped from Hawksworth's arms and wiped the moisture from her eyes. "Do you see what he thinks of me?"

"He thinks nothing of the sort. He desperately fears the worst, that he has lost you. And you have given him reason to fear. The way you regarded him at Lowick's, as if he were dirt beneath your feet."

"No. No, I did not. Not that. 'Twas I who felt dirty, filthy, and I could not bear to witness his disgust of me. I was ashamed, mortified that he had observed me . . . with—so vile a creature." All but mounted by that creature, she thought with inescapable and everlasting regret.

"Sabrina, he does not think badly of you. He is afraid, bitter, to see us like this, and hurt. Badly hurt. By you, and quite possibly previous to today, if I do not mistake the matter. Have you used him ill?"

"I have done nothing to hurt him. I have given him . . . everything." Sabrina refused to admit that until recently she had given him all but herself. The night before had likely been already too late.

She shook her head, repeating her silent denial. "Gideon hates me because of Lowick's accusations. I knew he would. He has taken a disgust of me. My association with such a horrid man is beyond scandalous; I always knew Gideon would perceive it so."

"I think you must look into your heart, my dear,

and discover the truth there, and then perhaps you should look into your husband's eyes—and discover the truth there as well. Learn to trust, Sabrina. Trust is everything," Hawksworth said. "Stanthorpe is a good man. He bound my wounds as best he could and held me as I lay dying, or so we both thought, making of himself a target on that bloody, deadly battlefield."

Hawksworth sighed as he looked into the teeth of hell. "He did not leave me willingly, but only when forced by circumstances to defend the members of our regiment against Boney's troops."

"I do not dispute that Gideon is a good man," Sabrina said. "I have had daily proof."

"He is the best of men. I would not have entrusted you to anyone less worthy. But even I know that you must earn love, and return it, if you wish to keep it."

"Fine words from a man who appears to be running away."

Hawksworth kissed Sabrina's brow, lowered his cane to the floor, and made for the stairs. "You mistake the matter," he said, turning. "I no longer have the ability to run."

Sabrina scoffed. "That is as blatant a falsehood as my saying I could not bear to regard your scars. Stephens Hotel indeed." Sabrina raised a brow.

Hawksworth smiled. "You have perfected Stanthorpe's arrogant brow, I see."

"Where will you go?" Sabrina asked, refusing to rise to his bait. "What will you do?"

"After I have said good-bye to the boys? I have not as yet decided."

"Have you at least informed Alexandra that she is not a widow?"

Hawksworth shook his head. "No."

"Then you had better, and soon."

Hawksworth regarded her sharply, and returned to her. "Tell me which is more important, that I tell Alex, or that I tell her soon?"

"Go and see her. Please."

"Perhaps I will," he said. "We do have a score to settle, her and I. She needs to be taught a lesson, I believe. Perhaps . . . Yes. I will strike you a bargain, Sabrina, my love. I will see my wife soon if you will tell Stanthorpe that you love him."

"I do not think I can," Sabrina whispered. "I am afraid he will not care—"

Gideon opened his study door. "Hawksworth," he said. "Do you mind if I have a word with my wife before you steal her away?"

There stood the man she ached to run toward, Sabrina thought, the man whose enfolding arms had once offered blessed comfort and a place of safety—if only he would open them now.

"Go," Hawksworth said. "I will be upstairs with the boys."

Sabrina raised her head and crossed the foyer on shaky legs, then she stepped into the study and shut the door behind her. As she and Gideon regarded each other, Sabrina damned near said she loved him, except that he distracted her by handing her the money canister that she had kept hidden in her desk since she moved in.

"Why were you hiding this from me?" Gideon asked.

Sabrina bit her lip. "I was not so much hiding it from you as I was hiding it *for* me."

He scoffed. "Always, you talk in circles. It is time for talking straight, Sabrina, for once, please."

"I suppose there does come a time to tell the truth," she muttered almost to herself, thinking she should come right out and say she loved him.

"From you, the truth would be a refreshing change."

Smarting from the sting of those words, Sabrina raised her chin and changed course. "I used to keep my money hidden, in the event I needed to get away from my husband—my first husband. Once, I did use it to get away from Lowick."

"And you hid it from *me* because . . ."

"Brian used to steal it, so I was forced to hide it. Once I was here, I continued to hide it because . . . I was used to doing so. Knowing it was available gave me a sense of safety."

"And you could n—"

"Though that was nothing," she said, stopping him. "It was nothing, I came to realize, compared to the sense of security *you* gave me."

Gideon opened his mouth to speak, paused to reflect, and firmed his lips. He paced to the window and looked out for a moment. "Thank you for telling me." He took a slip of paper from his desk and handed it to her.

"What is this?" Sabrina asked, stepping nearer the lamp to read the document.

"I had the full race purse, eighty-five hundred pounds, deposited into an account in your name this morning. That is a copy of the deposit order. The money is yours."

Sabrina sat. "You did this for me?" No one had ever done anything half so generous for her before. But then, Gideon had done so much, never previously attempted, including making her love him. She rose and approached him. "After today," she said, her voice suddenly as small as she felt. "You are especially kind to give this to me."

*"Kind?"* Gideon spat the word, as if she had insulted him. "I am not *kind,"* he shouted—roared, more like. "Damn it to hell, Sabrina." He grasped her shoulders. "Listen to me."

Her heart began to race and her palms to sweat. And Sabrina simply stood there, staring into his beautiful, dark eyes, aware, so aware that her love for him shone in hers, hoping that was love for her she saw in his.

But as if he could not believe the evidence before him, Gideon shook his head imperceptibly and stepped away from her. Then he ran his hand through his already mussed hair. "I love you," he said in a rush. "I love you in a way I never thought myself capable of loving. I love you so damn much that I am prepared to divorce you so you can have that former friend of mine, who gave you to me, only to take you away again."

Sabrina did not know which of them was more surprised by his words. Chagrin, bashfulness, of all things, seemed to color Gideon's features. He made to run his hand through his hair again, but dropped his hands to his sides. "I am sorry. I do not mean to act coercive or bitter. You deserve every chance at happiness with whomever you choose to spend your life." His voice was rising. "Though I honestly believe that I am the best husband for you, damn it." He took a breath. "But that is the last I shall say on the matter."

He loved her? After everything?

Gideon gazed out the window, traced the frost on the pane while seeming to look inside himself. "Sabrina. If you or the children ever need anything . . ." He turned to regard her, his obsidian eyes more beautiful than she had ever seen them, so filled with love, Sabrina was like to fall to her knees in thankfulness. "Anything," he said. "Ever."

Gideon, the man she loved, loved her in return. Sabrina could barely take it in.

But why, when he believed that she gave herself to Lowick? He did not even know the truth of it, that Lowick attempted to take her by force on two occasions and failed both times.

Could she be so fortunate as to be the recipient of such a love? Impossible.

Perhaps he wanted her merely because he could not have her. It was a disheartening thought, but she must know for certain. She must. "There is something you should know about Hawksworth," she said, "before we go a step further."

"Spare me. I know how much you love him."

"You know nothing of the sort," she snapped, getting his full attention. "Neither, I perceive, do you know that Hawksworth has a wife—though Alexandra yet believes herself a widow and is set to marry another."

"I thought—"

"I know what you thought, but you are wrong. It was never like that between us. Hawksworth was Brian's half brother. He was my brother-in-law. He became my best friend."

Did she see hope burning in Gideon's eyes? "Hawksworth is still a friend," she said. "But he is no longer my *best* friend."

"Then you have already been a duchess?"

"No, Brian was Hawksworth's mother's son, untitled and impoverished."

Bitterness dimmed hope in Gideon's eyes. "Ah, yes," he said with disgust. "And you will not be impoverished again."

"There is no danger of that. I have eighty-five hundred pounds."

"Yes, you do." Gideon sighed. "But let us not forget my situation."

"Your situation has no bearing on this matter, for I want our bargain done." Sabrina gave him back the document of deposit. "You said that money was mine to do what will make me happy."

Gideon nodded. "So I did."

"I sold myself to you, Gideon St. Goddard, and now I return your money. This negates my sale, does it not? It frees me?"

"Yes," Gideon said, closing his eyes against the pain of losing her, this agony infinitely more piercing than that from the pistol shot. "You are free to go."

"Good," Sabrina said, stepping closer. "If I am free to go, then I am free to stay."

Gideon could make no sense of her words. She was so close, he could touch her, but if he touched her now, he would never let her go.

He fisted his hands. "But I have lost all my money."

"You have not."

For a minute, Gideon thought she knew he had tricked her.

"You have the eighty-five hundred pounds," she said. "Money enough to keep us if we are thrifty. I am even better at economy than at horse racing, you know."

In Gideon's heart, joy sought purchase, yet too many questions lingered. "Why did you appear as if you hated me after I broke into that room? Why did you turn from me, after all was said and done and the Runners had taken the villains away? And why, by all that is holy, did you never tell me that horrible man was after you?"

Sabrina turned away from her husband's probing gaze. "It was so ugly, what you came in on. Previous to my coming here, people like Lowick, sordid, corrupt, are the kind I was forced to associate with daily. Such as them are so far beneath you that I knew you would take a disgust of me once you learned of my life with them."

"Do I look as if I have taken a disgust of you?" Gideon appeased his deep need to touch her by grazing her chin with his thumb. He wanted to haul her into his arms, but he was still afraid that if he did, really did, she would run screaming from the room, and straight into Hawksworth's embrace.

"I want our bargain done," she said again.

"Sabrina, you give me hope and take it away again. Please, you are killing me. If you must bury your knife, bury it to the hilt, now, with one thrust, and put me out of my misery. Tell me what you want of me."

"I want your purchase of me to be negated. I want you no longer to own me. I must own myself again, so I may be what I want so badly to be."

"What?" Gideon whispered.

"Your wife."

"Why?"

"Because you are a gentle man, and the best of papas. You are good, kind, mine. . ." Sabrina touched his face. "And I love you."

Gideon scanned her expression to see if he could read anything, anything to deny her words, his hope, but he did not, and he was humbled. "You love me."

"I do, but how can you want me, thinking me a whore and a schemer?"

"It never occurred to me to believe what Lowick said. I know who you are, Sabrina St. Goddard. I know you and I love you. But, Sabrina, tell me he did not hurt you. I have been so worried, but I dared not ask, because I was afraid you would consider the question a judgment on you. It is not." Gideon cupped her head to pull her near and press his face to hers. "You are so precious to me, I cannot stand the thought that you have been hurt in any way, and that you must suffer alone, because I am unaware of your pain. Did he hurt you, love?"

Sabrina was so touched, she pressed her lips to his ear before she could speak. "No, Gideon, not on either of the occasions he tried. I fought him off, though I might not have succeeded this time, had you not intervened. But if . . ."

Gideon straightened from their embrace and moved a curl from her eyes. "If he had hurt you, I would share your pain and we could heal together. Did he, love?"

"No." She shook her head. "I simply cannot comprehend that you would want me still if he did."

"Do you not realize that I have wanted you, any way I could have you, almost from the moment I walked into my kitchen and you threw flour in my face?"

"Any way you could have me?" Sabrina smiled through her tears. "The way you can have me, my lovable, undeniable rogue, is by your side, and in your bed, for as long as we both shall live."

Gideon kissed his wife the way he ought to have done weeks before, with all the love inside him. With his kiss, he told her how much he treasured her, and with hers, she proved the same. Love turned to passion and passion to desire and—

The world intruded with utter chaos . . . two excited little boys, and one crying baby, who shattered the moment's passion, but not the love.

The love, they deepened.

Sabrina and Gideon stepped apart, reluctant but smiling.

Damon and Rafferty whooped and charged Gideon, welcoming Papa home with kisses and hugs and questions and more hugs, until Sabrina once again sought Gideon's handkerchief, except that he had to use it on his own eyes first.

Hawksworth stood in the doorway, a screaming baby in his arms. "Help," he said.

Grinning, Gideon took Juliana, and the babe quieted and gave her papa her best grin.

Hawksworth chuckled.

Gideon extended his hand to his friend. "I apologize for thinking—"

"And I for doubting—" Hawksworth took Gideon's hand and clasped it firmly.

Gideon cleared his throat. "Welcome back to the land of the living."

"Thank you. If not for your care on the battlefield, I might not be here."

"I am glad you did not tell me so when I came in the door tonight."

The two men shared a smile.

Hawksworth nodded toward the baby. "Sorry to interrupt. I tried to hold them off as long as I could, but as soon as they knew Papa was home . . ."

Rafe slipped his arm about Gideon's leg and leaned against it. "Papa, Mincemeat went missing, but we found him sleeping in your bed."

"With 'his' kittens," Hawksworth said with a wry grin.

"Does that really mean he is a girl?" Damon asked.

Drizzle waddled in, went tail-wagging mad over Gideon and . . . drizzled, he was so happy.

Hawksworth laughed as he backed out the door. "As much fun as this has been, I must take my leave and allow you to recover."

Everyone followed him into the hall. "Hawksworth," Gideon said from the base of the stairs. "You will take the children at some point? You got us into this—for which we will remain eternally grateful—but we would very much appreciate a honey-month."

"Good God," his friend said, thunderstruck. "A month?"

Gideon chuckled as he slipped his arm around Sabrina's waist, and she slipped hers around him, and they started up the stairs.

Hawksworth remained by the open door to watch them, all five, make their undisciplined way up the stairs, happy, chattering, jumping, holding hands. A family.

"Can I have a pony ride, Papa?" he heard Damon ask.

"Lord have mercy," Sabrina said. "Your papa has a gunshot wound in his side."

"From saving me," Rafe said. "Thank you, Papa."

Gideon ruffled Rafe's hair. "Anytime, son."

"Can we do anything to make you feel better, Papa?"

"Why, yes, Damon, thank you," Gideon said. "I would like you and your brother and sister to spend some nice, quiet time up in the nursery, so I may take a nap—with Mama."

# About the Author

Annette Blair is the development director and journalism advisor at a private New England secondary school. Happily married to her grammar school nemesis—and glad she didn't know what fate had in store—Annette considers romance a celebration of life.

Always happy working on a new romance, Annette also loves hearing from her readers, antiquing, and collecting glass slippers. Contact her at: www.annetteblair.com or P.O. Box 302 Manville, RI 02838.

If you liked *An Undeniable Rogue*, be sure to look for Annette Blair's next release in the tantalizing Rogues Club series, *An Unforgettable Rogue*, available in bookstores everywhere October 2002.

Alexandra Huntington married for love once—and said good-bye to her war-bound groom on the steps of the church. Widowed soon after, Alex is penniless because the charming roué neglected to provide for her in his will. Of course, Bryceson Wakefield, Duke of Hawksworth, was always too aristocratically elegant for his own good, apparently far too much so to survive Waterloo. Now, with an aging aunt to care for, Alex is on her way to the altar once more, hang the fact that her groom is Bryceson's enemy, the Viscount Chesterfield. But the ceremony is halted by none other than Bryceson himself! Limping, bearded, and altogether more dear to Alex for it, Bryceson is definitely back, but he's not the man Alex has adored since childhood. What's more, she intends to show him that she is now a grown woman who will demand that her husband prove his love, as well as his loyalty. . . .

# COMING IN AUGUST 2002 FROM
# ZEBRA BALLAD ROMANCES

### __A FALLEN WOMAN: The Brides of Bath

by Cheryl Bolen        0-8217-7249-X        $5.99US/$7.99CAN

Since her husband's tragic death, Carlotta Ennis had hoped to attract a wealthy husband in Bath. Instead she made the ruinous mistake of loving a rake who was willing to seduce her, but not to marry her. Now she is certain no decent gentleman will ever marry her . . . until James Rutledge returns home from the war and offers his hand . . .

### __A DANGEROUS FANCY: American Heiresses

by Tracy Cozzens        0-8217-7351-8        $5.99US/$7.99CAN

Lily Carrington's ambitious mother had set her sights on a titled marriage for Lily. As honorable as she was beautiful, Lily vowed not to disappoint her family—even as she became the pawn in a sordid plot of seduction by the Prince of Wales himself . . . and found herself falling in love with a most unlikely hero.

### __KING OF HEARTS: The Gamblers

by Pat Pritchard        0-8217-7255-4        $5.99US/$7.99CAN

Wade McCord, a U.S. Marshall, poses as a gambler at a stagecoach stop to smoke out a notorious outlaw gang. But he never counted on his burning desire for Lottie Hammond, a woman who may be in league with the outlaws. Wade knows Lottie has secrets, but he also knows that the time has come for him to gamble his heart on the promise of love.

### __ON MY LADY'S HONOR: . . . And One for All

by Kate Silver        0-8217-7386-0        $5.99US/$7.99CAN

Sophie Delamanse envisiones a dull marriage to Count Lamotte, one of her twin brother's Musketeer friends. Her life took a tragic turn when the plague consumed her family. Her brother promised that Lamotte would come for her, but when he never arrived, Sophie vowed to go to *him*—disguised as her brother—and make him pay for his dishonor.

---

Call toll free **1-888-345-BOOK** to order by phone or use this coupon to order by mail. *ALL BOOKS AVAILABLE AUGUST 01, 2002.*

Name _____

Address _____

City _____ State _____ Zip _____

Please send me the books that I have checked above.

| | |
|---|---|
| I am enclosing | $_____ |
| Plus postage and handling* | $_____ |
| Sales tax (in NY and TN) | $_____ |
| Total amount enclosed | $_____ |

*Add $2.50 for the first book and $.50 for each additional book. Send check or money order (no cash or CODs) to: **Kensington Publishing Corp., Dept. C.O., 850 Third Avenue, New York, NY 10022**

Prices and numbers subject to change without notice. Valid only in the U.S. All orders subject to availability. **NO ADVANCE ORDERS.**

Visit our website at **www.kensingtonbooks.com.**

# Put a Little Romance in Your Life With
# Joan Hohl

__**Another Spring**      0-8217-7155-8      **$6.99US/$8.99CAN**
Elizabeth is the perfect wife and mother. Until she is widowed. Jake takes his pleasures where he likes—and to hell with tomorrow. Then he takes Elizabeth to bed . . .

__**Something Special**      0-8217-6725-9      **$5.99US/$7.50CAN**
Nobody spins a love story like best-selling author Joan Hohl. Now, she presents three stories, filled with the passion and unforgettable characters that are her trademark . . .

__**Compromises**      0-8217-7154-X      **$6.99US/$8.99CAN**
Now that Frisco's father has jeopardized the family business, it is up to her to prevent the takeover bid of Lucas MacCanna. But Lucas wants more than the business, he wants Frisco.

__**Ever After**      0-8217-7203-1      **$6.99US/$8.99CAN**
Cyndi Swoyer never expected her prince to arrive . . . in a late-model Buick! Now suddenly Bennett Ganster has driven into her small town to make her an offer no woman could refuse.

__**Never Say Never**      0-8217-6379-2      **$5.99US/$7.99CAN**
When Samantha Denning's father died leaving a will stipulating that she marry within five months or lose everything, she decides Morgan Wade is the ideal candidate for groom. It was supposed to be business . . . until Morgan made their marriage personal . . .

__**Silver Thunder**      0-=8217-7201-5      **$6.99US/$8.99CAN**
Jessica Randall managed her family's Wyoming ranch. She was a woman who defied traditional roles . . . until a handsome cowboy rode into her life. Duncan Frazer belonged to no one. But then he was Jessica . . . and wanted her with all his heart and soul.

---

Call toll free **1-888-345-BOOK** to order by phone or use this coupon to order by mail.

Name_____

Address_____

City_____ State_____ Zip_____

Please send me the books that I checked above.

| | |
|---|---|
| I am enclosing | $_____ |
| Plus postage and handling* | $_____ |
| Sales tax (in NY, TN, and DC) | $_____ |
| Total amount enclosed | $_____ |

*Add $2.50 for the first book and $.50 for each additional book.
Send check or money order (no cash or CODs) to: **Kensington Publishing Corp., Dept. C.O., 850 Third Avenue, New York, NY 10022**
Prices and numbers subject to change without notice.
All orders subject to availability. **NO ADVANCE ORDERS.**
Visit our website at **www.kensingtonbooks.com.**

# Discover the Magic of
# Romance With

# Kat Martin

## __The Secret
   0-8217-6798-4                                    **$6.99**US/**$8.99**CAN
Kat Rollins moved to Montana looking to change her life, not find
another man like Chance McLain, with a sexy smile and empty
heart. Chance can't ignore the desire he feels for her—or the suspicion that somebody wants her to leave Lost Peak . . .

## __Dream
   0-8217-6568-X                                    **$6.99**US/**$8.99**CAN
Genny Austin is convinced that her nightmares are visions of another
life she lived long ago. Jack Brennan is having nightmares, too, but
his are real. In the shadows of dreams lurks a terrible truth, and only
by unlocking the past will Genny be free to love at last . . .

## __Silent Rose
   0-8217-6281-8                                    **$6.99**US/**$8.50**CAN
When best-selling author Devon James checks into a bed-and-breakfast
in Connecticut, she only hopes to put the spark back into her relationship with her fiancé. But what she experiences at the Stafford Inn
changes her life forever . . .

---

Call toll free **1-888-345-BOOK** to order by phone or use this
coupon to order by mail.
Name_____
Address_____
City _____ State_____ Zip_____
Please send me the books I have checked above.
I am enclosing                                         $_____
Plus postage and handling*                             $_____
Sales tax (in New York and Tennessee only)             $_____
Total amount enclosed                                  $_____
*Add $2.50 for the first book and $.50 for each additional book.
Send check or money order (no cash or CODs) to: **Kensington Publishing
Corp., Dept. C.O., 850 Third Avenue, New York, NY 10022**
Prices and numbers subject to change without notice. All orders subject
to availability. Visit our website at **www.kensingtonbooks.com.**